BLIND
TARGET

A Codi Sanders Thriller

BRENT LADD

Archway Publishing books may be ordered through booksellers or by contacting:

Archway Publishing
1663 Liberty Drive
Bloomington, IN 47403
www.archwaypublishing.com
1 (888) 242-5904

ISBN: 978-1-4808-7843-3 (sc)
ISBN: 978-1-4808-7844-0 (hc)
ISBN: 978-1-4808-7845-7 (e)

Library of Congress Control Number: 2019906619

Print information available on the last page.

Archway Publishing rev. date: 06/10/2019

Dedicated to my wife Leesa, for whom
love has no conditions.

1

October 1957 – Umnak Island, Aleutian Islands, Alaska – 4:14 a.m.

Engineer Marshal Sergei Popov swallowed back the bile that pushed at the back of his esophagus. Twenty minutes of bobbing up and down in an inflatable raft waiting for the all clear was taking its toll. His moss green face seemed to glow in the dwindling moonlight, as he tried to concentrate on the nodding coastline in the distance. His round face and large eyes made him look frog-like, but his aberrant fear of the water had him clinging to the craft's seat with rigid white knuckles.

A thin, black, mottled silhouette in the distance buoyed up and down with the shadowy sea. It was a land beyond desolate, where few men came and fewer survived—Umnak Island. Popov's vision clouded with darkness in the periphery as his head started to spin. He blinked it away and sipped a lungfull of arctic air. Somebody next to him mumbled something and the raft started to move. *Thank God*, he breathed to no one. Popov was a holdout to the Russian Orthodox faith in an otherwise godless country, a place where the good of the state took priority over all. He turned back to see their leader, Colonel Tolya Alexeev, focused on the growing coastline. The man looked stoic and determined. If anyone could see them through this it would be the colonel.

The eight-man rubber raft pushed through the choppy water and pointed towards a small cove just visible ahead. *America*, Tolya, thought to himself. *Doesn't look like much.*

Tolya removed his goggles for a moment to rub the stinging sensation from his blue-gray eyes. Only moments before, the goggles had protected him from pelting airborne ice crystals. Five degrees below zero with a thirty-mile-an-hour wind was no picnic, but he had seen it all before. And if the reports were correct it was only going to get worse. He absently scratched at an old scar that ran along one side of his strong cleft chin.

Their eight-man state-of-the-art raft was made of a new synthetic rubber designed to provide twice the strength of any previous model. The compartmentalized air pockets allowed it to skim across the water with ease. But it was susceptible to wind, and Tolya struggled to keep it on course. His goggles immediately started to fog.

"Clear," Tolya said, and the raft picked up speed.

Tolya squinted through drifting clouds. Operation Blind Pig. Tolya smiled. It had to have been named after one of the politburo's wives. He looked over his squad. Three were well-trained men, all Alpha group, OBSP, formed by Minister Zhukov himself. Each had arctic training from the 379th special purpose detachment.

Corporal Misha Ivanov, a six-foot-one battle-hardened commando, had been under Tolya's command during the messy Hungarian Revolution a short while back. Misha's kind brown eyes belied the true fighter inside. He was a man Tolya could trust, an extremely rare trait in Moscow's current political landscape.

Sergeant Kazimir Yegor, or Kaz, as he was called, was the pessimist of the bunch. The man never smiled, but he made up for it by anticipating anything to go wrong at any moment. He was wound as tight as a longbow with a short string. His no-nonsense attitude kept everyone in line. Kaz was probably the most loyal comrade soldier Tolya had ever known. And one day, over several shots of vodka, he just might see the man smile.

Private Andrei Tatter was a promising cadet from the Suvorov Military School in Leningrad. He even spoke some English. The boy was from solid Russian stock, sinewy, fast like a cheetah, with a perfect smile and biting sarcasm. Something very few Russians seemed to have. He watched as the boy took a nervous swig of water from his canteen to wash the dried salt from his lips.

These were the best the Soviets had to offer. Tolya could have no better company on any mission, even to an island that time had forgotten.

The rest of Colonel Tolya Alexeev's team was a mixed bag of unknowns. He looked across the unit. Each wore snow camouflage outerwear with a large fur-rimmed parka hood, and had no identification of any kind. Identical all, except for one man.

Seated on the starboard second seat, looking more like a refugee from a comedy show than a squad member, was their guide, Chikuk, a Siberian Yupik Eskimo from Inupiaq Island off the coast of Siberia. Chikuk had refused the camouflage clothing in favor of his own winter gear of sealskin and caribou, and no amount of discussion could change his mind. The man had lived and thrived in some of the harshest winter conditions on the planet. He wore a perpetually disdainful expression, as though everyone around him was inept. But if anyone could guide them through this arctic winter operation on foot, it was he.

"Ah," a man called out.

The raft had hit a particularly large crest, and subzero-degree water breached over the gunwale. Tolya watched as the man next to Chikuk lifted his feet in the air, fearful of the cold. Zampolit Traktor Yashin was what every special forces squad going to America required—a political officer. Traktor was missing most of his hair and all of a personality. He wore a scowl he had been nursing since fifty-two. His beady black eyes seemed to take in everything around him and yet managed to see nothing. For Tolya, he was a 100-kg anchor on a 5-kg boat, and if he thought he could get away with it, he would have pushed the man over the side an hour ago. Ideology and indoctrination had no place on this mission, but the Deputy Chairman of the MPA in the Ministry of Defense had insisted. Tolya was almost positive Traktor was the man's nephew.

Good old Mother Russia, ever fearful of defectors and the bad press it carried, suffered from a terminal case of paranoia. Tolya scoffed at the thought that these men would defect. They were battle-hardened Soviet soldiers. They bled Russian red and would give their lives for the motherland.

The man who looked like he was about to vomit was Engineer Marshal Sergei Popov. A transfer from the science and engineering corps, Popov was the key to this operation, and Tolya's personal responsibility. In his arms Popov clutched a waterproof canvas package that held the latest in Russian technology. An electrical leach, he called it. No matter what lay ahead, Colonel Tolya Alexeev had one responsibility: make sure that leach was activated.

Visibility dropped to near zero as the clouds finally won their battle and filled the world with billowy cotton. It was a total whiteout with visibility mere meters. The new-generation optics was a joke. Sure, it helped block ultraviolet radiation, and the second-generation polarization cut snow glare significantly, but it was useless in these conditions. The damn thing kept fogging up. The GSS's science division was great at theory, but their lack of practical application often made men like Tolya guinea pigs. As he tried to navigate, he pictured the scientists here now giving their new equipment a try. His chapped lips cracked as he smiled.

"*Click.*" Chikuk made a soft clicking sound as the Yupik Eskimos do. He pointed with a flat vertical palm.

Tolya adjusted his course. Almost immediately, a dark mass pushed through the low clouds, and a small black rock cove covered mostly in ice appeared. The lava-strewn beach was a battle of black versus white, truly inhospitable. Tolya readied himself. This was what he was made for, the apex of extreme, living on the razor's edge with a life-and-death mission to fulfill.

He cut the engine and coasted towards the hummock-lined shore. They must operate in total silence.

Misha leaned over the front of the raft and, using an oar, broke through the hoarfrost to carve a path.

Once they reached more substantial ice, the team disembarked. Like a well-practiced drill, all gear and personnel was unloaded and moved across the frozen sea and up to the shore. The crunching of rocks and the cracking of ice underfoot was masked by the crashing of waves against the perpetually frozen barrier. A mix of stacked ice and frozen sea foam covered the shore, eventually transitioning to polished, rime-covered rocks.

Tolya glanced over at Chikuk who knelt briefly and mumbled some sort of prayer or greeting. The Eskimo then selected a smooth pebble, scraped the ice from it, placed it in his pocket, and stood for a brief moment, unmoving. Then, just as quickly, he was back helping the others drag the gear up the beach and onto the snow-covered landscape beyond the shore.

Traktor tried to stifle a sneeze as he moved empty-handed to the high-tidemark. He bent at the waist and tried to flick off the slush that had accumulated on his boots. He then stamped his feet up and down as though the American soil had tainted his soles.

Tolya looked around at the near whiteout conditions and felt confident their actions had not been seen. Given the choice, he would have approached this mission very differently, including the team selection. But the powers-that-be had turned a deaf ear to his ideas and dictated the terms. This was a "yes, sir" assignment right from the beginning. This new-fangled "cold war" was nothing like Tolya had experienced. He would have faced his enemy rather than steal around in the shadows. But different times called for different strategies. Still, he was not about to step foot on foreign soil without something to connect him to Mother Russia. He fingered his Order of Lenin medal he kept hidden away in his breast pocket, a reminder of home and why he was here.

His mind started to drift to a past mission—death, screaming, blood—so much blood. The screams of the innocent blended with the wind fighting its way up the cove.

"Colonel." Kaz was looking at him. "We're ready."

Tolya pulled himself back to the moment and gave Kaz a curt nod. Without hesitation, Kaz ran to the sea. He spun the black raft around, pointing the bow out to open ocean. He pulled out his DV-1 combat knife and made several slashes in the raft. He started the motor and released it.

The squad watched as the craft moved past the waves and finally succumbed to the impassionate sea, sinking out of sight with a gurgle and a sputter from the drowning motor.

The group stood in silence. They had reached the point of no return.

Colonel Tolya Alexeev looked at Engineer Marshal Sergei Popov. "You ready?"

His pale white face with nervous brown eyes nodded. Popov held his canvas bag close.

The squad reconfigured their gear and set off at a brisk pace with Chikuk in the lead, and Kaz, his bushy eyebrows already frosted over, taking up the rear.

Here at the top of the world, the wind and clouds were a living, breathing entity in itself. It was the ultimate hunter: cruel, unceasing, inescapable. The beast slowed the squad down, blowing and scouring the ground like a ravenous creature.

Chikuk looked back and called out, "Stay close. It's not the cold that kills, it's the wind."

The ground was relatively flat but frozen so hard it was like walking on slippery uneven concrete. The sun had risen to its pinnacle for the day, just inches above the horizon. It cast a greenish-orange anemic glow as it played peek-a-boo with the transient clouds. This time of year the sun was up for only a few hours, traveling low across the horizon and providing almost no warmth. The rock-covered tundra gave way to multiple snowdrifts that had to be skirted or climbed. After eighteen miles of dragging gear and coping with the bitter cold, the team's progress had slowed dramatically.

Tolya stopped them. He crept up behind a large volcanic boulder and took out his binoculars. He could no longer feel his fingers and wondered how the rest of his squad was coping. A large steel-gray monolith, near completion, stood in the distance. It was a testament to modern man. Here on Umnak Island, thousands of miles from anything, was the most sophisticated piece of electrical engineering in the world—the DEW Line, as the Americans called it, or, Distant Early Warning System.

Tolya was proud in his belief that it was the superior military strength of Russia that had caused the paranoid American bastards to build an 800-mile chain of radar tracking and alerting stations. With it they could detect a plane crossing the Arctic Circle out of Soviet Russia, and then scramble their jets to intercept. "All that ends today," Tolya said to himself.

He panned the binoculars and focused on the base where three men worked. He saw that a single guard was stationed nearby, his eyes glazed with boredom. Tolya turned and headed back to his huddled team.

Chikuk secured the last post on a black and white camouflaged dome tent. It was a new design that could withstand extreme weather. They had placed it in a small depression, and from fifty feet away, it was invisible. Tolya stepped through the flap and was greeted with a wall of warm air that smelled of burnt tobacco and fear, and for the first time in nine hours, no wind. It was a balmy minus five degrees Celsius inside, but it felt like summer to him.

Engineer Popov's color had returned to his face. He was hunched over, inspecting and organizing his gear: three gray boxes the size of a loaf of bread with odd connectors attached at both ends, two for the mission and one as backup. These were his charge and the entire mission depended on his unique skill set. Though not a social person by nature, Popov lived in the here-and-now of electrical science. Capacitors, resistors and circuits were his domain.

In the middle of the tent, Traktor was hunched over and scribbling in a little black notebook he kept in his breast pocket. His eyes darted from person to person, then back to his writing. The political officer's patented dour expression was relentlessly on display, a shield to keep the curious away.

Tolya moved to his second in command, Sergeant Kazimir, "How's the radio working, Kaz?"

"I'm getting a ping from our shadow."

Tolya nodded as he took off his arctic combat boots and rubbed the circulation back into his toes. The boots were made of a new kind of vulcanized rubber with an inflatable bladder to act as a weather barrier. There was little doubt of their effectiveness, but still, subarctic cold had a way of infiltrating everything, even your bones.

Chikuk was off to one side eating some kind of dried meat. He seemed unfazed by the day's activities and looked as if he could do it all again. Misha moved over and sat next to him. He held out his canteen and offered Chikuk a drink. In return, Chikuk offered him some of his mystery meat. Misha took the dark chunk in his hand and sniffed it.

Chikuk smiled at his hesitation. "Walrus mixed with crowberry. It's good."

Misha took a bite and tried to make a pleasant face. "Have you ever been to America before?" he whispered. He glanced over his shoulder, concerned that the political officer might be listening.

"I have cousins that live a couple of islands to the north from here." Chikuk gestured with his hands. "We have met for hunts in the summer. Good hunting there."

"I like to hunt," Misha said.

Chikuk reached over and squeezed his arm. "Hunting keep you strong." His cheeks spread into a smile revealing a missing front tooth and genuine care.

Misha returned it with an effervescent smile of his own.

Tolya was touched. Two men, worlds apart, finding common ground.

2

October 1957 – Umnak Island – 4:12 p.m. – That Afternoon

The wiper worked overtime against a losing battle, as a mix of airborne snow and sleet attacked the windshield. Four separate thousand-watt headlamps pierced the dusk as the last rays of the day's paltry sun dipped below the horizon.

Private Jenkins gazed out of the fogged-up side window of the Le Toureau Logistical Car VC-22 Sno-Freighter, as it moved along the ice and lava rock coast. It was a unique land train built to cross deep rivers and snow while pulling 150 tons of equipment. The cockpit of the VC-22 sat fifteen feet up in the air, and the segmented windshield angled forward, giving the vehicle the appearance of a praying mantis. But it was no insect, with eight-hundred horsepower powering twenty-four electric motors, one for each wheel including the five trail cars behind it. The VC-22 was truly a train without a track. The Sno-Freighter had high ground clearance, with eight-foot-tall tires that allowed it to clear debris up to four feet in height, and all at subarctic temperatures.

Jenkins had spent the last four hours wondering how he had gotten to this place in his life. Things used to be good for him. He was respected in certain circles of Chicago. Now he was a bottom-rung private caught up in some mad race against the Soviets.

As a flyweight fighter, Jenkins had proven himself in the ring. It was a skill brought on by desperation. He was the only provider for his family. His mother Agatha and little sister Penny depended on him for everything. Agatha had lost a leg from type-one diabetes and found work to be impossible for a one-legged black woman. And as much as she hated her son Jenkins fighting, she knew it was the street for all of them if he failed.

Jenkins had excelled for a time, eventually becoming a local favorite. He leveraged that success into a chance at the national stage. That was before a bad decision and trouble with the law left him a choice: jail or the army. Now, every penny he could spare from his private's salary went to his family. When his new orders came through to this posting, he'd been furious. But when he learned it meant a bump in pay, he was all in.

The Sno-Freighter jostled through a ravine, banging Jenkins back to the present. Up ahead he could see a massive, partially-illuminated structure. Towering sixty feet in the air, its concave surface was painted navy gray. A smaller column stood at its midpoint, pointing a receiver at the huge reflecting dish.

The tungsten work light rattled as the Sno-Freighter came to a stop next to the load-out area of DEW LRR Site 42. Jenkins climbed down the exit ladder from the cockpit and jumped the last two feet to the frozen ground. He stomped his feet and looked back up at the odd vehicle. Written in a mix of yellow cursive and block letters was the company's logo, Alaska Freightline Inc. With a practiced motion, he tapped out a single Lucky Strike from his pack and ducked behind the tall front tire to block the wind from his lighter. The sweet acrid smoke filled his lungs and calmed his frenzied nerves. He had arrived.

He watched as men and equipment unloaded the Sno-Freighter. The navy gray structure towered up into the clouds. It was constructed of individual steel plates making the surface look like a one-color jigsaw puzzle, where all the pieces were rectangles. Off to his right was an unpainted wooden building about the size of a four-car garage, and beyond that was nothing but ice and lava rock. Jenkins took another draw on his cigarette and exhaled decisively. The cold here made a bad Chicago winter look like swimsuit weather. He must have really pissed off somebody to deserve this posting.

Inside the wooden building was a common area with a small well stocked bar. The walls were unfinished plywood, and the floor was covered with thin green linoleum. There was a pool table and a reading area. The duty officer's desk was to the left. Beyond that, several doors led to sleeping quarters and a communal head. Jenkins reported to the commanding officer and was issued a cot and guard duty. Two shifts, four hours on, four hours off. Nobody stayed out in the cold longer than four hours. This was a standing order based on an incident three months back. His cot was a two-tiered affair that was shared with three other workers. Privacy was a thing of the past.

Chikuk leaned against the wind with his nose held high. He took a deliberate sniff. Then, with a curt hand gesture, pointed the squad in an arc around to the left.

The sun had long since gone down and the temperature was continuing to plummet. There were no workers on the grounds of the DEW LRR Site 42, only one guard.

Corporal Misha Ivanov stayed low in a crouch as he took

his time moving silently through the loose rock, his trusted DV-1 combat blade in one hand and a grapefruit-size rock in the other.

The silhouetted figure next to a burning drum was facing away. Tolya watched, longing for the man to stay just like that. The fifty-five-gallon steel drum popped and hissed as the fire devoured the wood inside. The wind had died to a constant thirty kilometers per hour.

The plan was simple. Misha was to take out the guard, making it look like an accident, and get Popov and his gizmo in and out of the facility as quickly as possible.

But plans have a way of falling apart the moment you make contact with the enemy. Whatever the reason, no one would ever know, maybe the man's back was cold, but the soldier turned from the fire and stared right at Misha.

Misha froze. At first the soldier seemed not to notice him in the dark. He continued to puff on his cigarette, staring out into the night, right in his direction.

Colonel Tolya Alexeev tensed as the squad helplessly watched the machinations play out from a distance. Kaz pulled his Makarov MP-71 and put the bead on the soldier's heart. Tolya raised his hand to stop him. The meaning was clear: no unnecessary gunplay or noise.

Private Jenkins paused to brush at a bit of tobacco stuck on his tongue, the cold nearly freezing his open mouth. The roaring fire did little to abate the encroaching chill. He imagined himself a rotisserie chicken roasting as it slowly turned in the flames. Only in this case it was to keep from freezing.

Jenkins leaned back, looking up at a spectacle of colored flames slowly dancing across the black sky. The collage flowed and wavered in an incandescent aura of azures and deep reds.

The local Inuit called them spirit lights, but he knew them as the aurora borealis. It was a spectacular sight.

Jenkins drew the last puff on the spent cigarette and flicked it. As he watched the glowing ember spin through the air, something caught his attention. Something was wrong.

Two human eyes with a feral look stared back at him in the span between flame and blackness. This was no fellow coworker. The man stood stock still, holding a large knife in his left hand. Jenkins quickly moved to unsling his M-1 rifle and call out an alarm, but his voice failed and only an unintelligible squawk came out that was quickly carried away by the wind.

The intruder didn't hesitate. Like a cat touching fire for the first time, he leaped headlong. But the loose rocks and ice gave way and he lost purchase. Jenkins reacted fast by pulling the rifle off his parka and taking a quick shot from the hip.

Click.

He quickly realized he hadn't chambered a round. If this was a drill, he just failed. In one practiced motion he put his mitten in his mouth, bit down and pulled it off. He racked the bolt on his rifle and chambered a round. He scarcely noticed the skin on his hand as it ripped free, sticking to the frozen metal of his weapon. But he did notice that this wasn't over.

The man hurled his rock attempting to delay the rifle's firing, but Jenkins feinted left and it flew past harmlessly. The man jabbed his blade, aiming for Jenkins' ribs, but ended up getting nothing but air.

Jenkins' mind and body instantly switched to autopilot. He dropped his stance, spread his legs and returned to his days fighting in the ring. His movements came without thinking. He used his rifle to parry the man and his knife to the side and swept the butt of the rifle around bringing it full force on the back of the intruder's head.

Gore and white matter from the back of the man's head was clearly visible. Jenkins stared down at the unmoving man. He tapped him with his boot, his stomach convulsing at the sight.

Suddenly, another man came from nowhere, followed by more men.

Jenkins spun around, still in shock. The world had gone deathly silent and seemed to slowly spin. He placed his now frostbitten hand up to his mouth to call for help. From some primitive place in his brain, there grew a crunching noise, but by the time he turned, the wind was pushed from his lungs as he took flight and landed hard.

He struggled against overwhelming odds. One of the men said something in Russian. The reality of it hit. This was no drill.

Tolya tackled the soldier at full pace, and five more of his men followed behind. The guard was immediately overwhelmed. They held him tight to the ground while one man covered his mouth and nose.

Within moments the team had suffocated the guard. They quickly moved to Misha and rolled him over. Tatter held the man's head in his arms. There was no movement.

Misha, the man who had been loyal to a tee, was no more. Strangely, he wore a slight smile on his rapidly cooling face. Corporal Misha Ivanov had died doing what he loved most.

Colonel Tolya Alexeev kicked the ground in anger and loosed a few choice words. It was an unimaginable disaster, but something they had all trained for. He would have to re-focus the squad quickly, or face losing them. Later he would grieve for his friend and one of the fiercest warriors he had ever known.

Suddenly, Chikuk ran off into the stygian night. "What is he doing?" Tolya asked.

"Taking a piss," said Tatter, ever the sarcastic wit.

"Unbelievable. Tell him to fucking hold it. We have a major problem on our hands." Tolya turned to Engineer Marshal Sergei Popov. "You have five minutes, not a second more. Understand?"

His tone left no doubt. Popov dashed off with his canvas bag in hand.

"Tatter, go with him."

Private Tatter gave a quick nod as he ran off in the engineer's footsteps.

"Colonel." Chikuk had returned and was motioning to the remaining team.

"What now?" Tolya said.

"Bring body."

The team quickly cleaned the site, grabbed the two bodies and moved off with Chikuk. There in the snow was a pool of frozen yellow. It took a second, but Tolya understood Chikuk's plan. They unzipped the soldier's parka, took off his gloves, and lowered his zipper. The next shift would find him frozen while taking a piss too far from the fire. They would claim it a rookie mistake and think nothing more of it. At least that was the hope.

Popov stopped at the bottom of the radar tower where a small pyramid-shaped structure housed and connected all the wiring before sending it to the building next door. He stooped by the metal double doors that held the wiring for the antenna's receiver.

The tall tower sprouted straight up from the roof of the metal pyramid. A highly-tuned receiving unit collected waves that reflected from the surface of the immense dish. It could pick up even the faintest of distant sounds and distinguish what they were through a collection of sophisticated vacuum-tube electronics stored in the nearby building. This information was then relayed to other stations along the chain and ultimately to a quick-response base located in Fairbanks.

Picking a simple padlock was easy, but not at minus ten in the wind. Popov finally heard the click as the hasp gave way. He quickly opened the doors and climbed inside. Tatter kept watch from just outside.

Popov pulled off his mittens and rubbed his hands together trying to bring them back to functionality. He clicked on his flashlight with the red lens to protect his night vision. Popov selected one of the gray boxes from his bag and began the process of installing it between the receiving console and the output cable. He stood on top of the radio box and unscrewed the twenty-eight-wire-pin coupling that attached the antenna to the console. He quickly inspected the pin configuration and admired the level of intel they were working from. Satisfied they were a match, he reattached each end of the connector to the electrical leach and hid the whole thing in a mass of wires that ran back to the receiver.

He climbed down to the floor and sat next to a console, and pulled out his portable battery-operated oscilloscope, a marvel of modern technology. He connected it to the wires leading to the transmitter and hit the selector knob. The signal coming into the unit showed a strong, consistent, cycling green wave, like a never-ending snake. Popov then flipped a switch on the scope and the same sine wave now had a small but definite spike on the upper arch of each wave. Satisfied that his job here was done, he packed up his equipment and left the compartment.

The squad met up back in the domed tent. Misha's body lay wrapped in a tarp off to one side, a sharp reminder of what was at stake for them all. Tolya knelt next to the body. He pulled back the tarp. A stone stared back at him. His friend was no longer human. The cold had claimed him. It would probably take them all before this job was done.

Tolya bowed his head in deep respect, thinking, "Of all the unlucky..." He stopped this train of thought, as it would do him no good. He slipped the red and gold medal with the profile of Vladimir Lenin from his pocket and held it in his hand. He whispered, "You deserve this more than I, Misha." He slipped his Order of Lenin medal into Misha's breast pocket, touched the dead soldier's face for a brief moment, and finally pulled the tarp back over his head.

"Comrade Alexeev," the political officer stepped towards Tolya, attempting to engage him.

"It's *Colonel* Alexeev." Tolya put his hand up to stop him from continuing. "And we can discuss this later."

Tolya turned to the whole team, and said, "I want everything packed up now. We must be miles from here when they find that body. We leave in ten."

Tolya looked to the now-stationary Zampolit Traktor Yashin, his face betraying the challenge he had intended for Tolya. "You best get a move on, 'Comrade,'" he said. "This is a bad place to be left behind." With that, he turned his back on Traktor and went to grab his gear.

"Colonel, what do we do with Misha?" Private Tatter asked.

"We bring him with us. No evidence of any kind gets left behind."

"Understood, sir."

The whiteout was complete. Snow, clouds, and wind mixed together against the black of night. Tolya reconfigured his parka for the third time in an attempt to block out the cold. The squad pushed against the merciless gale, their quick march doing little to maintain core temperature. And after six hours battling the harsh conditions it was taking its toll. Tolya could no longer feel his extremities.

The group had slowed, moving at about forty percent of their original pace. All except for Chikuk. He looked like he was just getting started. They had over twenty miles still to go and less than forty-eight hours to do it in. It was an impossible task. Tolya gave them a thirty percent chance of success. They were poor odds, but based on their situation and what was at stake, he would take them.

Sergeant Kazimir Yegor scooted next to Tolya and pointed a small flashlight covered with a red lens at his compass. "It says we need to go in this direction."

Tolya glanced down at the needle pointing off to his left.

"This far north the declination could be as much as seventy degrees off, Kaz. I recommend continuing up this grade." He pointed towards what looked like the beginning of a hill where, just visible through the gloom, was Chikuk.

"Just keep the wind on your left," said Tolya. "It's better than a compass up here."

Kaz nodded and returned the compass to his pocket.

Tatter abruptly appeared from out of the gloom, pulling a small sled with Misha's body, his red flashlight barely illuminating the ground around him. He bent at the waist trying to catch his breath. He wore a grim expression.

Chikuk, who carried no flashlight, suddenly returned. "We need to go around," Chikuk said. "Sludge ice ahead, very dangerous."

Traktor piped up. "What's sludge ice?"

Tolya looked to the political officer and said, "I don't know, and I don't want to know." Turning back to Tatter, he said, "Do what Chikuk says."

Tolya looked at his wristwatch and did a quick calculation in his head. "We have about two hours left before sunrise. And stay together. Do not lose sight of the man in front of you."

The team moved northwest in an attempt to skirt the problem that lay ahead, sludge ice. Each step was now labored as they moved against the heartless arctic wind.

"Comrade Alexeev."

Tolya kept marching, his eyes fixed on Tatter five meters in front of him, nothing more than a fuzzy red shape.

"Comrade Alexeev!" Zampolit Traktor Yashin ran forward, now matching his stride, huffing with desperation.

Tolya gave him the briefest of glances. "What do you need, Political Officer Yashin?"

"This is madness. We need to stop. My hands, the pain."

Tolya could tell the man was struggling, but had no sympathy for a government stooge.

"I'll decide when we stop. Let me know if the pain stops. That's when you need to worry."

"No mission is worth a man's life, comrade."

"Tell that to your uncle." Tolya glanced at the man.

Traktor fought for every breath. "He sent us here to get a leg up on the Americans, not to die on their soil and create an international incident."

Tolya trudged on mechanically. Finally, he stopped and turned to Traktor, freezing him in his steps. "Comrade, I have no plans to die here, but if you do, I'll be sure to put you on a sled and bring you back to your family."

Traktor stiffened. "You know I have orders to kill anyone who even looks at the Americans with envy."

Tolya let the comment sit for a second, continuing to move

forward. "Is that so? Well, I have orders to kill anyone who interferes with this mission, and right now that's *you.*" The wind howled, emphasizing that last word.

Tolya continued on, then looked back over his shoulder and called, "Besides, what do the Americans have to envy? More money than sense if they are wasting it on this silly endeavor. They will surely lose in the end."

The colonel stopped and looked straight at Traktor. "Zampolit Traktor Yashin, please get back in line before I put a bullet in your head. Oh, and please remember to put all this in your little report."

Traktor straightened and looked at Tolya with black eyes that could kill. He slowly reached for his pocket.

"Please try it," Tolya said.

Tolya shot a furtive glance just beyond Traktor, which made Traktor look over. Walking just off to his side was Kaz, and in his hand was a large pistol pointed straight at the Political Officer's spine.

"Now get your ass back in line, 'Comrade.'"

Traktor remained defiant and unmoving as he watched Tolya turn his back and disappear into the night.

Anger flushed Traktor's frostbitten face, focusing him to a single conclusion. This mission was doomed under the command of Colonel Tolya Alexeev. The arrogant ass was going to get them all killed. What Operation Blind Pig needed was the finesse and cunning of a man like himself. Not some blunt-nosed instrument like Tolya.

It was his duty to Mother Russia to remove that swine from command. He pondered at several possibilities, each ending up with the death of Colonel Tolya Alexeev. This made him smile as he savored the feeling, slowly lowering his pulsing blood pressure.

Traktor looked up. There was no one ahead in the gloom. Nothing but the unbroken parade of clouds as they whisked past the meager glow of his red-lensed flashlight. They seemed to be in a foolish hurry to some unknown destination. He blinked the frost from his eyes and spun behind him. No one behind him. Panic began to crawl up his spine as uncontrollable shivers set in. He called out several times, but only the lonely call of a howling wind replied. It seemed to laugh and mock him with its high-pitched scream. He looked to the frozen ground, but the blowing snow had erased any footsteps. How long had he been standing there thinking of Tolya's demise?

Traktor ran forward, shouting, "Comrades!"

Again, his words were grabbed and pulled away by the gale. He continued blindly forward as he pulled out his hand compass. It pointed off to his right. He adjusted accordingly and quickly trudged forward. As he moved he noticed a change in the ice. It had taken on a honey-like consistency. He continued through it, his rubberized boots temporarily holding the wetness at bay.

Then, for a brief moment, the blowing clouds parted and visibility jumped to nearly a thousand meters. A pool of moonlight speared what looked like the edge of a small shallow inlet in front of him. On the other side of the inlet was the red glow of his team's flashlights. The surface of the inlet was greasy in appearance, not solid. He screamed for all he was worth but the team continued on, unaware.

Traktor pulled his pistol out and raised it in the air. Then, remembering their strict orders about gunplay, he put it away. He quickly started moving through the slushy water around the shallow inlet to catch up with his team. It was only about twelve inches deep and his boots were holding up just fine. The Eskimo was an idiot. The political officer was saving significant distance by going this way. All he had to do was catch up before the whiteout returned.

Just as quickly as the team had appeared, the indifferent clouds once again swallowed them up. Traktor sloshed though the slushy conditions as fast as his legs would carry him. A surge of sudden adrenaline briefly warmed his core as he redoubled his efforts. He would not be left behind.

A sound like cracking ice came from behind him, spurring him on. Suddenly, the sound came from all around him. The slush began freezing at an alarming rate. Zampolit Traktor Yashin felt bile and fear stab at his guts. He panicked and sprinted for the shoreline. Then, like a shadow of a bird passing overhead, the slush transitioned from a semi-liquid to a solid. In an instant, Traktor was snared mid-calf, both legs gripped solidly by the ice. He tried to move, but he was caught like a fly in amber.

He thrashed wildly but his lower legs held firm in the grasp of the freeze. The cold fought through the layers of his clothing seeking warm skin. He screamed and pulled his Tokarev TT-30 from its holster with swollen, numb fingers. He emptied the magazine in the direction he had last seen the squad, secrecy be damned.

Tolya put his hand to his mouth and gave a quick whistle. The action caused a blast of pain across his cracked lips. The squad came to a stop and gathered together.

"Do you hear that?" he asked.

In the distance a faint clap of thunder popped. Kaz lifted his head. "Is that gunfire?" he said.

"Colonel!" Engineer Marshal Sergei Popov stepped over to

the group looking around. "Political Leader Traktor Yashin is missing."

"How is that possible?" Tolya asked Popov.

"I was just following the man in front of me and…"

Before he could finish, Tolya backhanded him across the face, dropping the man like a sack of rotted meat. Being new to Tolya's team, Engineer Popov didn't know his commander's dislike for excuses. In his squad you owned up to your mistakes.

"Form a search grid from right here, two by two," Tolya said. "Tatter, Chikuk, grid one." Tolya pointed in the direction they should search.

"Kaz, Popov, grid two. Be back here in ten minutes. Then we'll move to the next sections."

The men ran off, side by side, searching their quadrant. Tolya, as the anchor person could only pace and wait, muttering to himself, "Damn it, we don't have time for this." He looked down at the tarp that held Misha's body. The cost of this mission was already too high.

Traktor sat down on the now hard surface of the inlet. He processed his predicament. Luckily, he was actually feeling warm so he didn't have to worry about the cold anymore. He took out his knife and started chipping away at the ice that held his feet. As he worked, he felt his body get hot. He took off his parka so he could move more freely.

One leg was almost free; he could see the top of his shoe through the ice. He stifled a yawn; he was tired. This had been an arduous journey. After a short rest, he would start back up. He lay back on the ice and rested his eyes for just a moment. His hands felt too warm so he took off his gloves. *Ah, better.*

He thought of his summers back in Dzhubga, along the

Black Sea. It was a small town formed by Cossacks in the 1860's, and it was his family's favorite getaway. They had a small birch cabin on a hill that had the most incredible sunset views. He could picture the orange glow across the dark water as his mother and father sat side by side on a carved bench sharing tea as black as the ocean at midnight. He would run through the woods and pick wildflowers for the table. His mother was always so proud of him.

Traktor had an odd thought... *sludge ice very dangerous,* before drifting off.

After the second grid search, Chikuk and Tatter returned with the news. They had found their political officer.

Tolya looked down at their missing team member, lying on his back frozen solid. His feet were still trapped in the ice; his parka, gloves, and hat were off to the side.

Kaz mumbled, "Paradoxical undressing, one of the last signs of hypothermia."

Tatter looked confused, but he couldn't take his eyes off of the frozen man on the ice.

Kaz looked up at the boy and continued. "You think you're warm so you take off your clothes."

An awkward silence hung in the mourning wind. Tolya broke it. "Get him out of there."

Kaz looked at the Traktor's trapped legs. "What about his feet?"

"Cut 'em off. We've wasted enough time here." Tolya turned and walked away. He should have pushed the man overboard when he had the chance. Now they would have to drag two bodies with them.

Chikuk took out an ice saw and started on Traktor's left leg.

Two frozen corpses now rested outside the domed tent. They spoke volumes of the morale inside. Tolya sat with his hands to his head trying to relieve a headache that started back in fifty-six. The flap on the tent popped open and Chikuk and Popov entered. They had made camp just before dawn and managed to navigate within a mile of the next installation. All they had left to do was to insert the second electrical leach and evacuate off the island. The never-ending storm had taken its toll on the team, but had also made them invisible to the enemy. Every member was suffering from frostbite and exposure. The black skin on their appendages told of a future without those body parts, but going in they all knew what was at stake.

Tolya massaged his temples as his mind drifted back to Hungary where a T-55 battle tank rolled over bodies lying in the street like stacked cordwood. Sergeant Tolya Alexeev kept his men in tight cover behind the metal beast as it crunched along, pressing its advantage against the poorly armed resistance. His boots made a sucking noise as they slogged through the masticated gore left in the tank's tracks.

Moscow had changed its mind, and in an onslaught of overwhelming superiority had invaded Budapest to crush the Hungarian revolution. Nearly twenty thousand people had been killed so far and the number was rising.

Soviet soldiers were killing wounded civilians, and the atrocities were growing as many commanders turned a blind eye to their soldiers' actions. Some tanks were dragging the dead behind them as warnings to those still protesting. But Tolya had other thoughts on his mind. His OBSP team had been tasked with a very specific mission. Get to Prime Minister Imre Nagy and capture him alive if at all possible. Tolya knew that the powers back in Moscow wanted to make the Prime Minister's demise a very public event.

He tapped three times on the back of the tank's heavy armor plating with the hilt of his dagger. The tank turret spun to the command as bullets hopelessly pinged off its steel shell. The eighty-millimeter canon fired a shell at the heavily fortified entrance to the capital building. In an instant, the twelve armed men and mountain of sand bags blocking the entrance were gone. Tolya and his men dashed through the blood-spattered doors hanging loosely on shattered hinges. Bodies and parts were everywhere as poorly armed civilians had tried to protect the building. Inside, it was worse. Secretaries and paper pushers were willing to die, oftentimes with nothing but a coat rack or file drawer as a weapon.

Tolya's men made quick work of the hurdle as they moved room to room on their way to the top office. The lopsided battle finally ended with a very brave but stupid charge of eight men in suits wielding pistols. Tolya could take no more. He paused as his men and their Rexim-Favor submachine guns quickly shredded the small force, leaving nothing but carnage and moans.

Tolya sat up in a sweat, his eyes blinking the sight away. Breathing heavily, he remembered the moment he was forced to stand proud as he received his medal, The Order of Lenin, from Defense Minister Marshal Zhukov for delivering the Hungarian Prime Minister. That was nearly a year ago. It had launched his career like a three-stage rocket. Now he was here on American soil expected to do the impossible. And so far, he had.

He glanced at his Smersh watch, the radium hands ticking with a carefree precision. It was time.

The next infiltration into the American's station went much smoother. Popov had installed the electrical leach with the same exacting results—a specific spike in an otherwise perfect sine wave. They re-gathered at the dome tent, mission complete. All that was left now was to make one last push to the coast and evac. On the backside of Umnak Island, basalt rock gave way to large sections of snow-covered tundra and a small glacier that calved into the sea beyond. The plan was to exfil across the glacier and rendezvous with an old steel trawler that had been busy fishing and shadowing their movements from beyond five miles out to sea.

Kaz had tried to reach their shadow over the radio, but so far no reply. It made little difference to Tolya as their options were limited, to say the least.

All evidence was to be taken along, leaving only footprints behind to dissolve away in the snow flurries.

The wind subsided and the temperature rose to just below freezing as the beleaguered squad reached the coast five miles southeast of station DEW LRR Site 41. They had trekked a remarkable seventy-eight miles over the course of three days in some of the most brutal conditions on the planet. Truly a remarkable feat. Now, if they could just finish.

Kaz, while holding his headphones close to his ears, reached up with his other hand and waved it in the air. The radio had made contact. The remaining team leaned over to hear the one-sided conversation.

"Roger that, rendezvous oh fourteen hundred Walrus Bay," Kaz said. "That's a little tight for us..." And finally, "Understood."

Kaz put down the transmitter. "Another storm is coming. It's now or never."

Tolya glanced at his watch and calculated the remaining time: three hours. The arctic dash to the rendezvous site was taking too long. With the gear and the two bodies it was a struggle, and there was no way to bury the bodies and some of the gear, as the ground was rock hard. They were out of time.

Chikuk guided them at a brisk pace while pulling Misha's corpse. The man seemed impervious to the conditions and the weight of his load. Across the glacier was the most direct route to make their connection, but it was fraught with danger.

Tolya placed his hands on his knees as he huffed to catch his breath. The men were spent. The quick march to the coast had cost them all their remaining energy. The team would have to dig deep if any of them were to escape.

Chikuk gestured for them to go around the five-mile-long glacier, but that option died with the ticking clock.

"There's no time left, we go straight through," Tolya said.

Everyone knew the risks of crossing a glacier, but doing it in a hurry was madness. It was the Arctic's version of Russian roulette. Glaciers were constantly-moving creatures that had a way of cracking open into deep chasms hundreds of feet deep and then closing back up just as fast. And when the surface was covered with snow, there was no way of spotting the dangers below without using extreme caution, which meant taking extra time.

Tolya didn't wait. After catching his breath, he jogged with his heavy load out onto the moving ice field. The rest of the team hesitated but then followed behind. Tolya called behind him, "Follow my tracks!" He figured that if something happened, at least they could learn from his error. The cove, just six hundred yards on the other side, was their destination.

A scream died in the wind as a crack and rumble shook the ground. Tolya looked back and did a quick head count. Kaz was missing. He ran back to investigate.

One hundred feet below in a narrow ice chasm lay the crushed body of Kaz. His folded remains were illuminated by impossibly blue ice that lived at the heart of the glacier.

Kaz had followed Tolya's footsteps but the snow that had covered the chasm had given way under his load.

With no possibility of getting down to him, Tolya made the only choice he could to save the rest. "Everything over the side."

The men stared numbly.

"Move it!"

They pushed all that they were carrying over the ledge and down into the ice crevasse. Tolya moved to Tatter and put his gloved hand on his shoulder.

"Even them." He gestured to the corpses. "Hurry now, private."

The men, as reverently as possible dropped the two wrapped bodies into the crack. The wind sang a sad hymn as they stared down at the jumble of bodies and gear lying in the bottom of the gap.

"Now run!"

Chikuk watched as the small group of men ran recklessly across the uneven surface. He removed his glove and reached into his pocket. He pulled out the small pebble he had collected when they first came ashore. "Thank you for keeping us all safe," he said. He bent to the ground and carefully placed it down on the ice. "It is finished."

Three desperate men sprinted across the rest of the glacier without incident. Once on the other side Tolya paused to take in his crew. They were a mess. Tatter's nose was black with frostbite, and Popov was running stiff legged. He was probably going to lose his feet to the cold.

He waited, but there was no Chikuk.

Tolya called to Tatter, "Where's Chikuk?"

"He left."

Tolya looked confused. "What do you mean?"

"I mean, he waved at me, turned, and disappeared into the

storm." To himself, he muttered, "I guess he decided to move to America after all."

Tolya stared off into the distance, a view that included every possible shade of white. "We're done with him anyway," he said. "Come on."

The three men climbed down the embankment towards the cove. From out of the gray gloom came a black rubber raft puttering to shore. Tolya took a shallow breath of the arctic air. This mission, though critical to his superiors, had been costly. In the end, he could only hope that the evidence they had left behind would never come to light. Three of them, against all odds, had made it. Honestly, he was surprised.

3

CHERSKY, SIBERIA – 7:31 P.M.
– TWO WEEKS LATER

The Tupolev TU-16 Badger accelerated down the unmarked runway outside Chersky, Siberia. It was a cold but clear night with nothing but good news for the weather that lay ahead.

Radioman First Class Vaughn Pankiv, who everyone called Panky, warmed his hands with the heat generated by the vacuum tube radio in the aft cabin. He was a scruffy man in appearance and attitude, with large ears and a squared chin. The tiny room buzzed with an electrical hum competing in volume with the two large Mikulin AM-3 turbojets' roar.

Sitting in the forward cabin in nylon-mesh seats were Doctor Grigory Nepein and his demure, nervous male assistant, Shura Mosin.

Grigory was the genius behind Operation Blind Pig. He had spent the last three years developing a counter to the Americans' defensive string of early warning radar stations across the Arctic. And the result was the GN01, a transmitter capable of sending out a very specific signal. He was one of the Soviet's best and most guarded secrets. His heavy brows and obsidian eyes were so intense that the average person often found themselves looking away rather than at the man during a conversation.

With the apparent success of the ground mission, all that was left was for him to test the GN01 transmitter. Grigory had spent most of his life at his well-stocked lab, having little contact with the outside world. The lifestyle suited him well. Five years ago, he had lost his wife during childbirth, and now his work was all he had to keep him warm in the cold Russian nights.

As with most governments, the Soviets demanded progress from their science divisions. They had been patient with Grigory, but it was now time for him to prove his worth. He was personally going to show them what a true electrical intellect could do. Success would mean unlimited resources and possibly a little more freedom to pursue his other pet projects.

His assistant, Shura Mosin, was busy with three boxes of electrical equipment stacked nearly to the ceiling. Red and green lights blinked in a systematized array as he went through a precise checklist mounted to his clipboard. Shura was the son of Polish parents who, early on, found a place for their son's exceptional intellect and had used it to better their own stations in life. His round thick glasses and perfectly parted hair contributed to his intellectual look. The flight suit they had assigned to him hung loosely on his small frame, as though he had borrowed it from a big brother. But the man was so task oriented he didn't even notice. He leaned to his left trying for a more comfortable position that would work with the Makarov in his back pocket. It was loaded with specialty ammunition deemed safe for use aboard airplanes. The minister had personally given it to him with explicit instructions to shoot Grigory in the head should anything go wrong. There was no way they could risk him being captured, should the plane go down on American soil. Shura had taken on the task like he did everything in his life, with a scientific coolness.

The skies remained clear, and the first taste of dusk was

still two hours away. The TU-16 was a cigar-shaped long-range bomber that could reach speeds of 990 kph with a range of 58,000 kilometers, the pride of Soviet bombers.

It had a large cockpit and three cabins, each the size of a small shed, running in parallel from front to back. The bomb bay could hold two nuclear weapons and deploy them both at once or one at a time, depending on the requirements of the mission. The cockpit sat on top of a bulbous nose that gave the plane its unique look and nickname, Badger.

Captain Yana Shchavelsky leveled off and set their course for ninety degrees due east. "Attention: radio silence from here on out. We have approximately," he looked at his watch and calculated speed, distance and headwinds in his head, "three-and-a-half hours to target."

The captain was a large man with even larger hands. He double-checked all the gauges. Yana's natural instinct to always plan for the worst had served him well on over fifty sorties of this type. To him, this mission was nothing more than business as usual. But the higher-ups had seemed unusually paranoid, calling it off twice before giving the final go-ahead.

Yana looked over at his first officer, a man named Toma Fukin. He was busy at his station and was certainly competent enough. "Toma, take the controls." As he turned the controls over to the co-pilot, he whipped out a dog-eared book that he had been working through, and picked up where he had left off. Toma smiled at his captain; this was a regular occurrence.

"So did she kill him or was she framed?" Fukin asked.

Without looking up, Yana answered, "I will happily loan you the book when I'm done."

"Who has the time to read these days?"

Yana gave his co-pilot a sideways glance and shook his head. *Oh the youth of today.*

This particular Tupolev bomber had been modified. The

standard, somewhat prominent nose cone had been replaced with a concave transmitting dish covered with a Plexiglass cone to protect the bomber's aeronautics. Attached to the dish was a thick braid of wires leading to the forward cabin.

Doctor Grigory Nepein wiped the sweat from his face and readjusted the wispy blond hairs that occupied parts of his scalp. In spite of the outside temperature of well below freezing, the electronics in the cabin radiated heat like a furnace. All systems had checked out and there was nothing left to do but wait. But this was not the doctor's way. So he did a double-check for the third time, running through every possible scenario, just to be sure. He knew failure would most likely result in his death and possibly global war. Everything had to be perfect, as well as himself and every crewman aboard.

"Shura, let's run the sequence again."

"Fifteen minutes to target," was broadcast throughout the cabin in an impassive female voice. The navigator, Natasha Zykin, was a highly decorated officer, with the most flights of anyone on the jet. The Soviet Union had many females in key positions throughout their military machine. Seldom were they given command, but many excelled beyond their male counterparts.

Natasha had proven herself extremely competent, and that information had leaked up the chain of command. It won her a place on Captain Shchavelsky's crew. The captain, though a bit protective of her, was always impressed with her dead-on navigation skills. She never faltered.

She was a short woman with a curvaceous figure and an ever-present smile. Her curly auburn hair was kept short. A smattering of freckles was the source of the nickname she had very slowly come to accept, Nushki.

Two years previously she managed to keep a mission on course in spite of a hurricane-level storm and a lightning strike that caused a complete electrical failure on the plane. The crew panicked and assumed the worst. But when the clouds parted to reveal the runway, she was declared a hero.

She scratched absently at the nape of her neck as she buried her face into the green glow of the radar screen in front of her. The scope's spinning light saber swept the grid-patterned screen with mechanical repetition. Nushki picked up the mic and spoke without looking at a small metal chessboard that was attached to the wall next to her with magnetic chess pieces strategically placed. "Bishop to queen three."

Panky looked at an identical board in the aft radio room. He moved the white bishop and pondered. He tentatively moved his black castle. "Castle to pawn three."

Captain Shchavelsky put his book away and took the stick. "Toma, I'll take her from here."

First Officer Toma Fukin relinquished control. He was starting to feel the tension in the air as they drew close to their primary target. "Yes, sir. You have control."

The captain looked out at the vast sky beyond. "American airspace… Well, this is a first."

Toma swallowed hard and squeaked out, "Yes, sir." Get ahold of yourself, he mouthed with mock bravery.

In the radio room, Panky reached over and flicked several switches. "Powering down the radio and radar," he announced.

"Roger that, radio and radar powering down," came a reply from the co-pilot.

"Resetting speed and altitude, Doc. It's all in your hands now," the captain said.

Panky looked back at the board and concentrated.

"Pawn to castle four," Nushki called from the cabin next to his.

He nodded at her play and moved the piece.

The captain pulled the throttle lever and adjusted the flaps as he spoke to the copilot directly. "I sure hope they know what the hell they're doing back there," he said to Fukin. He gestured with his head to the two scientists in the cabin behind them. "Or this is going to be a real short trip that ends in a ball of fire."

They shared a concerned look but moved past it, focusing on their duties.

The TU-16 decreased its altitude to 10,000 meters and slowed to 750 kph. There was more turbulence at this altitude, but the height and speed were critical for the success of the mission. The captain had flown this route many times, but had always turned around at the 190th parallel while still over international waters.

This operation was as black as they got and he only hoped they would live through it. The pride and brilliance of the Soviet Union was at stake and he would make damn sure to fulfill his role.

"Five minutes to American airspace," Nushki broadcast. She was feeling the tension grow with every mile.

"Disconnect transponder," said the captain.

Panky followed his orders. There was no going back now.

"Queen to bishop four. Queen takes knight," Panky called out. He smiled as he took Nushki's knight.

Nushki moved the corresponding pieces and called out over her shoulder. "You're getting reckless, Panky."

Panky rubbed his fingers together in an anxious fashion. Even the plane seemed nervous as it bucked and trembled trying to shove through the subzero air.

Grigory pushed a small green button on a metal console and glanced to his assistant for reassurance. A signal traveled at lightspeed to the dish in the nose of the jet. The dish amplified the signal and broadcast a very specific high-powered frequency to the world ahead.

Shura nodded timidly while readjusting his glasses on his sweaty face. "CCI is broadcasting," he croaked.

CCI was the Russian acronym for Focused Frequency Emitter. Grigory pushed the intercom and announced, "Captain, maintain this heading and airspeed. We are broadcasting."

The captain confirmed the information and then snapped his oxygen mask into place. Toma followed his lead.

The Tupolev bounced, then settled, as it held its new bearing. Nushki, while keeping her head buried in the optics of a slightly forward magnified view of the ground below, began the countdown. "Two minutes to target."

Toma and the captain could see the outline of an ice-covered island approaching in the distance.

Shura answered with, "Signal strong and steady."

Grigory rubbed his hands against his pants in an unconscious circle. He stared at the lights on his console—all green. Theoretically, the plane's broadcast frequency, in concert with the planted electrical leaches' specific frequency filter, would blind the two radar installations below to their approach.

Grigory had built a full-scale replica of the Americans' radar station based on plans smuggled out of General Electric, the company that had won the contract to build the DEW Line radar stations across the Arctic. The replica had been tested and retested against his CCI unit and leach, until Moscow was satisfied.

"Sir, I see the target now," Nushki announced.

Everyone held his or her collective breaths as the bomber passed overhead. Through her field of view Nushki watched as the shadowy silhouette of Umnak Island passed underneath.

She could just make out the Americans' gray radar installation set against the snow below.

"Passing target now."

The building fled from view.

"Target passed."

She looked up from her scope and tried to swallow, but her throat was dry. They were through, but had they been detected?

Doctor Grigory Nepein allowed the breath he had been holding to release. "Captain," he said, "you can return to our normal altitude and speed." He flicked off the green button and sat back in his seat, barely hearing the words the captain spoke in return.

"Copy that, Doc. Let's hope your little gadget worked. Nushki, set a course for our next target, and Panky, you can turn the radio back on. I want to know if you hear anything."

The navigator consulted her chart and worked out their next bearing. "Roger that, sir; course nine eight degrees, Seattle," Nushki said.

Panky returned the power to the units and concentrated on his headphones. "No contacts, sir."

"Let's hope it stays that way," the captain said to himself. "Panky, let me know if you see so much as a gnat coming our way."

Grigory leaned back and put his hands behind his head. If he had done everything right they should be completely unseen in the American airspace. Grigory allowed a rare smile to form; it had been a long time coming. With this successful test he would be a household name in the Kremlin. Good things were to come, perhaps even a summer cottage on the Black Sea.

"Target distance, ten miles," Navigator Nushki announced.

The captain repeated the information and squinted ahead

through the hazy atmosphere as the skyline of Seattle slowly grew. A sequence of events started to unfold as the crew went through the final preparations to drop their bomb.

"Ready for final bomb check."

"Final bomb check."

"Bomb fusing master safety on."

"Fusing master safety on."

"Target distance, seven miles."

The sequence continued like a well-choreographed dance, each playing their part in time with the other. At the same time the chess game between navigator Nushki and radio/bombardier Panky continued.

The young Shura Mosin removed his glasses and rubbed the lenses on his sleeve. He was no longer involved in the current mission. "Professor," he said to Grigory, "I was thinking we might be able to use the CCI technology for other applications."

"I see you have been reading my book, Shura." Grigory focused on his assistant. "What did you have in mind?"

Shura broke eye contact with his boss, now unsure of his idea. "If there was a way to remotely implant the filter without actually being there."

Grigory wrinkled his forehead at his assistant's idea. The voice over the speaker interrupted his thoughts.

"Target distance five miles."

"Open bomb doors."

Grigory held up his hand to pause Shura's words, his interest piqued but not above the current action. "Perhaps we can talk about it after we have a successful test here."

Shura fingered the gun in his pocket while he nodded.

"I have visual on the scope," Nushki announced as she began a countdown.

The TU-16 buffed slightly, then smoothed out. Everyone

was at the ready. This was what the months of training was all about, right now, this instant. Time seemed to slow for the crew as they neared the drop point. Even the sound of the roaring turbines seemed to fade away.

Then, in a clear and precise voice, Nushki called, "Release bomb."

Panky answered. "Bomb away."

As Captain Yana Shchavelsky heard those last words, he put the bomber into a hard 180-degree turn. "Let's get the *suka blyad* out of here."

Nushki watched on the aiming scope as a large metal-cased bomb dropped, ultimately making contact with the sea some quarter-mile from the city. And harmlessly sinking from sight. Seconds ticked by and still nothing happened.

"Well, Doc," the captain said, "looks like you have your proof of concept. Radar screen evaded and test bomb run successful."

"Thank you, Captain. Excellent crew you have here."

He had to agree. They had all done a great job—so far.

"Now get us back home safely so we can tell someone about it."

"Roger that," the captain replied.

Everyone stayed alert and at the top of their game as the TU-16 reversed its course and moved back through the radar gap they had created in the DEW Line. Once again the CCI had performed perfectly, and they left US airspace without consequence.

Once over international waters, Nushki worked her way to the cockpit and popped the cork on a bottle of champagne she had brought along. "Captain, do I have your permission to pour?"

Captain Shchavelsky glanced over his shoulder. "I don't think one bottle divided by six will hurt. Please do the honors, Nushki."

Nushki made the rounds for all to share. Even the doctor was in a celebratory mood. The morale was high and they were all feeling invincible. After all, they had duped the Americans' radar defenses and even dropped a practice nuclear bomb on their doorstep. All without the capitalist pigs even knowing. It was a good day for the Soviet Union.

Nushki made her way to the aft cabin and handed Panky the nearly empty bottle. "All yours."

He grabbed it and pointed to the chessboard on his wall. "Castle to king five."

Panky guzzled the remainder of the bottle. Nushki looked at his move and then a broad smile spread across her face. "Bishop to rook six. Checkmate."

Panky spit out the remaining champagne and stared at the board, his mouth agape. Nushki smiled and returned to her seat in the next cabin. She looked down at the simple red star with the crossed gold hammer and sickle on her uniform. Had she made the right decision? It was too late now.

Within five minutes the plane seemed to wander. She glanced in the aft cabin at Panky doubled over in his chair motionless. Nushki quickly moved past Doctor Grigory Nepein and his assistant, both unmoving in their chairs. Once in the cockpit she struggled to remove Captain Yana Shchavelsky from his seat, his dead weight making it a real chore. She ended up grabbing his hair to get a good hold and heaved. Once he was on the floor, she sat in his seat and belted herself in. The freckle-faced navigator would no longer suffer the stupidity of men. She said goodbye to her long hated nickname and said softly, "Captain Natasha Zykin."

She looked around one last time and pushed the control stick forward, dropping the bomber into a steep dive straight for the Bering Sea.

4

PRESENT DAY – Washington D.C. – 12:57 p.m. – FBI Headquarters – 5th Floor

Special Agent Collette Sanders, Codi, flowed with a sea of bodies exiting the glass doors of a large meeting room. She moved away from the stale air and bad cologne. Her insipid expression clung to her like a sloth gripping a wobbly branch. She was wearing a white blouse and matching navy pants and jacket. She glanced down at the pamphlet in her hands, *FBI Rules and Regulations—The Do's & Don'ts of Social Media*. It had been three painfully long hours that she would never get back.

For Codi, social media was easy—don't say anything about your work to others, ever.

And when it came to her personal life—don't post anything while drinking or that your mom wouldn't approve of, well, most moms, anyway. The fact that some idiot agents had recently posted a picture of themselves next to a mutilated body on an ongoing investigation had the entire FBI in panicked damage control. Now, every agent and employee was required to take this course. It was always that way, she thought. A few imbeciles ruin it for the rest of us. She deposited the pamphlet into the nearest circular file and headed for the exit.

She checked the time on her phone—perfect—just enough time to eat and change.

At five-foot-eight, Codi could hold her own with most men. She was an avid swimmer and took physical fitness seriously. She had even competed in college in both relay and as an individual.

After several career side trips, Codi accepted a position at the General Services Administration, or GSA, as a federal agent. She handled cold cases involving fraud and tax evasion, effectively a paper-pushing cop. She embraced the job with fervor and quickly got the attention of her superior, Director Ruth Anne Gables, a politically connected strong leader who took Codi under her wing. She pushed Codi when needed and supported her when there was trouble.

Codi was assigned to work with Agent Joel Strickman, a computer savvy agent with a heart of gold. His wiry frame and unkempt blond hair framed his normally positive curiosity for life. They had found success bringing to justice several individuals who had defrauded the US government. But it took a cold case from the forties to really test them. It had started benign enough but quickly escalated to international implications and ultimately global terror. It pushed Codi to her breaking point, unleashing her full potential. She fought through the impossible to stop a madman bent on global destruction.

It seemed that the harder one pushed her, the harder she pushed back. It wasn't stubbornness but determination born of a confidence her father had instilled in her at a young age. In the end, she was credited with saving hundreds of thousands of lives.

The case got her noticed at the FBI, and now she found herself about to go to work for the special projects division as a special agent. For Codi, her career was back on track, but her personal life was still a mixed bag.

She looked at her phone hoping for a text from Matt, Dr. Matt Campbell, a man whom Codi had become involved with on her last case. Twice, they had nearly died at the hands of that madman, but the resulting stress had formed a bond that was stronger than either was willing to admit.

After the case, they had spent nearly a month together convalescing. During that time Codi and Matt had time to heal their physical wounds and discover a love neither was expecting. Eventually, work pulled them in different directions, becoming the norm that stunted the growth of the relationship and left little time for maintenance.

Matt was away in some remote lab up near Boston. At first, the work limited his ability to reach out. Later, his compulsion to finish what he had started became all-consuming, taking over his life. Ultimately, they had a hard time connecting, with voicemails and texts often slow to return. With each passing week the fire between them dimmed. Codi bit back on her emotions as she pushed her phone back in its hip holder. She knew Matt loved her, but careers and relationships always seemed to be at odds, and this was no different.

She took one last look at her old office at the GSA as she turned out the lights for the last time. The General Services Administration had been the place where Codi found her moxie again. After a bout with depression and a downward spiral in her life, she had rediscovered her strength right here on the second floor.

She would never forget her boss, Ruth Anne Gables, the woman who had pushed her and encouraged her to be her best.

She flicked her shoulder-length brown hair and turned her trim figure out of the office door. She moved down the narrow hallway with a languid stride, just in time to see her partner, Agent Joel Strickman, come out of his former office.

He was holding three cardboard boxes precariously. He had his phone in his mouth and was trying to close the door with his foot.

"Need some help?" she asked.

"Codi. Hi. Sure," he mumbled through lips pressed against his cell.

She reached up and took the phone from his mouth and continued down the hallway. Joel looked over his stack of boxes, at her receding form. She wore black patterned fitness leggings and a casual white tee shirt that read, *Bloody Difficult Woman.* But her movement is what he noticed most—athletic, like a cat on the prowl. A beautiful cat. One that intimidated the hell out of him.

"Thanks, I guess," he said.

She glanced back with a smirk. "Hey, somebody's gotta hold the door open. Come on."

Joel hurried to catch up to her, his black wingtips tapping loudly on the marble floor. He used a corner of the top box to push his black-framed glasses back in place. Joel was computer savvy but his social skills were another thing. It was all topped off with a healthy dash of germaphobia. None of that mattered to Codi because Joel was one-hundred-percent trustworthy and loyal. That was a rare commodity in this world that made for an unbreakable bond.

Joel's expertise fell more to the technological side of their partnership. He had proven a solid performer, even in the field where germs always seemed to seek him out, or so he believed.

Codi held the trunk lid as Joel loaded his boxes into his Prius. She plopped into the passenger seat and, as Joel clicked his seatbelt in place, looked over his new Dunhill suit and tie combo. "It's moving day," she said. "What's with the getup?"

He smoothed the seatbelt across his suit. "Just wanted to make a good impression."

Codi's lips turned up. Though Joel would never win Man of the Year, he was still the perfect partner. Seventy-percent brains, twenty-percent brawn, and ten-percent social skills. He was also a completely-by-the-book agent, but Codi was working on that.

Their last mission had put them both in mortal danger. Both had been shot and, in Codi's case, also nearly drowned. They had been at odds with an FBI task force and ultimately one-upped them. Since that case, she had been offered a chance to join the special projects team as a full-fledged FBI special agent. Codi had jumped at the opportunity. But Joel needed some convincing. His overactive sense of low self-worth was not ready for the big time. But, as usual, Codi had gotten her way.

Some may have said that Codi and Joel's rise in the FBI had been meteoric, but she claimed it was more of a wrong place at the wrong time sort of thing.

The Prius pulled away from the loading zone, and Codi's phone started to buzz. She glanced at the text screen: "My office in 10 please." Codi showed the screen to Joel. "Better step on it," she said.

Joel tightened. "But this is a thirty-five zone."

Codi's eyes narrowed. "Seriously? We're FBI special agents now."

Joel looked a bit flummoxed. "But that means setting an example."

"Right, by kicking the bad guys' asses!"

Codi flicked her eyes forward and Joel reluctantly stomped on the accelerator. "I was hoping to stop for a coffee," he said.

"I know a good drive-through on the way."

Joel made a face at the thought of drive-through coffee, but held his tongue.

Twelve minutes later, Supervising Special Agent (SSA) Brian Fescue stepped around his desk to greet Codi and Joel. "Sorry to interrupt your moving day, but cases rarely take time off. Nice suit, by the way, Joel."

Joel's face beamed. He shot Codi an I-told-you-so look.

"So spill, Brian. What is it?" Codi blurted out in an attempt to change the subject.

Brian was their boss and head of the special projects task force. Officially, he was Supervising Special Agent Brian Fescue, but to his team he was just Brian. The casualness was born of too many times in the trenches together. He was a highly decorated agent with a long list of convictions to his record. He had said goodbye to field work when his wife Leila became pregnant with their second child and subsequently gave birth to a beautiful little girl named Abigail. Brian spent as much time as possible trying to be an active parent while still taking his time at the office very seriously.

Brian's island roots were only evident in his slight Jamaican accent. His piecing dark amber eyes were set against cappuccino-colored skin, making him stand out in a crowd. He was about an inch shorter than Joel but he was built like a tank. His no nonsense approach to management had made him a rising star at the FBI. The rumor mill had him in line for an assistant directorship.

Brian scratched at his close-cropped hair as he sat back at his desk. "What do you two know about the Aleutian Islands?"

Joel, a wealth of knowledge, piped up. "It's a chain of islands extending from mainland Alaska, separating the Bering Sea from the Pacific Ocean. Oh, and it's bitter cold there."

"Thanks to global warming we have a curiosity that's been pushed in our direction."

Codi and Joel shared a glance.

"I need the two of you to pop up there and do your thing." He opened his drawer and removed a flash drive. "Everything we know is on this file. I'm sorry. It's not much." He handed it to Joel. "See Mindy for your travel arrangements. And before you ask, the family's fine."

Codi and Joel snickered and Brian unleashed a smile that covered his entire face. It was a running joke that the three shared.

"Wasn't gonna ask," Codi said as she started to leave his office.

"Sure," Brian said. "Tristan scored a goal on Saturday."

Codi stopped in the doorway. "Tell him good job, from me."

The main room for the special projects division was small by FBI standards. It was a square bullpen-style room with nine desks set within tall office cubicles forming a rectangle. There was a hallway down the middle, and Codi's office was straight across from Joel's. Daylight glowed from windows on one wall where a small glass conference room was housed.

Joel dumped his boxes on the frosted glass surface of his desk just in time to answer a call from Mindy in transportation.

"Now boarding group D."

Joel listened as the airport speaker called his group, but he was in no hurry. The last-minute arrangements had gotten them tickets in the very back row of Alaska Airlines Flight 1 out of DC's Reagan International Airport. Gate C18 was a zoo. As he and Codi made their way through a sea of bodies to access the jet way, Joel kept his hand on his wallet pocket, always careful in a crowd.

Codi had been right to check as much luggage as possible because, by the time they got to their seats, there was no more overhead space available. Joel had the window seat and Codi the middle. They sat and tried to get comfortable for the long flight with multiple layovers.

Once the jet took off and reached the required ten thousand feet, Joel opened his computer. "What do you know about the DEW Line?" he asked Codi.

"As in 'I do,' the words spoken in a marriage ceremony?" Codi had her eyes closed and peeked over to see that Joel had opened up his laptop.

"No, D. E. W., Distant Early Warning System. It was an integrated chain of early warning radar and communication stations constructed across northern Canada and Alaska from 1953 into the early sixties."

Codi looked bored. The man sitting on the other side of her was just big enough that he was hanging over the invisible line separating the two seats. He was wearing oversized headphones and a red hibiscus-print Hawaiian shirt. The headphones were blasting Latin jazz that could be heard three seats away. Codi was trying her best to ignore him, and, to be honest, Joel too.

Joel continued. "It was specifically designed to detect Soviet bombers coming out of Russia in time for us to scramble fighters to intercept. During the cold war, it was a huge deal and probably saved us on some level from getting a nuclear bomb dropped on our heads." Joel read on. "General Electric won the bid to build it and the Air Force ran it."

"What's that got to do with our John Doe?"

"Doe's, as in three bodies."

This got Codi's attention. She sat up and leaned towards his screen. The plane bucked slightly as it passed through a cloud.

"Nothing," he said. "It's just the only thing that has ever

happened on this forgotten island we're heading towards, except for seasonal muskox herding."

Codi scrunched her face at the thought of a wild goose chase so far from home. She took a slow calming breath. Only fifteen more hours to go.

Joel added, "Here's something interesting. There's a small town at the bottom of the island, Nikolski. Its population swelled in the fifties when the DEW Line was being constructed, but now it's down to only eighteen."

Codi laid back in her seat thinking, "Joel you lost me at… What was the name of that town? I can't even remember where you lost me." She closed her eyes.

"Nikolski is reputed to be the oldest continuously-occupied community in the world."

"What? How is that possible? The Aleutian Islands off Alaska?"

Joel read on. "They have found archeological evidence dating back eighty-five-hundred years."

Codi processed the information. "That's before the pyramids."

"Right."

"And only eighteen people live there now? Crazy."

Joel cleared his throat, "Well, whatever it is, it must be important enough to call the FBI."

Codi tried to recline her seat, then remembered the last row sat against the back bulkhead and didn't recline. "Or we're just getting jerked around."

She tried to ignore the man's flesh pressed against her arm from the neighboring seat. Then the man let out an enormous sneeze. She closed her eyes again, thinking, "This is gonna be a long-ass flight."

"Can I get you anything?"

Codi stabbed a look to the aisle where a flight attendant was waiting, cart in hand.

"I'll take three of those." She pointed to the Jack Daniels mini bottles on the attendant's cart.

Salvation.

5

Umnak Island, Alaska – 10:06 a.m. – The Next Day

"Thanks for coming, and welcome to Umnak Island, by the way. We tried to keep the bodies untouched as soon as we realized we had something…uh…" The man searched for the right word. "Unusual." Lieutenant Silla Dobkins of the Alaska State Police seemed almost giddy to be talking to FBI agents all the way from DC. He shook their hands vigorously as Codi and Joel exited the boat, and pointed them towards a hill.

The trip to Umnak Island had been agonizing. Once they got to Anchorage, Joel and Codi had flown in a puddle jumper to Driftwood Bay, then in a floatplane to Nikolski Bay on the island's southern end. From there they took a trawler around the leeward side of the island to a small inlet. The total travel stint was over sixteen hours, and the two bleary eyed special agents were living off caffeine and borrowed time. For Joel, the exit from the boat was timely, as he'd started to turn a shade of green during the crossing.

The frail sun did little to fight the chill as it moved parallel to the horizon. Codi checked her phone to find no signal as she moved up from the shore. Her head seemed to pound in time with her footsteps. She was wearing jeans and several layers topped by a dull green parka.

Lieutenant Dobkins was a short round man with Eskimo blood and a fast pace. He led them up a small game trail alongside a dying glacier. Joel was glad to be on land, but puffed at the sudden exertion. The air was crisp and smelled like rain. His boots struggled for purchase on the loose lava rock. In his panic about the arctic cold, he had layered up until he looked more like the Michelin Man rather than an FBI agent. His movements were forced and clunky.

"One of our part-time residents found them, Bert Yazzie. He runs muskox up here in the warmer months. Says he was looking for a lost calf when he found the first body. Called us up and we got busy. Turned out there were three, all buried together. At first it looked as if a lost hunting party fell in one of the glacier's crevasses. No biggie, right? But then a few strange things popped up."

"Strange like what?" Codi asked.

"Let me show you."

As they came over the rise, Codi could see men and equipment gathered around a large blue pop-up standing at the dirty edge of the glacier, its blue heart exposed to the elements. Joel pulled up his parka hood against the sudden icy wind that assaulted them.

Dobkins made the introductions and took them to the bodies. Under the pop-up three bodies were laid out on the ice. Surrounding the bodies was an organized and tagged pile of old and mostly smashed gear. Codi could see where they had chipped some of the ice away to free the bodies. The corpses were in varying conditions. Two of them looked like they'd been ground up, frozen, and then pulverized again for good measure.

The other was in remarkable condition as though he had just died.

Lieutenant Dobkins looked down and spoke reverently. "A

glacier is a funny thing. It can grind you up, or keep you just as you were. There's no love in the ice, only cold."

Codi stepped over to the corpses and knelt for a closer look. "And all three of these…" she looked closer at the two masticated bodies "…men, were found in the same place?"

Dobkins broke out of his reverie. "Yes mam, they all went into the ice at once, and I'm guessing by the age of this gear… mid-fifties?"

Codi stood back up. "I still don't see why we were requested."

Dobkins paused; he kicked at the ground with his boot. He looked hesitant but continued. Well, it's really more of what you don't see. Looky here."

He moved to the body that was still intact, bent over, and pointed to the man's boots. "These here vulcanized boots were developed by the Russians. We get a lot of their surplus stuff here nowadays, but not in the fifties. This was state-of-the art equipment back then."

He moved over to the tagged and piled gear. "And this radio, what's left of it, definitely looks Russian."

Dobkins pulled something shiny out of his pocket. "And the *piece de resistance.*" He held up a red and gold medal with the silhouette of a man in the middle. It was about the size of Post-it note. "This, definitely is Russian."

He handed it to Joel for a look. Joel looked it over. "The Order of Lenin, their country's greatest award."

Dobkins nodded. "Right. And if you look at the date it was issued…"

Joel looked closer. "1957."

The date hit him like a gunshot. "That's when the DEW Line was built."

Dobkins nodded, and pointed away from the glacier, "There's an old abandoned station just across on the windward side from here."

Lieutenant Dobkins moved over to stand between Codi and Joel. "So the question is?"

Codi answered. "What were Russian soldiers doing on a US island during the cold war right in the middle of the DEW Line."

Dobkins held his index finger in the air. "Bingo!"

"It has fifty-six reviews on Yelp." Joel was struggling to keep up with Codi while looking at his phone and stumbling across the uneven ground. "Even a few four-stars. That's a lot for up here."

The mile-long spit extending northeast made the town of Dutch Harbor, Alaska, a natural port. Now famous for its crabbing, it was once the location of the Battle of Dutch Harbor where a Japanese carrier strike force unleashed a forty-eight-hour battle against the US Army and Navy stationed there. It included several air battles and a loss of over twenty-three US soldiers killed and ten MIA. The highlight was the recovery of the first intact Japanese Zero. The plane was shipped to US Intelligence where it was later dissected and analyzed.

After they had finished up on Umnak Island, Codi and Joel took a floatplane back to Unalaska Island to the town of Dutch Harbor for the night. There they checked in to their hotel and changed for dinner. Joel wore a pressed, new plaid flannel with jeans and boots, while Codi kept it simple, jeans and a faded purple Henley with the sleeves pushed up. They both carried their weapons, but that seemed to be the norm for the islanders.

"I'm sure it will be fine," she said to Joel.

She glanced up at the sun, which was not due to set until after one a.m. and then rise by 4 a.m. This was a strange part of the world. She would hate to have to spend the winter here where sunlight was weak and very brief, if at all. As a Southern California girl, she was all about sunshine.

Joel continued to read from his phone. "There used to be a saloon here that was rated the roughest bar in the US."

Codi looked a bit forlorn. "Too bad it's gone."

Joel looked like he'd bitten a lemon. "You wouldn't seriously go into a place like that."

Codi gave him a *heck yeah* look, to which Joel had no response.

He pushed open the swinging doors of the restaurant to reveal a pitted wooden floor. It was interrupted with white vinyl tables and chairs. Plastic red gingham tablecloths were decorated with paper plates and plastic utensils. But the real attention grabber was the rustic room's patrons. Craggy, blue-collar workers all covered in job-of-the-day, each hopped up on testosterone and alcohol.

"You really know how to show a girl a good time," Codi said out of the corner of her mouth as eyes from everywhere undressed her. Joel looked worried at his choice of eateries. He found an empty table and quickly sat down.

As he stared nervously around the room, he noticed they had entered a literal hole-in-the-wall restaurant. The south-facing wall of the room had a hole clear through it with a view to the outside. He lifted his hands from the sticky surface and used some paper napkins to try to clean the tablecloth. "We have arrived," he whispered to Codi pointing at the feature with his eyes.

The humor wasn't lost on Codi. "It was probably made by someone's head," she said.

An older stout woman with an elongated face and a wrinkle for every pore, approached their table. She wore a stained brown apron that had once been white. "Whatilitbe," she said as one word.

"Can we see a menu?" Joel croaked as he looked up to meet the waitresses' mostly toothless smile.

"Fish or crab. Name's May. Welcome to The Borealis. Fish or crab?"

She gave Joel a look that dared him to test her. Joel withered from her glare and turned helplessly to Codi for reinforcements.

"One of each, please, and two beers," Codi responded without hesitation.

Joel tried to repeat the order to May, but it squeaked out all wrong.

May gave him a concerned look and lumbered off to another table, shaking her head.

A buzz from Codi's phone pulled her attention. She read the incoming text to Joel: "The autopsy is complete. The bodies will be ready tomorrow a.m."

"Good. Then we can finish up and get the hell out of this town." Joel said the last part with a little too much enthusiasm.

That brought a sudden silence to the room, and a very unwelcome focus on Joel. As he looked around, he saw a virtual Who's Who of the mangy and rugged. He tried to swallow but his throat was unexpectedly dry.

"What's wrong with our town?" said a particularly large man with a beard that nearly touched his belly. He stood up and eclipsed half the room. Greasy black spots decorated his XXXL flannel shirt.

Joel seemed to shrink three sizes.

Codi burst out laughing. This was more to her liking, but Joel couldn't decide if he should cry or run to the bathroom. Her laughter, however, was contagious, and soon others started to join in. This made the big man turn a little more red. He zeroed in on Joel. After an uncomfortable moment, he gesticulated with his arms to quiet the room. "Quiet down, all."

He looked Joel over and shifted to Codi. A slight twinkle formed in his eyes. "You seem like good people. I will let you buy me a beer."

Just then May returned with their food and beers. "Corky, stop clowning around or I'll throw your ass outa here."

The behemoth of a man looked properly chastised as he sat back down. "Yes, May," he mumbled.

May turned and plopped the food on their table. "Don't mind him," she said. "He's always looking for a way to get free beer. And you're lucky."

"How's that?" Codi asked.

"We'd all love to get the hell out of this town if we could. Enjoy." With that, May spun on a heel and left.

The seafood was probably the best they had ever eaten, and the patrons, compliments of a few rounds of Moscow Stout, soon found a comradeship in the two FBI agents. Codi had threatened to shoot the big oaf a couple of times but she was pretty sure the bullet would never penetrate deep enough to do any good. By midnight they were all singing, laughing, and telling stories.

Codi looked up at the old gray-painted metal hangar. It was the size of a flat-roofed four-car garage. It had one rollup door wide enough for a small plane that was closed and looked rusted shut. Large chunks of gray paint were peeling off the walls and littered the ground around it. As the two agents entered a side door the hinges protested, announcing their arrival with a squeaky wail. The rotary Pratt Whitney engine of a Beaver De Haviland rushed down the nearby runway drowning out the sound of the door closing.

Joel quickly covered his ears as the noise cut through his hangover. The smell of formaldehyde and carrion hit him like a monologue from a B rated movie. He almost turned around and left. He tried to breathe through his mouth, but the stench made its way into everything. He held his sleeve against his nose as a filter and tried to focus through teary eyes.

Sitting on three steel tables in the middle of the open space were the partially covered bodies from the glacier. On a long metal table off to the side was the collected gear, tagged and organized. As Codi approached, the smell intensified. She noticed that the two corpses that had been ground up had been carefully put back together. They looked like bad Frankenstein jigsaw puzzles. The other had the traditional Y-cut from an autopsy.

Lieutenant Silla Dobkins turned and called out. "Great. You're here. We can get started. I was just starting to get used to the smell, and that's never good." He shook their hands just as vigorously as he had before.

"Lieutenant Dobkins, good to see you," Joel said.

"Please. We're past all that. Call me Sil."

"Okay, great. That's Codi and I'm Joel."

"Here, this will help with the smell."

Sil handed them a jar of Vicks Vaporub. Joel watched Codi expertly put a dab under her nose. He did the same and his eyes immediately started watering again. He blinked rapidly and suddenly a ridiculously loud sneeze took over his entire body. The glob of Vicks shot from his nose onto the floor. Codi handed him a small rag from the corner of the table. "Here"

He put it over his mouth and breathed through the cloth instead of using the burning ointment. Sil introduced them to the M.E. and his assistant. Codi shook their hands and stepped over to get a better look at the bodies. The medical examiner filled Sil in on his findings.

"I did a DNA test to determine origin. It's pretty simple really, they're all Russian."

"See, told you." Sil looked proud, like he'd just won a bet.
Joel spoke up. "Have you determined cause of death?"

The M.E. walked over like he was about to deliver a lecture.
"John Doe number one was impaled by what was most likely
an icicle at the bottom of the crevasse he fell into. Number
two died from a blunt force trauma to the back of his head,
and number three froze to death."

"Where's the rest of him?" Joel was referring to the third
cadaver that was missing his calves and feet.

Codi was carefully inspecting the stumps. "It looks like
they were cut off, no, sawed off."

"Yes, post mortem," the ME added.

Joel made a face.

"Okay, why?" she asked.

Sil moved around the table to Joel's side. "We can only
speculate at this point."

Joel nodded thoughtfully. "Do you have an approximate
year or day when this all happened?" he asked.

"The best I can give you is Fall 1957."

"How did you come up with that?" Joel asked.

"The USGS has been measuring glacier migration and
melt in this area since the first satellites went up. Glaciers are
like tree trunks in that they keep track of their environment
at the time within the ice. And then there's this." The doctor
lifted a boot from the nearby collection. "They were new and
dated."

The boot clearly showed its manufacture date of August
12, 1957, in Cyrillic.

Codi paced between the bodies as she processed the information. "So Russians, most likely Special Forces based on
their gear, were here in 1957 to do what?"

"That's why we called you folks," Sil said.

Joel took a picture of the three men's faces, as he spoke.

"I'll see what I can dig up, but I'm betting it's related to the DEW Line. They were undoubtedly spying on one of the installations to see what they could learn."

He checked his camera to make sure the pictures turned out okay.

"A long forgotten operation," Sil said, "and therefore, I'm betting, of no real consequence today."

"I'm sure you're right," Codi said hopefully.

6

Washington D.C. – 10:08 a.m. – FBI Field Office – 3rd Floor

"The Dew Line?" SSA Brian Fescue looked up from his desk, confused.

"US fifties technology used to track incoming bombers over the Arctic Circle." Joel had this part down cold.

Codi massaged the bridge of her nose. Last week had been a grind. As far as she was concerned the incident was old news and a waste of their time.

"As in *nineteen* fifties?" Brian asked.

"Exactly, sir."

"You can just call me Brian, Joel."

Joel nodded nervously at the familiarity.

Brian looked at the puffy bags under his agent's eyes. He stood up and walked around to the front of his desk. It was clean and organized just like his mind. A place for everything, and everything in its place.

"Okay. I don't see a reason to spend any more resources on this case," Brian said. "Whatever happened out there is long forgotten and has no implications to national security or anything else. See if you two can identify the dead. We'll notify the state department and see what they want us to do next. Hopefully we can then close it out or shelve it."

Codi was the first to stand.

As they left the office, Brian called out to them, "Good job out there."

The week had been a total bust. First, Codi lost half-a-day in some worthless CYA seminar, and then she was sent on a wild goose chase in the Arctic. If bad things happen in threes, she couldn't wait to see what was next.

The text alert on her phone announced an incoming message. Codi scrolled to read: "Codi, been buried trying to re-configure the output signature on my 'Project.' Won't be able to make it this weekend—SO SORRY—XOXO Matt."

She lowered the phone in slow motion. It had taken two months for them to block out the upcoming three-day weekend, and now, the day before it was supposed to start, it was over. Maybe, so was their relationship. She turned in the hallway and headed for the exit thinking, "There we go, number three—*damn.*"

She heard a muffled voice call after her, but ignored the instinct to answer. For her, this was the worst news yet.

Joel called her name one more time, but she continued to walk away. He let her go and shuffled back to his office. He took his phone and transferred the pictures he'd taken of the three dead Russian commandos to his computer. He then went to work tracking down their identity. He knew the chance of them being on a US database was slim, but every in-depth search had to start somewhere. He lifted his cup and sipped the freshly brewed dark Ethiopian Hambela roast coffee with its fruit and chocolate undercurrents. It was good to be back home. He looked around his cubicle and imagined ways he might personalize it. Perhaps a plant.

Park Je Kwan had effectively trained his whole adult life for the next forty minutes. He lowered the sun visor in his blue Hyundai Kona and looked himself over. He flicked a few stray hairs from his forehead and licked his dry lips. The forgettable twenty-seven-year-old South Korean was ready. He took a deep breath as his eyes defocused briefly, then flipped up the visor and left his car. He followed a coworker across the sunny parking lot to a waiting conveyance, his crisp steps in tune with the fresh alpine air. He wore khaki Dockers, a blue tee shirt, and a lightweight black coat.

Kwan took the stairs to the blue-gray military bus two at a time and headed to an empty bench seat near the back. It was important to make today look like any other. He pulled out his phone and pretended to check his Instagram. He needed to blend in, and over the last year, Kwan had collected 112 followers.

The diesel pusher lurched forward and trundled up a narrow switchback road, leaving Colorado Springs in the distance. He glanced up as the bus entered the manmade domed tunnel with the words Cheyenne Mountain Complex stamped into the steel rim opening. He watched as his phone's signal dropped from three bars to zero, the ambient daylight quickly replaced by the harsh glare of sodium vapor bouncing off the carved granite walls.

Inside the mountain the bus pulled to a stop and the passengers shuffled out. Kwan stowed his phone into his worn backpack and set it in a nearby locker along with the other workers' personal belongings. He then walked over and joined the queue to the advanced security checkpoint, just like he did every Monday through Friday.

Only today was different. Today Kwan had an organic memory chip imbedded in his right palm. The technology was new. It used his body like a battery to keep the stored information active. Once removed, it almost immediately started to lose data. But the organic material made it non-magnetic and completely undetectable, something that was most important today.

No electronics were allowed in the facility. In fact, every thing and every person had to go through a very sophisticated scan that not only detected metal but also degaussed electronics that passed through, leaving them blank and useless. If you forgot to leave your cellphone in the locker it would be dead the moment you entered.

The same was true for exiting. That's because the entire facility ran on a sealed operating system with no outside connections to the Internet or computers of any kind so that no hackers or spies could get in or out of the system. The old movie *War Games* was the genesis for the sealed and specialized operating system. It was critical for America's security and safety. But organic data was something new, experimental, and impervious to magnetism.

Kwan stared listlessly ahead at the open blast door entrance to the facility. It was three feet thick and over twenty feet tall with giant hydraulic pins that could lock it in place when shut. It was a sight he never tired of—a truly incredible feat of engineering born of fear.

One by one, the workers filed through the scanning process.

"Morning, Kwan. What happened to your hand?" The guard scrutinized Kwan's hand.

Kwan was shaken from his thoughts. He instantly became self-conscious and tried to downplay it. "Just a stress fracture, no big deal. Got it playing baseball on Saturday."

Kwan made a halfhearted fake swing with his arms.

"I didn't know you were a baller."

Kwan held his hand up, showing the metal splint that surrounded his thumb. "Apparently, I'm not much of one."

The guard nodded subtly. "Well, you know the drill. I'll have to personally search you or that splint will set off every damn alarm in the system."

Kwan stepped through the side gate and over to the guard who moved his wand over Kwan's entire body, slowly and carefully. Kwan fought to remain calm and pretended to scratch an imagined itch in an attempt to wipe away a bead of sweat that had formed along his hairline. The wand squawked loudly as it passed over the metal splint in Kwan's hand, causing him to repress the desire to run. But the guard didn't linger and instead he simply waved Kwan through.

"You're good. Next!"

Kwan walked briskly through the huge degausser and over to the changing room, where he took a few calming breaths. His legs felt leaden. He needed a second to compose himself before donning his maintenance uniform and heading out to work.

The simple blue coveralls were well worn and hung loosely on his thin frame. He glanced down at the embroidered badge on his left chest—twin eagle wings wrapped around a globe showing North America. They were split with a sword and two lightning bolts, all displayed against a blue shield. A ribbon below identified it as North American Aerospace Defense Command, commonly referred to as NORAD.

It was a large complex built in the center of a granite mountain in Colorado during the late 1950's, a joint operation between the US and Canada, tasked with detecting any airborne or space-borne threats to the two countries. The five-acre facility was completely self-contained and could be locked down against a conventional nuclear attack. Once locked, it became one of the most hardened command centers on the planet.

But since the advent of smart nukes, the facility was no longer as safe as it once was. Now, less than a hundred people worked in the mountain. Most of NORAD's essential functions were relocated to Peterson Air Force Base in Colorado Springs. But not all of them.

Once beyond the blast doors, Kwan stopped to get his electric maintenance cart. The high ceiling and walls wept with water that had seeped through the many layers of rock above. Rusty bolts and pipes snaked in all directions like a jungle with no blueprint. Kwan drove his cart past the mostly abandoned town that sat in the heart of the mountain. The paint- and steel-sided buildings showed their age. The entire city was built on a foundation of hundreds of thousand-pound springs that allowed it to move in order to withstand even the most extreme earthquake or bombing.

Kwan glanced over at the cement-encapsulated command center as he drove past. This was the heart of the NORAD system, and this was his mission. Day after day for the past twenty-eight months, he bided his time until they were ready.

Inside the open floor plan was a bevy of terminal stations that faced a wall covered with large monitors. They displayed maps and technical information, all used to pick up and track anything, from a small plane flying low out of Mexico to an ICBM traveling in the stratosphere out of North Korea. Their main purpose was to detect and give enough advance warning to dispatch the appropriate response to the threat.

Kwan unlocked the door to the storage room and stepped inside. Fluorescent tubes winked on, casting a greenish glow in the room. Because the Navy built the facility, everything had a battleship style to its architecture: steel beams, exposed pipe, and hatch-style doors.

Kwan's workbench was immaculate with everything in its place. He placed his hands on the worn steel bench and paused for a moment. It had been a long process to get here, requiring a lot of patience and even enduring some racism along the way, but his chance to prove himself had finally arrived. He had trained with a friend named Jin before coming here and he was looking forward to sharing a beer with him in celebration if all things went well today.

Kwan was born in the south section of Seoul known as Suwon. He had enjoyed a normal childhood with dreams of college and a promising career that he had a passion for. But an unexpected train accident took both his parents. The accident was blamed on poor maintenance by the Ministry of Land, Infrastructure and Transport, an unwieldy bureaucracy that swept the incident under the rug.

He was left with nothing but a life on the street, his dreams of being a civil engineer gone forever. He joined the military to escape his predicament and endured the cruelty the armed services dealt. As an orphan with no pedigree, he was given the worst of everything. When his enlistment was up, he left vowing to never look back. He traveled around the country looking for what was next.

On a cold rainy night in a small bar in the port city of Pohang, he reconnected with his estranged Uncle Hanja, or, as Kwan soon began to call him, his Funcle. The man made light of any situation. It was so contrary to the way Kwan had been raised where every step was planned, and discipline was the word of the day. Uncle Hanja enjoyed life. It was a breath of fresh air for Kwan, and it wasn't long before a smile returned to his face and he found himself feeling normal again. Things were looking up.

Until his uncle died in a shoot-out with the KCS, Korea

Customs Service. It was then that Kwan realized the life his uncle had led was not at all what it seemed to be.

Shortly after Hanja's death, Kwan found himself starting to flounder again when he was approached by a very tall, lean man who introduced himself simply as Lee. The man had worked with Kwan's uncle a few times. He opened a new door of possibilities to the disillusioned young Korean, one that set Kwan on his current path. It was a path that would give him purpose, and allow for a small measure of revenge against a status quo that had taken away everything important to him.

Kwan slid the top of his workbench back, revealing a hidden compartment below. He pulled out a small module that he had smuggled in piece by piece and then reassembled. It looked like a metal pack of cigarettes. One end contained a multi-pin connector and there was a small sliding door on the top. Kwan pressed his thumb and forefinger against its sides and the box powered up. A subtle green LED glowed on the top and the door slid open. Kwan then quickly removed the splint on his right hand and took a penknife from his bench. He gently pushed the subdural organic chip out of his hand with the point of the knife.

Blood followed but Kwan didn't seem to notice. He placed the organic chip in the box and quickly closed the door. The green light started blinking as ones and zeros flowed from the organic chip into the unit, converting organic ones and zeros to magnetic files.

Kwan let out a sigh of relief. The experimental technology had maintained its data. It had used his body to keep the chip alive until the transfer could be made. The organic chip first uploaded its own operating system onto the module, enabling the device to download specific files required for his mission. The green light stopped blinking and remained solid. It wasn't a huge file, but the information it contained was some of the most important for the cause that had ever been written.

Kwan pulled the multi-pin from the box. It looked like a small USB thumb drive with an oversized connection. He slipped it into his pocket and returned the small box back into its hidden home in the workbench. His last step was to rewrap his bleeding hand. It was time.

He exited the storage room, nearly running into Carl.

"Whoa there, K-boy, what's the rush? Afraid those toilets are gonna clean themselves?" Carl was a perfect example of everything that was wrong with America. And the redneck oaf was his immediate superior.

"You said it," he replied. "Gotta get there quick."

Kwan grabbed his cleaning cart and tried to push it away. Carl held onto it, looking like he didn't trust letting Kwan go. They shared a brief struggle before Kwan glanced up at the security camera to remind Carl it was there. Carl immediately let go, pushing the cart in Kwan's direction. The cart nearly ran him over, with the diminutive Kwan barely staying on his feet. Carl stifled a snicker as he watched the retreating form of the small Korean, and shook his head. A few derogatory words flowed silently past Carl's lips.

Kwan pushed his metal cart down the side tunnel towards the famous blast doors of the command center. Each weighed over twenty-three tons and used twenty-two hydraulic pins to lock it down. The doors had remained open since 1992, except for a brief period during 9/11. Kwan nodded to the guard posted outside the first portal as he wheeled his cart past the massive door. He swiped his ID card through the slot reader next to a recently installed electronic entry door. It opened to reveal two heavily-armed men staring him down. He used his cart like a battering ram to push past the two men, just like he did every Wednesday at this time.

The room smelled of ozone and body odor, awaiting a third smell provided by Kwan—bleach. He efficiently made his rounds cleaning, wiping, and dumping, slowly working his way to the server room. As he approached the entrance, a third guard stood near the door. He smiled at Kwan, and seeing his bandaged hand, opened the door for him.

"Thanks, Marv."

"Sure thing, Kwan. Looks like you're a bit hobbled today."

Kwan told him the same story he gave to the main-gate guard and entered the room. The hum of the electronics was mind-numbing as Kwan went about his regular duties. Marv watched his every move, but after months of uniformity the sharpness fades from even the most attentive of guards.

Kwan turned his body to temporarily block the guard's view as he stealthily slipped the thumb drive onto the multi-pin diagnostics port. The drive took over from there, uploading its contents into the sealed system.

"Hey, what are you doing!"

Kwan almost jumped out of his skin as Marv approached with purpose.

"What?" he managed to squeak out.

"You're going to ruin the electronics."

Kwan pupils instantly dilated with fear. Then he noticed Marv was pointing to his hand.

"You're dripping."

Kwan quickly realized his hand was bleeding through the bandage. "Damn it. Stupid thing won't stop."

He used a cleaning rag to wrap his hand, keeping his body between Marv and his device. He made a big show of cleaning up the mess. Marv chuckled to himself as he turned and headed back to his station. Kwan glanced at the thumb drive. The LED was no longer flashing. He yanked it out it and headed for the door.

Marv re-secured the door to the servers as he watched Kwan leave the area. "You should get that looked at," he said.

Kwan gave him a bloody thumbs-up.

Carl sat at his usual chair of stacked shipping crates. He carved on a small piece of wood while he enjoyed a large chaw of tobacco, spitting the residual with deadly accuracy into an old no. 10 can. The storage room was his domain, and he let everyone who worked for him know it. As he whittled away, he glanced over at Kwan's workbench and his mind started to drift. What would be a good prank he could pull on the little gook. He stood up and saw that there was blood on the bench surface. He moved to investigate. It was not like Kwan to leave a messy workspace. The blood looked rather fresh. He noticed that it seemed to disappear through a seam he had never noticed before.

Carl jimmied the top of Kwan's workbench. Suddenly it slipped open, revealing a hidden compartment.

"Well, looky here."

Kwan burst into the storage room holding the rag on his bleeding hand. He looked up to see Carl with a sneer on his face and with Kwan's electronic box in his hands. *Shit.*

Kwan's mind spun, trying desperately to figure out what to do.

Carl's head tilted and his eyes narrowed. "Looks like I found us a spy, K-boy."

"E-cigarette, dipshit."

"What?"

"It's an E-cigarette. I've been trying to quit and this helps."

"Bullshit. You think I'm an idiot? What's with the secret

compartment?" He motioned to the hidden space in Kwan's workbench.

"It's not mine. I found it by accident. Somebody before you or me put it there."

"And you just happen to keep this little gizmo hidden in there?"

"I didn't want it to walk away on its own, what with the people who work around here." Kwan gave Carl a hard look. "But seriously, go ahead and take it to the base commander. You'll be the laughing stock, not me."

Carl re-inspected the small metal box. Now he wasn't so sure.

"Here, let me show you how it works." Kwan stepped over and held out his hand. "It holds almost any flavor of tobacco you could think of—razzleberry, cardamom."

Carl scrunched his nose at the mention of a razzleberry-flavored cigarette. He hesitated a beat longer, then gave it to Kwan. Kwan set the device on his workbench and waited for Carl to focus on the box.

"You turn it on by pressing here."

He squeezed his fingers on the box and it powered up. The little door slid open. Carl dropped his head to get a better look inside. There were traces of blood and a round device inside. This was no E-cigarette.

With his free hand Kwan fingered a crescent wrench hanging on the pegboard. He brought it down with all his strength across the back of Carl's head. The big man dropped to the floor with a muted thud.

Mindful of the security cameras outside the room, Kwan pulled his cart into the storage room and stuffed Carl inside.

The lower section of Cheyenne Mountain City holds a crawl space that is unlike anything on the planet. The entire city's foundation is made of thick steel plates that are supported by a forest of thirteen-hundred giant springs anchored into the granite base. Each building is free-standing, all connected by hallways and ramps. Kwan rolled his cart holding the unconscious Carl along the stone floor. He found a spot to dump him deep under the mostly abandoned city. He positioned the man who had been a brutal boss just so. Then he lifted Carl's head up and slammed the back of it against one of the thousand-pound steel springs that attached to the subfloor, disguising his previous blow from the wrench with the steel of the spring. The tyrant's head made a cracking noise, ending him with a twitch.

The rest of the day was uneventful for Kwan, and he actually smiled as the transport bus exited the tunnel into the waning daylight. He watched his phone as the signal returned to three bars and then four. He selected a happy face emoji and texted it to a prearranged number. Kwan leaned back and stared at the ceiling of the bus. What was next for him, he didn't know, but after today he was ready for anything. Destined for greatness, if you will. His mind drifted to his very close friend Jin, back in China. Maybe now he could refocus on something he hoped would bring joy to his lonely life—a true friend.

Kwan pulled his blue Hyundai Kona into the narrow lane heading out of the parking lot and down the rest of the mountain. His finger drifted to the volume on his radio. He turned it up. It was celebration time, and tonight he was going to make the most of it. K-Pop blasted from the speakers as his lips curled up and his head bopped to the beat.

As he came around the first switchback he noticed his brakes seemed mushy. He pumped the pedal several times with little result. By the next hairpin turn, his brakes were nonexistent. He quickly pulled the emergency brake to slow his increasing speed. Nothing. He tried down-shifting but the transmission was locked in place. He grabbed for the key and turned it off. Again, nothing. The key turned back and forth with no effect on the engine. This was first-rate sabotage. He considered bailing out, but his speed was now too great.

Kwan held onto the steering wheel tightly as his speed and panic surged. He tried to track the dangerous curvy road to the best of his ability, anticipating the corners and using both lanes to stay on the road. The car wobbled, having trouble tracking the bends as his speedometer passed sixty. He prayed for no oncoming traffic and perhaps a miracle. Tires squealed and smoked as he fought for a semblance of control.

In a last desperate move Kwan slammed the passenger side of his vehicle into the mountainside to slow his speed. The Hyundai bucked crazily but finally started to slow. As sheet metal met the granite mountain all Kwan heard was grinding metal and popping tires. He took a small breath as a modicum of hope built. But the road suddenly turned sharply back to the right leaving him no mountain to rub against.

The blue Hyundai Kona, its steering now damaged by the mountainside tussle, headed straight for the road's edge. Kwan sailed off the road and through the meager guardrail. He took a sudden breath with the weightlessness and gripped the steering wheel as if it might provide some salvation. His car's nose tilted downward into a three-hundred-foot nosedive to the rocks below. Kwan knew who had set this up. But the memory was fleeting. His last thought was of his friend Jin and what might have been.

Lee watched through his binoculars as the Blue Hyundai accordioned on the rocks below. The impact was so violent that the engine ended up in the trunk. He felt a brief pang of regret for having to end young Kwan's life. He had been a good recruit and soldier, but there could be no loose ends on a mission as critical as this one. He lowered the glasses and looked once more at the smiley face emoji texted to his phone. Lee smiled as he flicked away a toothpick he'd been nursing and deleted the text—no lose ends.

"Watch out, driving can kill you," Lee mumbled to himself as he headed back down the trail that overlooked the road, his memory of Kwan quickly fading.

Time to head back home. His work here was done.

7

WASHINGTON D.C. – 10:08 A.M. – FBI FIELD OFFICE – SPECIAL PROJECTS – 3RD FLOOR

Joel lifted his spectacles and massaged his eyes with his thumb and index finger. He'd been staring at the screen in front of him for too long. Maybe a short break was in order. He stood to leave, and his computer gave a short tone. New email. Like Pavlov's dogs, Joel turned back around reflexively and clicked to open the file.

"Finally," he said to himself, as a long-awaited response popped up. The email was short but it promised to close out the last case: "Hope this helps," GeneralVladstoff@MinisryFA.Ru.

He sat back down and pounded out a message to the man at the Russian Ministry, double-checked it, and blind-copied both Codi and Brian. He leaned back for a second and then hit send.

Joel had grown up in the suburbs of Chicago. He had excelled in both the piano and his love of computers. He spent most of his youth on one keyboard or another. It had earned him a full ride to MIT at the age of seventeen. But Joel struggled to fit in with the social side of the college experience. He often would find a corner of the library to hide out in on

Friday nights, doing homework or gaming. His parents were both professionals that were happy to see their only son leave home and go off on his own. They had a once-a-year perfunctory Christmas get-together and they rarely talked or chatted with their son in between.

Joel had what it takes to be liked, with his quirky, uptight humor. He just wasn't comfortable around strangers. It was something he couldn't quite get past. So he ended up spending more time alone than not.

His career and naive view of the world changed dramatically when he was hired on at the GSA. He was assigned to a desk in the technology division where he chased fraud leads electronically. He excelled at his job, but his coworkers seemed to not even know he was alive. It took a bold move from his boss, pairing him with a newly-minted agent, Codi Sanders, to change that. The chemistry worked, and like Yin meeting Yang, they formed a solid partnership.

Joel and Codi had been thrown into a case that forced them to fight for their very lives. Joel, surprisingly, stepped out of his comfort zone and became a solid team member, integral in helping solve and stop a terrorist threat. Along the way he found the first love of his life. But sadly, he had to watch as she died in his arms. That moment changed him in a way that could not be quantified, but he was now a man driven by purpose. Even if he was still a giant nerd at heart.

Cody's fingers absently toyed with the zipper on her gym bag. She stared out across the pool as swimmers worked through their laps, each in their own lane. The one exception was lane three. It was empty and calling her name. She refused to listen. She just sat on the blue fiberglass bench by the side of the pool and watched.

The Art Deco-style pool was cocooned within gold and blue tile columns surrounded on three sides by large arched windows. The ambient light squiggled off the rippling liquid as swimmers mechanically pressed through the water following their daily routine.

Codi had taken to the water at an early age, both swimming and surfing along the coast north of San Diego where she grew up. After losing her father, she gave surfing, but swimming became an obsession. It was a fading connection to her father that she fought to keep. She had excelled at the crawl and the butterfly in high school, and had leveraged that into a way to help pay for college and to escape a home life that was cracked and flawed. She represented UCSD in the nationals three of her four years there.

Now, starting her day doing laps in the pool was ingrained into her routine as much as eating or sleeping. Every morning at 6:30 a.m. she would push herself through the water with the determination and stamina that defined her.

But after her last case where she had drowned and been resuscitated she no longer had that desire. She knew the traumatic event was controlling her actions and she knew it was just psychological, but right now it was okay with her to just let it go. Maybe today was the day. She could go into the locker room, put on her suit and hit the water. She breathed in the humid, chlorinated air, a smell that signaled comfort to her.

She reflected on the moment right before she had regained her life. She had literally been plucked from the depths of the Thames River. A white light had welcomed her. She felt joy. It was followed by a great shot of pain as it was all taken away. Theologians and scientists disagree on what causes people who are technically dead and then brought back to life to experience this. But for Codi, the memory of seeing blue sky and the man she loved, Matt Campbell, kneeling over her was better that any white light.

She believed in a higher power, but her experience with organized religion and how it often treated others had left her tepid on the subject. But to each his own. If only the rest of the world felt that way.

Codi released a breath she didn't even realize she'd been holding, picked up her bag, and left the building. Maybe tomorrow.

As Codi cleared the security gauntlet at her building, she looked up to see her partner Joel waiting for her. He was wearing his usual perfectly pressed suit, and was carrying an anxious smile along with two cups of gourmet coffee.

"Kenyan Roast. Undoubtedly the best of the African coffees," he said, as he passed a cup to Codi. "Medium roast with a sharp tang, good body, and yet a smooth winy finish."

Codi looked up with indifference, *seriously*? "Is it hot and black?" she asked.

"I waste my coffee talents on you."

She took a long sip. "Hmm, tastes great. Thanks."

Joel looked at her skeptically.

Codi turned up the corners of her mouth. "See, not wasted."

"Boss wants to see us right away."

"Good, we're probably fired. *Finally,* some good news."

Joel went rigid at the thought, as Codi turned and walked away. He was still getting used to her sarcasm. He took a calming breath and hurried to catch up to her. "Hey, that's not funny."

SSA of Special Projects Brian Fescue set his reading glasses on his paper-strewn desktop as Codi and Joel knocked and entered. "Please sit," he said.

He quickly tidied up his desktop without looking up. He

then fingered through a stack of file folders that were neatly stacked behind him, rejecting the first three, until he found what he was looking for and pulled it out. He handed over a thick faded file with tattered edges. "Your next case," he said. "Hopefully you'll have more luck with it than the last one."

He said that last comment with a straight face. Codi and Joel shared a look, not sure if that was meant as a jab or not. But the smile that grew on his face, told them the truth.

"Hey, a little boss humor for you," he said. "What do you expect? Special Projects Division means we get all the oddball and cold cases. We expect your close rate to be dismal."

Brian's smile never wavered as he changed the subject back to the file Joel was now holding. "That file," he said, pointing, "is just the overview of the case. There are twelve boxes that I had sent to your office, Joel. Sign here for them while I got you." Brian pushed a chain of custody form over along with a pen.

"But I haven't verified the contents."

"Just sign it," Brian said as he leaned back in his chair and stared at his two agents.

Joel looked like it was the hardest thing he'd ever done, signing for documents he hadn't double-checked first.

"What do you know about a man named Dan Cooper?" Brian asked them.

Codi had a blank look on her face. Joel perked at the mention, finishing off his slow-moving signature with a flourish.

"You mean D. B. Cooper, the most famous skyjacker of all time?"

"That's the one," Brian said, as he pointed to the file.

"That case was never solved as far as I know."

"Right, and it's been a stain on the bureau's record since the seventies."

Codi felt useless in the conversation, so she took the file from Joel and started to peruse it.

"Some kid found a wad of bills that match the missing serial numbers," Brian said. "I want you two to check it out and see if you can shed some light on a case that's been a total dead end and a black eye for the FBI for more than..." he looked up as he did a quick calculation. "Forty years."

Codi sat at her desk and checked her email. She pulled at the elastic that held her hair up. A familiar address caught her eye and she opened it with a click. An image of a large bouquet of red roses appeared with a note that read: "I am an idiot! But at least I realized it. Please accept my apologies and this symbol of my love (roses) and if you scroll down, a first class ticket to come and see me this weekend. Please accept! Love, Matt."

Codi's heart skipped a beat. She couldn't contain a smile that filled her face. She clicked reply and started to type: "I would love to spend the weekend with a known idiot," when a cry from Joel's desk got her attention.

"Hey, Codi, got a second?"

She paused mid-typing and left without finishing.

One side of Joel's office was packed to the ceiling with twelve very old cardboard evidence boxes. He'd done a quick count when he first entered, worried it wouldn't jibe with the count on the chain of custody form he'd just signed.

Codi plopped into his extra chair and then began to slowly spin as she looked through the folder Joel gave her. "So D.B. Cooper's a skyjacker?" she asked.

Joel referred to a large stack of old files he'd been going through on his desk. "1971. A man boards a flight to Seattle."

"D. B. Cooper?"

"Right. Well it was most likely an alias but that's what we know. He boards a 727 Boeing, Flight 305 from Portland to Seattle. Shortly after takeoff he tells the stewardess..." Joel shuffled through some papers. "...Florence Schaffner, that he has a bomb. He shows it to her. It's in his briefcase. He then makes her write a note to the pilot. They force-land in Seattle and trade the hostage passengers for $200,000 and four parachutes. At some unknown point after takeoff, he jumps out of the plane with the money and vanishes."

Codi looked up from her reading. "Nice, but only $200,000?"

"1971." Joel ticked off his fingers while he did a rough calculation. "That's like 1.3 million today."

"Okay, so this guy is a genius," Codi said.

Joel countered, "Or just really lucky."

"Or dead. Says here, he's suspected not to have survived the jump."

Joel leaned over Codi's shoulder to see what she was looking at. "Sounds like a hopeful agent trying to close a case," he said.

Codi held up the file. "I say we just show Brian this section: Case Closed, and we don't have to fly to Oregon. Besides, I have very important plans this weekend."

Joel's phone buzzed and he grabbed it. "Agent Strickman."

He listened to the brief message and hung up. He looked at Codi. "Our tickets are booked. We're on the next flight to Portland."

Codi slapped the file she was holding down on Joel's desk with obvious frustration. "They couldn't wait till after the weekend? This case is like forty years old. It isn't going anywhere."

Joel sympathized as he watched her leave his cubicle.

An unexpected crushing sensation took hold of Codi as she sat back down at her desk. She looked at her unfinished reply to Matt. After a moment she hit delete. Her second-chance weekend with Matt had just evaporated like a drop of water on a hot skillet. She grabbed her things and left the office.

8

Hong Kong – 3:12 p.m. – The Abattoir – 3rd Subfloor

Jin was a member of a hacking team—F1-Firefly. It had originally been formed as part of the technology and science division directly under the office of General Wang Sun, one of the leading up-and-comers within the party. The team was responsible for gathering intelligence and classified data, all under China's cyber-espionage program, and they were very good at their job.

Over the last five years, however, the politicians had been dealing with serious blowback over their diverse government-backed hacking and cyber divisions. In an effort to calm competitive fears and increase their deniability, a change was needed. Finally, eleven months ago, a breach of their internal systems had shut down part of the government's computers for three days. That was the final straw. It pushed the powers within the party to discontinue all cyber-espionage divisions. What the public didn't know was that the Chinese government simply moved the hacking teams out of their organization and into private hands.

The set-up was simple. Just like in America, the Chinese government contracted with independent companies to provide information and access to the same classified data they were getting before. Contracts were handed to loyal party members, only now with an arm's length between them. Information still flowed just like it always had, but without the bad press. The difference was that an enterprising contractor could use this same information for himself as well.

General Chow Phun was just such a person. He had taken the elite F1-Firefly team and completely rebranded and re-located them. Chow was an old-school red communist and had been in charge of many different divisions and programs over his years with the party. After the onset of Guillain-Barre Syndrome left him with numb hands and feet as well as a partially paralyzed face, Chow left his position in the government and continued on in the private sector. Through his many contacts, he had taken several of his pet projects along with him. He ran a host of off-the-book operations for both himself and the Chinese government, making a bigger name for himself now than what he had before. And with it, a seemingly unending flow of currency.

Chow operated everything from a seemingly abandoned building right in the heart of Hong Kong—The Abattoir, a five-story Plain Jane, faded, white-walled concrete structure. Chow had purchased it for a song from the government, and left the visible parts in its original abandoned state. It was surrounded by a high stone wall and concertina wire. Modern stainless-and-glass high-rises looked down on the dreary, often-considered-haunted derelict. Chow used the people's natural superstitions as well as a few heavily armed guards to protect it.

A close inspection would reveal weathered, peeling walls and old rusted machinery once used to butcher livestock. Part of the roof had collapsed and the rest was unstable. It stank of mold, rat feces, and long-dried blood with standing water in several rooms.

What the public could not see was that below the crumbling façade was an underground three-story high-tech complex called the Red Baks (box). It was Chow's pride and joy. And since losing his wife and daughter to a bird flu epidemic, it had become his life. Each level was given its own personality. A Thai beach theme for the first floor held his personal offices and operations for his more legitimate businesses. A bamboo forest theme for the second floor below held his pet projects, some held over from when he was working for the party, and some more recent, each with enormous promise. And an urban jungle theme for the third and lowest level was where the once-known F1-Firefly team operated, now rebranded the Cathay Dragons. They kept as low-profile as possible. Each employee was well cared for, and Chow was proud of his team. Though they were often scrutinized by ever-present security, each had a sense of pride that they were part of something special—the elite.

Chow paid handsomely because he wanted the best. Anything less was dealt with harshly. He had no time for incompetence, and everyone who worked for him knew it.

Jin watched as his personally written program bombarded the Safran Group with a uniquely devised scrolling password. The French aerospace company had recently announced a new design for a prototype turbo-shaft engine that could produce more horsepower on less fuel. It would be worth a fortune to both the helicopter and jet industries. Chow wanted that design. Jin sipped his tea as the first firewall dropped. *Finally*, progress, he thought to himself.

The third floor was a large open oval with thick concrete beams that supported the two floors above. The walls were decorated in modern graffiti complete with neon signs and streetlights. The flooring looked like street pavement, complete with painted street lines. The cubicles were made of aged steel and smoked glass. The room's ambient glow changed with the passage of time, getting darker at night and brightening with the new day.

The only entrance to the room slid open mechanically with a slight *whoosh*. Chow stepped inside and scanned the perimeter like an owl hunting prey. He was a short man with round features, pushing sixty. Due to his illness the right half of his face drooped like a partially melted wax sculpture. There were times when drool would weep out of the downturned corner of his mouth. It was something Chow could neither feel nor control. He carried a handkerchief in his right hand and had become obsessive about patting his right chin to keep it dry. Over time, a harsh red rash had formed along the dribble line.

He walked past the cubicles of hard-working hackers bending the world to suit his and his beloved China's needs. "Jin," he said.

Jin looked up as Chow approached his cubicle. He quickly stood to greet his boss, trying not to look at the man's damaged face. "Sir."

"Lee contacted me and said the worm has been loaded. He also told me that there was a terrible accident. I'm sorry, son, Park is dead."

Jin sank back into his chair, the disappointment clear on his face.

Chow put a fatherly hand on his shoulder. "He was a good comrade and we were lucky to have been part of his life. They sure could use your help up in 212."

Jin blinked his eyes several times against rapidly forming tears. He had trained Park for this operation and they had become close. "An accident?"

"Car crash. Drunk driver ran him off the road."

Jin nodded absently. Park was never coming back.

"It's tragic," Chow said with forced remorse.

Jin tried to keep his emotions in check. He gripped his hands tightly, letting the pain focus his mind on the information while he nodded absently. After a pause, he said, "That's great news, sir, about the worm." He looked up to his boss. "212? Right away. I'll take care of it."

He left without looking back as he headed to the second floor.

Room 212 held a project Chow had inherited from a former party member. It had been an on-again, off-again operation depending on the powers and desires in charge. After a sensationally successful double-cross with the Russians back in the late fifties, the division had acquired and developed a system to make approaching aircraft completely invisible to the enemy. It wasn't stealth technology where you were still vaguely visible, just hard to see and track, but completely invisible. With the help of a female agent, a Russian airline navigator, whom they had recruited, the Chinese managed to collect the two main scientists behind a daring Soviet Union project known as Operation Blind Pig. With a little coercion, they had convinced one of the Russian scientists to work for the Red Army of China.

The result was a technology that could blind the enemy's early warning systems against a Chinese attack. It had been very popular with the higher-ups early on. Throughout the course of its development they had experienced many test successes and only a few failures. But the people in charge had never followed through and used it. Eventually time and new technologies had made the project outdated. Chow initially had planned to scrap it until an unexpected breakthrough was brought to his attention.

Jin slumped into a vacant seat next to the electronic hub. He quickly logged on and opened the program he had personally written. Doctor Shura Mosin, a sixty-eight-year-old Russian scientist-defector-turned-Chinese-asset looked over his shoulder. There was pallor to his saggy round face. Thick round glasses and a short bowl-cut hairstyle had become his trademark.

"This shit doesn't go faster with you lookin', Doc," Jin said to the man.

Startled, Shura stepped back. "Sorry, it's just that we are so close to success. I cannot begin to tell you the path I have traveled to be here right now."

"Let's not get carried away. Success is what you get when it works, Doc."

Shura nodded as he shuffled away to check on another project.

Doctor of Electrical Engineering Shura Mosin, had inherited this project after waking up in a Chinese prison in 1957. He had been welcomed to his new home and offered many things if he would cooperate. It was something he considered, but his boss, Doctor Grigory Nepein refused. After weeks of torture without success they killed his unyielding mentor right in front of him. The psychological blow made Shura jump to accept their offer.

His first assignment was to oversee the reverse engineering of the captured Tupolev TU-16. They took it apart piece by piece and then made molds and copies of every part. That design was then merged with the current Chinese Hong T5. China had just pushed their aerospace program forward by ten years. Next, Mosin was put back into a lab to refine the GN01 Transmitter that Doctor Grigory Nepein had developed. Over the years the technology had improved and had been successfully tested on many other countries, like Japan and Russia. As the computer age advanced, Mosin became one of China's bright stars for a time. But technology is an evil mistress, and ultimately Shura was left behind.

It took the creativity of General Chow Phun to put a modern day hacker like Jin together with the mind of Doctor Shura Mosin and come up with an outside-the-box solution. A way to get the same results in the modern world of satellites and computers.

The familiar blue shield of NORAD popped up on the screen as Jin opened the benign public access web page. He slid his cursor over to the far right where he selected the French tab, *Francias*. He then followed the dropdown menu to: Contactez Le NORAD. He searched the bottom links with his curser. As it moved across the empty bottom section to the right, a hidden icon popped up, Plus. Jin couldn't believe his eyes. He leaned back to take it all in. *Park had done it.* He had uploaded the worm. It wouldn't allow them access to the closed system, but it would now be blind to a very specific frequency. After all their training and practice...

They had built a mockup of the server room to practice on, piggybacked onto the latest organic storage technology hacked from a lab in Des Moines, Iowa, and deeply planted their man inside NORAD. It was years in the making, and it had worked.

"Hey, Doc!" Jin called.

9

VANCOUVER, WASHINGTON – 11:48 A.M. – WASHINGTON STATE

Codi trudged up the berm that led to the wide river's shoreline. A liquid border divided Washington State from Oregon. Here, the Colombia River flowed north along Caterpillar Island.

Jimmy Paulson was a talker. The thirteen-year-old redhead kept his lips in what seemed constant motion. Two weeks ago he'd been fishing along the gap between Caterpillar Island and Kadow's Marina. He noticed something half-buried along the shore and dug up a wad of old twenty-dollar-bills totaling $6,800. It wasn't until his mom found them stashed under his bed, along with a huge hoard of candy bars, that the discovery was reported.

The serial numbers matched the ransom paid to skyjacker D. B. Cooper. This set off a whirlwind of action as local authorities and then state police got involved. The FBI was next on the list and special projects was given the nod. Soon, news stations got wind of the story, and by the time Codi and Joel landed in Portland the story was everywhere.

"They can't keep the money," Jimmy said to Codi and Joel. "I found it. It's mine. I know the law. Statue of limits is up and I want it back."

Joel tried to get a word in to correct him. "It's evidence now and it's called statute of…"

Jimmy popped right back in. "Plus, I ain't tol' no one about where I found it. Fact is, I should be chargin' you to take you there at all."

He suddenly stopped. Joel almost ran into the back of him.

"Yeah, I should be chargin' you." Jimmy turned around. "What's the goin' rate for information nowadays? Times two." He moved an accusing finger to both Codi and Joel.

Codi pushed past him. She was at her limit. She followed the small game trail to the top of the berm, her boots digging into the soft loam. At the top, she froze.

"Hey, I'm talkin' to you, lady fed. What's the goin' rate?"

"Zero," she said.

"Wait. What?"

Joel and Jimmy ran to the top of the berm to join Codi. The Columbia River was a stunning blue-green as it moved along a deeply forested background. But as far as the eye could see, holes had been dug into the ground all along the shore, even up the bank and into the forest. There were literally *thousands* of holes. "Didn't tell anyone about where you found the stash, huh?" she said to the kid.

Codi knew that any trace evidence was long gone. Jimmy looked crestfallen and was thankfully, finally silent.

"We should charge you for wasting our time," she said.

She turned and left. It was a bitter pill, especially considering what this trip had cost her. Would Matt ever forgive her or could she even forgive herself. Codi had never responded to his email, partly because of her situation here, and partly because deep down she was still mad at him for cancelling on her before. It was petty, she knew, but the right man for her was one who was willing to do the hard stuff and make a friggin' effort.

Now that time had passed, it may be too late. Honestly, she was a little embarrassed to reach out now. She could just play it off like she'd never opened the stupid email. But that left them at an impasse, one she couldn't see around at the moment. A myriad of thoughts coursed through her head, swinging back and forth like a pendulum as she stormed back to their car at the trailhead.

After a check-in with the boss as to their dead end on a cold case that was still unsolved, Codi and Joel had a somber dinner at a fish house back in Portland. The beautiful city sparkled against the slow-moving Willamette River. Codi was wearing a slimming black dress with a slight scoop neck and three-quarter sleeves. Joel was dressed in his patented two-piece suit with a blue collared shirt.

Joel spent a good portion of the dinner talking about the D. B. Cooper case and how he was excited to be part of its history. Codi stared at her phone trying to figure out what to text to Matt, if anything. She had started several times but each time had deleted her words. Finally she put her phone away. A gentle rain followed the sun's dip to oblivion behind the mountains. It seemed to wash away the events of the day, and after a cold local beer, Whole in the Head, Codi was feeling herself again.

A chime sounded on Joel's phone and he looked at the message.

"What gives?" Codi asked.

"Finally heard back from the Russian Defense Ministry."

That piqued her attention. "And?"

"They are neither confirming nor denying knowledge of the bodies found on that island."

"Sounds about right. What about the medal, the Order of Lenin?"

"They say the recipient…" Joel looked down at his screen,

"Colonel Tolya Alexeev is buried in Saint Petersburg, so the medal must be a fake."

"You and I both know that was no fake," Codi said.

Joel nodded. A moment of silence lapsed.

"So what now, Codi?"

"I say we ship the bodies and the medal back to Moscow and say goodbye to this area." She wiped her hands together as she said, "Both cases unsolved but closed for now."

"I'm for just shipping them as well," Joel added.

Codi nodded.

"Unfortunately," he said, "it's not up to us."

She ordered another round.

The Finnair jumbo jet leveled off at forty-two-thousand-feet. Codi glanced at the state department slacker who had been assigned to them. After a short flight and two days waiting in Seattle, the bodies and the assistant-to-the secretary of something-or-other (she had stopped listening) had arrived. Nolan Pierce, a blue blood butt-sniffer for sure Codi thought, was immaculately dressed in a Brooks Brothers custom tailored suit and had his hair coiffed to perfection. A resolute expression crossed his face as he met Codi and Joel for the first time. Immediately, he tried to take control and Codi was torn between letting him hang himself and squeezing the life out of him with a single hand. The thought made her smile. Joel had picked up a nervous twitch since the arrival of the politically charged assistant.

Nolan seemed to be in everyone's business at all times. Codi thought he would make an excellent helicopter mom.

At one point, Joel leaned over and whispered in her ear, "Nothing good will come of this."

He was probably right. But there was nothing they could

do about it for now. Maybe some sleep would help. Codi reclined her seat and closed her eyes, trying to tune out the events of the last week.

Diplomacy was never Codi's strong point. She would rather bull her way to a solution than talk about it. She'd always been driven to cut to the heart of a situation and felt like she had something to prove. Her father had been one of the Navy's elite divers and had specialized in deep water recovery. It allowed time at home in between missions and training. And when home, he'd been a solid father figure in her life. During a routine deep-water dive, unexploded ordnance triggered unexpectedly leaving three families without fathers.

Afterwards, Codi became a latchkey kid. Her mother, Carolyn, struggled with the loss and dipped in and out of depression. Twice she disappeared for days at a time, and Codi was sure she wasn't coming back. They moved every year or so, her mom in search of a new job, a new boyfriend, or greener grass.

In time, Codi found that the only person she could really count on was herself. She used that as a motivator to find her independence. She would not follow her mother's path, and instead blaze a new one she could call her own.

After graduating college with top honors, Codi received several promising opportunities. But she left them all behind and joined the Marines as an enlisted soldier. She had something to prove to herself and to her father. After three arduous years she was one of the very few females ever admitted to BUDs training. Becoming a SEAL was something she had set as a do-or-die goal. Nothing would stop her from achieving it. Nothing except an all-male "boys club" that conspired against her. She was forced to tap out after a tragic injury left her ankle shattered, along with her dream.

Codi had spiraled down into a dark place that put her out

of the military and practically on the street. But she found her-self, once again, after accepting a job as a GSA Agent where she was responsible for tax and fraud cases, essentially a paper cop. Though feeling like she had let herself down, Codi put her best foot forward.

Ultimately, she was teamed up with Joel, and after follow-ing up on a cold case from the forties the two had been swept into a tidal wave of espionage, international crime, kidnap-ping, even a bioweapon, all part of the case. The two had been integral in bringing it all to a close and stopping a madman willing to massacre for his agenda. Their success had put them on display and the FBI had recruited both to work in their special projects division.

Along the way, she met and saved Doctor Matt Campbell. They forged a special relationship that was full of promise. But lately it seemed to be dwindling with every day they spent apart.

Codi felt vindicated from her past and even proud of the things she had accomplished. All that was left now was to close their current case and then figure out what was happening in her personal life.

After an unusually long taxi on the macadam, the Finnair Airbus A300, came to a stop and powered down. Joel looked at his phone through bloodshot eyes.

"We are here. Only eighteen hours and thirty-eight min-utes. We're early. I sure hope I get to see some real Russian countryside. But first I need a good cup of coffee."

Had Codi possessed the energy to roll her eyes she would have. Instead she tried to extricate herself from her seat and come to a standing position.

"Follow my lead," Nolan commanded, as he started down the aisle. "There will probably be dignitaries, news coverage, and maybe even a parade."

Nolan stepped outside and started to wave from the top of the jet stairs. He quickly realized there was no one there and put his hand down. He just stood staring blankly as Codi passed him and headed down the stairs.

"The parade must be running late," she said to Nolan as she passed.

"It's because we're early," Joel added, as he passed by.

The air was cool, and a light mist danced in the air before finding the ground. As Codi got to the bottom, a black Mercedes G wagon pulled up in front of her. A man in a gray suit that matched his hair stepped out of the back. "Pierce?" he said with a thick Russian accent.

Codi thumbed behind her to the man at the top of the stairs. "He's up there."

Pierce suddenly hurried down the stairs almost tripping and falling the last three steps. He quickly recomposed himself and shook the man's hand. "Assistant Deputy to the Secretary of State Nolan Pierce at your service," he said in flawless Russian.

The man said something in Russian back and then said, "Fedot Sokolov, Administrator to the Head of State," in equally good English.

This elicited a mutual nod.

Codi thought to herself, perfect, these two were meant for each other.

"I have car service for you, Assistant Secretary. Colonel Galkin will take possession of the bodies." He gestured as a green canvas-backed Kam AZ, a heavy-duty military transport vehicle, pulled to the rear of the plane. Several soldiers exited out the back.

Nolan got into the rear of the G wagon with Fedot and they sped off, leaving Codi and Joel behind.

"I guess we're with the truck," she said.

Joel followed her as she marched to the back of the jet.

The room smelled of old cigarettes and cheap furniture polish. It was done in heavy wood and had a definitive masculine touch. Codi sat next to Joel in the overly firm leather chairs that faced an empty desk bathed in slotted sun lines from the shutters on the window. The rain had traded places with an intense sun. Two military guards with Kalashnikovs slung over their shoulders watched from either side of the entrance door. Joel jumped as the doors burst open revealing a large bear of a man in full military dress. The guards tensed and gave a quick salute, which the man ignored.

Codi and Joel stood to greet the man.

"Thank you for coming," he said in nearly perfect English.

As if we had a choice, Codi thought to herself.

"I'm General Vasily Sokolov."

The introductions went around and they all sat down.

"It was good of you to escort the bodies of our comrades. I thank you."

An awkward moment hung in the air.

"So, what now? Why are we here?" He said, raising his hands for emphasis.

Joel cleared his throat trying to bolster his courage. "We, General, as you may know…"

"Please call me Vasily."

"Yes, well, your comrades were found on US soil, and so, just like with every government, we have to close the file on this situation. So anything you can add, we'd be grateful for."

The man looked on, unmoved.

Codi leaned in and put on an air of earnestness. "Honestly, Vasily, we are talking about a case that is more than sixty years old. No one cares who was spying on whom. We just want to close the file," Codi pantomimed a file closing action, "and go back home."

Vasily leaned back in his chair and stroked his chin. He appraised the two agents with care.

"I have read your files, and I was impressed. Your military gave you a raw deal."

Codi had a flash of panic nearly overtake her.

"But you are right to not get caught up in the current politics that are going on over at the Kremlin right now. I'm sure your associate is getting the Russian circle."

Codi and Joel looked confused.

Vasily leaned forward. "Where you talk in circles." Now it was his turn to pantomime and he did so with a rotating downturned index finger. "Nothing gets done."

Codi always believed honesty was the best policy. "Yes, we have that in the US, as well," she said.

"The American circle?"

Joel covertly kicked Codi in the shin, but she continued unfazed. "We call it shoveling bullshit."

The general paused for a moment. The corners of his mouth suddenly sprang up. "That is good. I like it!"

He paused one more time, then let it all out as one continuous thought. "So here's the deal. Yes they were spying on your early warning system looking for a weakness and, yes they must have been caught in a storm, as they were never heard from again. We apologize for doing it and we thank you for delivering the bodies back to their homeland."

He paused again. "But, as you say, those were different times. Drink?" He reached into his credenza and pulled out a bottle of Krupnik vodka, along with three glasses.

Joel mumbled, "Actually, we're still on duty and not allowed to…"

Codi elbowed him mid-sentence. "That would be great, Vasily," she said.

They finished up mostly listening to the general talk about his passion for fly fishing. Then suddenly he stood and spoke to the two guards. "See that they get safely to their hotel."

Codi reached in her pocket and pulled out the Order of Lenin Medal and handed it to Vasily. "I'm sure you'll know what to do with this."

He inspected the piece with reverence, finally looking Codi square in the eyes. He gave her a slight nod, turned on a dime and left the office just as abrupt as he had entered.

As Codi and Joel clamored out of the drab green military sedan, she said, "What was your deal back there?"

Joel looked over. "What?"

"The shin kick."

"Oh, I was sure you were going to say, circle jerk."

"To a Russian general? Give me some credit, Joel."

Joel nodded almost imperceptivity. "Sorry." He turned and looked up at their hotel. "Whoa, this place looks really nice."

He double-checked his paperwork. "This is not the hotel I have in our itinerary. To their escort, he said, "Sir, I think you brought us to the wrong hotel."

Now it was Codi's turn to kick Joel in the shin.

Before he could complain, their guard escort motioned with his arm. "Compliments of General Sokolov." He led them up to the entrance.

The Hotel National is a grand building set against flowing park-like grounds. It is the best of old and modern Russia combined. And it has a reputation for only the best.

The guard walked them through the marble and polished wood lobby and made sure they got checked in. Then, in broken English, he said, "For dinner, from General." He handed Joel a business card with a restaurant logo on it.

Joel and Codi each had a room on the top floor with private balconies and a spectacular view of the city. After all the horrible places this job had sent him, finally, Joel felt he had arrived. He lay out in his bed and took it all in. He did a quick almost reflexive clean of his glasses with his tie. As he put them back on, his view opened to fine linens, gilded moldings, a domed ceiling. This was the life. He let his mind wander, hoping Assistant Deputy to the Secretary of State Nolan Pierce was staying in a hostel. With a shared bathroom down the hall. This thought sparked a smirk on his face so big it almost hurt.

Chun Lee entered the restaurant. It was a small room with ten tables, like many along the busy Hong Kong street. He nodded to the owner and then headed to the rear of the building. A small door marked storage opened to a larger than expected space. It was filled with boxes and supplies stacked to the ceiling. There was an old rusty rollup door on the back wall that leaked light around the edges. Lee pressed a hidden button by an old sink above a crusted floor drain. A stained panel slid to reveal a freight elevator. He punched in a six-digit code and the doors opened. The elevator took him down to the first subfloor where a long stone arched hallway led him under the street to the offices hidden below the abandoned building next door. He passed through the security checkpoint where two heavily armed guards behind an armored door processed him. Once inside, Lee moved to an office at the end of the hall.

He tapped on a teak carved door and proceeded, following an "enter" from the other side.

The unusually tall, bald-headed Lee entered a

warm, cream-colored room with carved beams and an intricately-patterned bamboo floor. He ran his fingers across the belly of a golden Buddha sitting on a pedestal by the front door. Lee noted that his boss was looking worse since the last time he had seen him. His face showed signs of a complete loss of control.

General Chow Phun popped to his feet and stepped over to congratulate Lee. He shook his hand and patted him on the back. "Chun Lee, good to see you again. Nice work in Colorado. Please sit," he said as he returned to his desk, dabbing at a small rivulet of drool on his chin.

Lee sat in one of the overstuffed chairs next to Chow's massive desk. The chair was designed purposefully to be lower than the desk, but Lee's height, at just over six-three, countered the boss's ploy.

"The Dragons have picked up some chatter," Chow said, "from one of their Russian partners on an old mission that connects directly to one of our current operations. It may be nothing, but I didn't get to this position in life by taking chances."

Lee looked on with concern. "Which operation? Do you know what kind of leak? Tell me and I'll plug it."

One corner of the old general's mouth upturned. "There is something you might not know, and it could be relevant." Chow said this last part looking off into space.

A moment of silence ticked by.

Chow stood and started to pace, his numb fingers fighting to find each other and interlock behind his back. It was the simple things that Chow missed by losing his sense of touch, and it seemed to affect everything he did. Muscle memory was great, but without continuous feedback that memory fades, and with it, coordination.

"Many years ago," Chow said, "during the cold war, I

was involved in a very bold operation. The Soviets called it Operation Blind Pig. We called it… well, it was all very classified and ultra-top-secret.

"I was just a young up-and-coming officer then. But our division had managed to snatch some very cutting-edge assets and technology from the Soviets. This led us to major advancements and, for a time, we actually had the ability to cross the sovereign airspace of any country without their knowledge, the US and Soviet Russia included."

Chow continued to pace as he thought back to those times. He ran his fingers numbly across his golden Buddha, hoping for some miracle that would return his sense of touch.

"And?" Lee prodded.

Chow looked back to the man who had been like a son to him ever since the death of his wife and child. "Unfortunately, the powers at the time were too spineless to act. Imagine a competitive advantage like that and not using it. Such a waste."

"What's that got to do with our current op? The cold war, that was a long time ago. The technology has got to be archaic."

"Well, it just so happens that our little trip to NORAD is a modernized reincarnation of that same technology. Soon I will have the ability to give our comrades the power of invisibility when breaching enemy airspace."

"But we are not at war."

The comment elicited a focused stare-down from Chow. "That is a short-sighted view, Lee. There is always a war, even if it is economic."

Lee nodded to his boss, as he watched him return to his chair.

"I can't have anyone putting the pieces together before we are ready to act." Chow leaned forward with his fingers splayed flat on the desk. "Right now, there's a situation happening in Moscow and I need you to take care of it."

10

KALUZHKOE SHOPPING CENTER – 8:45 P.M. – MOSCOW, RUSSIA

"Should be right around the next corner." Joel led Codi with his smart phone along the sidewalk. They were headed to the address indicated on the card given them by General Vasily Sokolov's guard. Joel had been using his translating app to decipher the Cyrillic names on the street signs. Codi was wearing a light blue sleeveless dress with a slight shimmer and fringed bottom. Joel had changed up his usual outfit with a peach collared shirt.

Codi was smiling to herself as they strolled along.

Joel looked over at her as they passed stoic Muscovites out for an evening amble. "What?" he asked.

"Oh nothing, just thinking."

"Come on, I know that look. What gives?"

After a beat, Codi opened up. "I was just thinking that I can now cross it off my list."

"Cross what off?"

"Drinking vodka with a Russian general."

Joel stopped mid-step. The old woman behind him barely avoided a collision. "Wait," he said to Codi, "how is that even on a list. I mean, who has a list like that?"

Codi regarded Joel for a moment, and continued walking. "You'd be surprised what's on my list, Joel."

Joel hurried to catch up. "Like swimming with sharks, or bungee jumping from a helicopter?"

"Been there, done that," Codi deadpanned.

"Seriously?"

Codi flashed back to a dark time in her life. She had left the military and had healed enough to walk without a limp. Her dream of becoming a Navy SEAL was gone and she became reckless. In hindsight, it was most likely her need to prove that she could still do anything. Her outlet was almost always dangerous and life threatening, extreme versions of extreme sports. She had even tried sky surfing. That ended when she was forced to use her emergency parachute seconds before taking the big bounce. After three months of essentially failing to kill herself, Codi found an even more destructive state, a deep dark depression that threatened to consume her.

"We're here," Joel said.

The words snapped her from her thoughts.

The LavkaLavka was a farm-to-table restaurant located in a bright yellow neoclassic building on Petrovka Street. Codi and Joel passed through the gated wrought-iron archway that led eight stone steps down to the entrance. Once inside, Codi did a quick look around. The old brick walls, red painted milk-can lights, and kitschy Russian memorabilia plastered everywhere screamed bad Applebee's. The *maître d'* had their names on his list and led them past a small bar and a large family-style seating area. The smell of fresh seafood and fragrant spices filled the air. He turned left and opened two maroon doors that led down into a small cellar seating area.

He gestured, and in very broken English with an over-the-top smile said, "You sit here." He then turned and left.

Joel stepped down into the small domed room. There were

three four-person tables but only one had been set up. "I'm guessing here," Joel said, as he took a seat.

The room was decorated with large stylized food icons, comfy upholstered chairs and a modern lighting grid. The floor was polished stained concrete and even the slightest whisper echoed around the room.

"This must be where they keep the foreigners," Codi said as she checked out the empty space.

The sommelier came a few moments later and took their order. Cody and Joel sat uncomfortably alone once again. They could hear the muffled sounds of happy patrons on the other side of the wall. "This is weird," Joel said, "let's see if we can get moved to the main dining area. I feel like I'm being watched."

"Relax Joel, we are here for a reason. Give it time. Besides, we undoubtedly are being watched. If nothing comes of tonight, you can tell everyone you had a romantic dinner with me in a Russian cellar."

Joel tried to smile but it came out more like a grimace. "I should probably make a list so I can put that on it."

"The point of a list is to remind you to do things you want to do but haven't done yet. Not to fill it in *after* you do something."

"Hey, you do your list your way and I'll do mine."

The sound of high heels on tile caught their attention as a tall model-like blond flowed into the room. She wore a skin-tight red cocktail dress, cut in all the right places, and moved with a purpose. She walked up to the table and before Joel could stand, took a seat.

"Good evening, I'm Sasha, and I am pleased to make your acquaintance Agent Sanders and Agent Strickman." Her accent was just the right amount of charming.

"Hi," was all that Joel could manage, as he gawked at the buxom beauty in awe.

"Pleasure," Codi voiced while reaching out her hand.

The two women took stock of each other and shook hands. Codi smacked Joel on the shoulder to get him to snap out of it and follow suit.

They ordered dinner and made small talk, most of which seemed forced and meaningless. Codi got the white fish and Joel the Kamchatka crab salad. Both were delicious. When the meal was about halfway through, Sasha leaned forward and said, "I am here at the bequest of General Vasily Sokolov."

Finally, Codi thought to herself.

"He has instructed me to give you a message."

Joel anxiously glanced around the otherwise empty room.

"There is a person you must see before you go."

She reached inside her purse. Both Codi and Joel tensed. Then, palming her hand across the table, she pulled it back revealing the Medal of Lenin that Codi had given the general. Codi placed her hand on top of it.

"Why are you... is the general doing this?" Joel asked.

Sasha paused before saying, "Men who die in honor for their country should have their story told."

"I agree," Codi said as she turned the medal over and glimpsed a name and address taped to the back. She slid the medal into her purse.

Sasha suddenly stood up. "I must go."

Joel finally found his voice and squawked out, "Please stay. And have a drink and maybe some dessert."

Sasha's lips parted into a dazzling smile. She walked over to Joel who suddenly looked a bit shell-shocked. She ran her fingers through his hair and whispered into his ear. His skin prickled as he turned the color of the Russian flag. "Maybe next time *Lyubimiy,*" she said. "You are very cute, but I prefer a man in uniform."

With that, Sasha spun and left, clicking her way out of the room.

Joel's glowing face practically lit the whole table. "I have a uniform," he said to himself.

Codi tried to keep a straight face for her partner's sake. "Easy there, Don Juan."

"It means, 'my love.'" Joel read the definition of *Lyubimiy* from Google Translate on his smart phone.

"You're supposed to be navigating, lover boy."

"Oh, ah, turn left in five-hundred meters."

Codi turned the rental car, avoiding a bicyclist and a roving street vender. Moscow traffic had been painful but the E115 North had opened up to some beautiful countryside.

The town of Pestovo located on the Moscow Canal was a modern looking city with none of the trappings of classic Russian architecture. Even the Soviet-era block housing had a modern spin.

Codi turned down a tree-lined gravel road that led south away from town. It paralleled the famous canal that was built in the late thirties, connecting the Volga river to the Moscow river, and was used as a major thoroughfare for goods coming to and from the great city. A mixed forest grew along this side of the waterway providing breathtaking glimpses of the slate blue water between the trees.

The road continued to deteriorate, finally ending in a small parking lot where Codi pulled to a stop and killed the engine. There were several older vehicles parked haphazardly in the lot, including an old Russian Gaz-51 pickup. A faded wooden footbridge crossed a small stream leading to a mostly-white steel building that was connected to a battered dock that floated in the channel. The words on the building were in unreadable Cyrillic but the hellish potpourri of gasoline and rotting fish said Bait Shop.

Codi and Joel stepped into the small shop and looked around. The walls and the shelves were filled with a kaleidoscope of colors and shapes, everything geared towards fishing. There were mounted trophy fish everywhere and faded pictures with grizzled men holding record catches.

Codi walked up to the counter and spied the old man behind it. He seemed to pay no attention to the visitors. He had his back to them, focused on some task.

He asked a question in Russian that neither Codi nor Joel understood.

"Are you Andrei Tatter?" Codi asked.

The man paused what he was doing and turned slowly towards Codi and Joel.

Codi could now see that he had been tying a fly to a hook that was mounted on a small vise. He was wearing a ridiculous looking magnifier on his head and one eye looked enormous through the convex glass. The man took off the headset and looked at his two customers with neutral curiosity.

Codi could see that the man was very old and had spent a good part of his life in the outdoors. His skin was mottled and saggy. He had large ears, but the most defining feature was the end of his nose. It was missing. You could see right into his nicotine-stained membranes.

He narrowed his eyes and took a guess. "English?"

"No, American," Joel said.

He looked them over one more time.

"Da, Americanski. You want fish?"

"Ah, no."

Codi and Joel glanced at each other and then back to the

man. She was beginning to regret coming all the way out here. This guy was going to be a waste of their time.

"We were hoping to speak with you about this." Joel said the last part slowly, over-enunciating every syllable. He gestured for Codi to show him the medal. Codi passed the Order of Lenin medal over to Tatter. He picked it up and eyed it suspiciously. Flipping it over to read the name on the back.

Joel played a prerecorded message translated into Russian on his phone:

> Can you tell us something about this. It was found thawed out, along with three Russian Special Forces members from the nineteen-fifties on a glacier on Umnak Island, Alaska.

Tatter slumped noticeably. He used the counter to hold himself up. He whispered three names in reverence.

"Misha, Kaz, Traktor."

"You knew them?" Joel tried to write their names down on his phone.

Tatter looked up. "Come. I make tea," he said in broken English.

Tatter led them to a small room in the back. It looked as though he'd been living as well as working at the bait shop. Joel and Codi sat hip-to-hip on a small couch covered with an old blanket, waiting patiently as the proprietor made tea in silence. Joel didn't know where to put his hands as he was afraid to touch anything in the room. Ultimately he decided on his lap.

Finally Tatter brought a chipped and worn tea set over and passed cups around. He sat in a dog-eared chair across from them and took a cautious sip. The afternoon sun filtered through a small window providing the room's only illumination. Nicotine stains covered the once-white walls. Dust motes danced in the air as Andrei lit up a filter-less cigarette and breathed in the pungent smoke. He held it in his lungs as though his life depended on it, before releasing a puff through his missing nose. The smoke shot out and up in an uncontrolled spiral. A short coughing spell followed.

Andrei Tatter then began to tell them the story of a top-secret mission he had been a part of over sixty years ago, Operation Blind Pig, from the moment they landed on Umnak Island to the installation of two electrical leaches on the island's resident radar towers. He spoke of the dead in a reverent way including the gruesome task of cutting the legs off of Political Officer Zampolit Traktor. Finally, he told them about the dash over the glacier and their trip back to Russia. Only three men had survived, and all were left with a reminder of the trip.

Andrei gestured as he spoke. "Popov lost left foot and three toes on other. Colonel Alexeev lost two fingers and half an ear. And I, as you see, lost nose. Not good for army or woman."

Tatter stared at the floor for a moment, as he picked a loose bit of tobacco from the tip of his tongue.

"So I am here." He shrugged at the way his life had turned out. "How you say, frost tip?"

"Frostbite."

"Yes, terrible word."

"What was the purpose of the electrical leach?" Codi asked.

Tatter took another puff on his cigarette. "We were never told."

A long pause followed, which made Joel antsy.

"But I might have means to help," Tatter said. "Before I leave service I take papers of mission. I put in bank box."

"What do these papers say?" Joel queried.

"I never read. Too much pain." Tatter spoke the last part more to himself. He took another slow breath drawing on his half-burnt cigarette. "It has been…hard to relive."

He dropped his head, his eyes tearing up with emotion. His hand shook as he tried to put the tip of his cigarette back in his mouth.

"I'm so sorry," Codi said.

Tatter regarded her briefly and nodded in thanks. "Come tomorrow, noon, I get you... papers."

Codi and Joel said their goodbyes and left Tatter to his memories and despair.

They bounced along the gravel road north, back to Pestovo. "Come back tomorrow? Are you kidding me? I say, come back *never.*" Joel said aloud their common thought.

"Exactly," Codi said. "It's a hell of story, but who gives a crap. I mean it happened so long ago. It's just a piece of history now."

They drove in silence for a bit. The sunlight through the trees created a moving dappled pattern on the windshield.

"Do our clothes smell like dead fish?" Joel asked, as he wrinkled his nose.

"I thought that was your cologne." Codi hit a pothole as she said it and they both jarred in their seats. She lowered the windows to a much-needed breath of fresh air.

Codi's hunger got the best of her. "I bet the vodka and caviar are good in Pestovo," she said.

"The caviar here is probably radioactive."

"That's what gives it that extra bite that I love. Joel, live a little." Codi's grin was infectious and growing.

Joel slowly nodded in agreement, trying to psych himself up for what he was sure to be a disappointment. This just made Codi laugh.

"Hey," she said, "you wanted to see the Russian countryside."

11

MOSCOW CANAL BAIT SHOP – 11:28 P.M. – PESTOVO, RUSSIA

Lee watched as the last light blinked out in the small bait shop. The location and target had come from one of their connections higher up in the Russian military. It was the way of the world. Countries spying on countries, each with its own agenda, each trying to one-up the other. It was a vicious loop, but it kept Lee busy. He moved cautiously across the footbridge, staying near the edge to keep the planks from squeaking. The tall and lanky assassin was like a wraith in the night, as he quickly slipped up to the front door. He kept his back to the wall, reached out with his right hand and tested the handle. He was surprised to find it unlocked. His sixth sense alarm went off.

Was this guy careless or was it a set-up? Caution had served him well over the years and tonight would be no different. Lee pulled out his silenced Russian SR-1, a gift left waiting for him at his hotel. He slowly turned the handle and let himself in, staying low as he entered. He was assaulted by the aroma of stale cigarettes and day-old fish. There was a slight blue glow from moonlight peeking through murky windows. It cast an assortment of shadow and light patterns across the stocked shelves and wall-mounted fish. He pressed forward, pistol leading the way as he began to clear the room. Each step slow and purposeful, his eyes and ears tuned to the slightest anomaly.

After a short stint in the PLA, People's Liberation Army, Special Forces, Lee had found himself at the wrong end of Chinese politics. After a bar fight with a privileged officer that had left the man blind in one eye, Lee became a guest at the Qincheng Maximum Security Prison. It was a modern prison with old world practices. Torture and threats of execution were on the daily menu, and food and water were often neglected.

But Lee held firm and never let them see weakness. Once, after two days without food or water he had been dragged into one of the various rooms used to taunt the prisoners. He acted hollow and pretended to be desperate for water. He used the ploy to draw the guard closer to him, one who had been particularly mean. Lee used the opportunity to break the man's nose with a head-butt. He was beaten severely as a punishment but the satisfaction it gave him put a smile on his face as he was pummeled and dumped back into his cell.

This information made its way to a General Chow Phun, a man always on the lookout for special men for his black operations.

Over time and many missions, Lee and Chow formed a unique bond. Chow used Lee as his personal wrecking crew, which resulted in many untraceable deaths—key deaths that moved Chow up and up the ladder of success. Soon, he had a solid reputation and a fear built around him—don't mess with General Chow Phun and, more importantly, don't fail him. Even after Chow left the military, the two continued in their prosperous association. And after Chow's family died, they developed an even stronger relationship.

Lee took his time as he stepped through the shop. He was in no hurry. A swooshing sound briefly filled the air as Lee moved next to the checkout counter. Before he could react, a huge fishhook impaled his gun hand and yanked. His gun skittered across the weathered floor and disappeared. Lee instinctively grabbed the monofilament attached to the hook and pulled with all his might as he jumped over the counter to safety.

Tatter knew every sound and squeak in his world. As he had put down his last cigarette for the night and closed his eyes, he knew immediately something was wrong. Not by any noise that he heard but from a lack thereof. Crickets were singing their nightly song and then they were not. Tatter worked his way to a dark corner of his shop, grateful that he had on his dark blue pajamas.

He quickly cobbled together a weapon. A nine-aught treble hook tied to 100-lb. test line. The hook was roughly the size of a man's hand, with three very sharp barbs. He silently watched as a tall slightly hunched stranger moved like a cat through his shop, a silenced gun in his right hand. This was no ordinary burglar. This man was here for one purpose, to kill him. Tatter flung the hook with deadly accuracy, catching the man's gun hand and setting two of the three barbs deep into his flesh. With a snap of the line, he disarmed the assassin. But the man's reflexes had surprised Tatter. The assassin jumped over the counter and pulled so hard on the line that Tatter crashed to the floor, the rod and reel yanked from his hands.

Lee gritted his teeth and jerked the large hook free of his hand. Meat and blood flew from the back of his palm and wrist. He ignored the pain and peered over the countertop in time to see an old man scramble back up to his feet. Lee pulled his Kukri, with its unique curved blade, from his belt. In one fluid movement, he moved back around the counter and took an aggressive stance.

His target tensed, like the last lamb to notice a wolf. Lee let loose a sneer as he closed the distance, eager to exact a measure of payback for his damaged hand.

Tatter backed up, looking around for something to fight with. In the pile of products that had spilled when he was pulled to the ground was a gaff hook used to hook large fish and pull them into the boat. He grabbed the large stainless hook mounted on a three-foot pole. He then grabbed a long black fishing rod that was still clamped to a display next to him. He squared his body and prepared to defend himself, one in each hand. Using the fishing pole in his right hand he was able to keep the killer at bay. He flicked it like a whip with the precision of a lifelong fisherman.

The tip of the black pole smacked Lee's face and arms repeatedly, leaving welts, and forcing him to defend himself rather than attack. It was impossible to see in the darkness. Lee tried to protect his eyes and bull-rush the man but the wizened man maintained his distance and matched Lee's moves with surprising skill. Lee feigned to the right, then pulled back left just in time to feel the whack of the pole's tip on his arm.

He tried throwing several cans of oil that were stacked on an end-cap at the old man, but they were parried away by the gaff pole.

The battle continued for several minutes like that, cat versus old mouse.

Finally Tatter stumbled and fell backwards over a metal hand net while trying to back-pedal. Lee jumped at the opportunity and moved inside the effective range of the pole. He sliced down, severing the fishing pole at an angle, then swung the blade, clanging off the steel hook from the gaff pole. He pressed his advantage on the fallen man who was unable to find an opening to get back on his feet and had to fight from his back. Lee used the blade expertly to keep the man pinned, the poor visibility on the floor finally declaring a winner as Lee's blade found its mark.

He parried the gaff hook and countered, plunging his knife towards the old man's larynx, while at the same time pinning the gaff hook to the floor with his knee. But the old fisherman was surprisingly strong and stopped the blade right at the skin.

In a desperate move Tatter removed one hand and reached for the severed fishing pole that lay next to him. He shoved it at the assassin's ribs for all he was worth. But the man barely seemed to flinch. Instead, he used the moment to finally plunge the tip of his Kukri deep into Tatter's throat.

Lee held the pressure on the knife until there was no struggle left. He rolled over onto the debris-littered floor to catch his breath while the body next to him twitched and gurgled. He felt a sharp pain in his side and looked down to see the handle of the severed fishing pole sticking out of him.

Lee lay there trying to catch his breath, waiting for the pain to subside. He moved to a seated position with a bit of a struggle. He pulled the pole from his side with a gasp, nearly passing out from the pain. He tried to breathe through the agony as he took a rag and put pressure on the wound. A wheezing sound was heard as air escaped through the wound with each breath. Gradually Lee stood on shaky legs and stared down at the old fisherman who had been so hard to kill. He spied his gun and collected it. Then, with much pain and effort, Lee spread gasoline on the corpse and room. He flicked a lighter he had taken from Tatter's pocket and stumbled out of the burning building.

"Eventually, smoking will kill you," he said with a rasp and a pained smile.

After much debate, Codi and Joel decided to stay the night in Pestovo. Even their boss Brian was good with the idea. But to Codi, it seemed like more trouble than it was going to be worth. They should undoubtedly turn the whole thing over to a military historian.

The rainy evening had been uneventful. They found a nice bed and breakfast just outside of town and the quiet evening had been a good calming influence. But after a breakfast of fried eggs with Russian *kolbasa* and dill, Codi and Joel were Jones-ing to get going, finish with Tatter, and head back home.

An intense sun had scattered the clouds from the night before creating a clear, beautiful Russian day. They rode in silence, each waiting for the coffee to kick in. Joel drove, tapping his hands unconsciously on the steering wheel to the beat of an unknown song. Time on the road allowed for a closeness you didn't get with your average coworker. Joel and Codi had been through a lot together, including being shot, kidnapped, and the subjects of a massive manhunt in England. It had formed a bond few share. They were starting to think alike, and moments of silence were no longer awkward.

"So what's with you and Matt?" Joel said. "I haven't heard you talk about him like you used to."

Codi took the words in and let them brew for a moment. Recent events seemed to be going against her. "I don't know, we're both so busy. We've tried to get together and make it work but we keep failing. Maybe it's not meant to be."

Matt had been the closest thing to real love she had ever

found. An unexpected case had thrust them together and pushed their limits. They found each other capable partners. The relationship had excelled under the immense pressure of life and death, but the real world seemed to lead them down different paths. No longer needing each other to survive, they had drifted apart. Maybe the effort it took to keep it going was more than they were willing to expend.

"Work."

Codi glanced sideways at Joel and his comment.

"You have to work for love," Joel added.

"Sounds like a bad eighties song."

Joel smirked but continued. "Maybe it is but it's still true today, maybe more so. What with all the social media, no one talks anymore. And sharing emotion through a text? It seems shallow, without feeling."

Joel selected an emoji on his phone and showed it to her. "A heart emoji is nice but doesn't cut it. It takes work."

Codi let the comment simmer.

"Heads up," she interrupted.

As they came around the corner to the Bait Shop's parking lot, they were met with fire and police vehicles. They could see the blackened, smoldering remains of the bait shop. A charred body was being carried to a stretcher, and a policeman was walking their way. He signaled for them to turn around and yelled something in Russian.

Joel hit the brakes and flipped a U-turn, following the officer's instructions. The policeman watched them return to the tree-lined gravel road before turning back to his job.

Codi and Joel drove back in silence as they processed what they had just seen.

"Damn, what a waste," Joel said. "I guess we'll never know the purpose of Operation Blind Pig."

"Yeah, breaks my heart. Now let's get the hell out of this country and go ho–"

Before Codi could finish her words an old tow truck T-boned them from a side trail. The impact was so sudden, Joel had no time to react. His head hit the side window smashing his glasses and skull. Codi was slammed towards Joel and recovered just as the vehicle's passenger side tires caught on a small berm along the canal, forcing the car to flip through the air and into the water.

Almost immediately, the car began to sink, first on its side, and then it righted itself, the curved roofline of the Russian rental disappearing last under the water.

Lee stepped slowly out of the tow truck, still holding his wounded side that was now leaking again after the impact of the crash. He was covered in sweat and struggled to remove his silenced pistol. Everything hurt. His right hand was bandaged, so he used his left to hold the pistol. He watched the water with the focus of a blue heron searching for fish.

Codi rolled down her window and grabbed at Joel to follow her. Water quickly filled the vehicle. She fought a rising panic that had gripped her ever since she'd drowned on her last mission. For her, the water now held only terror. She briefly flashed back to the incident and felt panic's cold fingers take hold of her body. The experience of drowning a second time was too much. She fought to gain some control, as water filled the car around her.

Certain death sometimes has a way of jumpstarting the antidote for fear—adrenaline. Codi fed off it like a hungry infant with a fresh bottle. She pinpointed her focus to her days competing on the college swim team. She needed to deal with the first problem at hand, get out of the car.

She started to swim for the surface, feeling her confidence in the water return. Just before surfacing she looked up. The silhouette of a man with a gun standing at the shore rippled above her. She grabbed Joel and shoved him back down. Joel fought the panic at being pulled away from the air that he needed so desperately. Codi pointed to the man with the gun on the shore. Joel, who was just about to exhale reflexively, nodded with bulging cheeks and eyes as big as saucers. They were trapped.

Lee looked on, as the water's current erased all evidence of the incident. He felt a slight disappointment at not being able to finish them off when they came to the surface, but the results would be the same.

Cody pulled Joel back inside the car and up to the ceiling. The curved roof of the Russian rental car held about four inches of trapped air. Codi and Joel arched their necks and gasped what little oxygen they could glean from the small reservoir.

They wouldn't last long.

"Stay here," Codi motioned with both hands, before dropping back into the water.

Joel raked his eyes over to the side to see what on earth Codi was doing, afraid to leave the security of the air pocket.

Lee lowered his weapon as a slow-moving boat came into view. He could smell it almost before he saw it. A garbage barge. He backed away from the shore but never took his eyes from the water.

A moment later, Codi returned. She could tell that the air had begun to stale. They had but a few viable breaths of oxygen left. "We've got a bit of a swim. Follow me." She pulled as much air as she could into her lungs and dropped back into the water. Joel sucked in several gulps and followed.

She stroked for the other side of the river, staying deep as she went. A dark shadow came over them and she started for the surface. The air she had taken into her lungs was already depleted of much of its life-giving oxygen and she was struggling much sooner than she expected. Her body fought and spasmed to breathe in but sheer force of will kept her going.

Lee watched the barge carefully as it moved up river. No human could still be underwater and live. But a few more minutes wouldn't make a difference. He considered swimming down to the car and checking it for bodies, but the wound on his side was getting worse. The wheezing intensified with every breath. He needed medical attention, and soon.

Codi surfaced on the far side of the barge with a desperate gasp, and heaved air in and out of her exhausted lungs. Joel popped up right behind her and looked like he might not be able to continue. She quickly stroked to the passing hull and clung to a line buoy that was dangling. She grabbed Joel as he tried and failed to do the same, and pulled him to her.

Lee watched the barge pass and, finally, after nearly ten minutes of waiting turned back to the tow truck. Smiling to himself, he murmured, "Careful, water can kill you."

Codi and Joel clung to the buoy on the far side of the garbage scow. They waited for their strength to return and then climbed up onto the deck. Both collapsed and just lay still for several minutes, until the surrounding smell reached their consciousness.

Joel made a face. "We're laying in garbage, aren't we?"

"Yep, and there's a sun-ripened, poop-filled diaper awfully close to my face. But, hey, you wanted to see the real Russia. This is pretty real."

Joel started to laugh at the ridiculousness of it all and Codi couldn't help but follow. Somehow, they were still alive.

"Privet!" A voice yelled from behind them.

They turned to see a man yelling at them in Russian from the raised bridge of the barge. Another man was climbing down a ladder and moving their way.

"I guess this is our stop," Codi said, as the two agents stood on slightly wobbly legs and jumped off the barge back into the water. They swam to shore amid Russian swear words coming from the moving vessel.

Joel crawled up next to Codi on the shore.

"Just another day in paradise." She huffed between words.

Joel looked over skeptically. "We need to get to a phone."

"Ya think?"

Lee checked in with Chow, giving him an update. The loose ends had been tied up and there was no possibility any blow-back would come their way. Chow loved how efficient Lee worked and made a mental note to congratulate him upon his return.

Chow arranged for him to meet a doctor they knew who worked off the books. "But first," he said, "get well, my friend."

Chow looked down at the only picture he kept on his desk. A gold-framed moment with his wife and child. They were all smiling, a task he now found difficult. It would be a dishonor to them to not leave a legacy, something to keep their memory alive, a place of honor for him and his family's name. Chow didn't think of himself as a psychopath, more a determined man with a plan. And he was a firm believer in the end justifying the means. And finally, the end was in sight; he was close. After many years, Chow would leave his China a better place. A place of power and strength. Where foreigners would no longer subvert their culture and traditions. His China would have the world powers trembling in fear.

The two drowned rats finally stood and walked along the shore, following the now distant barge. The beautiful Russian countryside of white birch and Olgan larch eventually gave way to a small town. They were able to find some local clothes, a disposable cellphone, and a rental car to get them back on their way. Joel navigated while Codi drove.

"How you doing without your glasses?" Codi asked.

"Fine. Just don't ask me to read any street signs."

"Noted."

Joel was wearing a black tracksuit with gold tennis shoes. Codi wore a yellow collarless summer dress with a muted floral print, and a white sweater.

"All you need is a gold chain," she said to him.

"What do you mean?"

"You look like a Russian mobster in that outfit."

"I'll take that as a compliment, coming from Maria Von Trapp," he said, citing Julie Andrews' character from *The Sound of Music*.

They headed south back to Moscow. The traffic was light and they were making good time, as Joel dialed up their boss.

"Fescue." His voice was thin and distant.

"Hey, it's Joel and Codi."

They brought him up to speed and both parties came to the same conclusion—someone doesn't want this story getting out.

Was there a connection? If so, what was it? There were too many unanswered questions. But something about this case was still active and someone didn't want it made known.

"Look, I need you both to get back here to DC," Brian said. "I can't have you creating another international incident."

Codi couldn't imagine how an international incident could be her fault, but she let it go.

"I have a few friends in our counterintelligence division. I'll see if they can take it over. We'll close our side of the case from here and set up a meet so you can turn over everything you know."

Codi hated the idea of unfinished business, but the FBI had its own way of doing things. As an agent, you followed procedure or found another line of work.

"Besides, I have something a little more current I need you on," Brian added.

Joel couldn't agree more. He gladly redirected Codi to the airport. The thought of a case that was more current helped Codi accept that she would be letting go of this one.

Once in the terminal, the two agents purchased enough personal items to get them home, all on the company credit card. They used the bathroom to freshen up and rendezvoused back at their gate. Codi settled next to Joel for the hour-and-a-half wait before takeoff. She had ditched her dress for slacks and a blouse. Her hair was up in a ponytail and she had found some more comfortable Nike's, most likely Chinese knock-offs, to wear for the long flight home.

Joel leaned back in his chair and crossed his arms over his chest. He let his eyes close and tried to tune out his surroundings.

"You're right."

Joel's eyes cracked opened, waiting for what came next. Codi repositioned herself in her chair, pulled her legs up, and turned to face Joel. "Love does take work. And lately, I've been doing too much regular work to put the time into making what matters most work."

This made Joel think briefly about the love of his life, Agent Annie Waters, and how she had died on a recent mission in spite of his best efforts. It had left him hollow for some time. He had yet to even consider dating again.

He looked over at Codi. "It would be terrible to lose something so precious without trying your hardest."

Codi nodded almost imperceptibly. "That's why when we get back, I'm going to take a week off and make the trip to Boston. Matt and I are either going to work things out, or move on."

"Good for you," Joel said.

He handed her their recently purchased cell phone and Codi started in on a carefully worded text to both Matt and her boss. After several moments of personal debate, she hit send on only one text. She needed a clear head for Matt and now was not the time. She would find the right words on the flight back home.

The flight out of Moscow Domodedovo Airport finally boarded. Codi and Joel had been late to book the flight and had their usual back section of the plane, each in middle seats, separated by three rows. But the thought of coming home seemed to make up for the lack of leg and arm room. Joel seemed to have finally perfected sleeping in an upright position. Codi was seated in between a husband and wife that refused to sit next to each other but continually chatted across her in a language she couldn't understand. Her best guess, Mongolian. It took some doing, but finally she tuned them out and got some sleep.

They dropped out of the clouds into Shanghai's Pudong Airport eight-and-a-half hours later. Codi could make out the distinct glass and steel wave-like roofline of the terminal as a light rain fell. She rubbed a kink from her neck and managed to look back over her shoulder to a sleeping Joel. A three-hour layover was to be followed by business-class seats for the rest of the journey. She watched as he jolted awake to the double impact and squeal of tires hitting the tarmac. It gave Codi her first reason to smile in many hours.

They waited interminably for their chance to exit the jet way, all so they could stand in another line at customs. In an attempt to get through the wait faster, Codi and Joel chose different queues but gave that up when a new line opened up.

Codi slid her passport to the officer in the booth. He swiped it with bored efficiency. A slight negative tone sounded and he re-swiped it. Again, a negative beep. Without emotion he pressed a button on his desk and handed her passport to the responding agent.

"You go with him."

"Is there something wrong?"

"No wrong. Go with him."

"Next."

The customs agent looked to Joel who was next in line and saw the concern on his face as Codi was escorted to a nearby room.

"No problem, random search. Passport, please."

Joel fumbled for his passport.

Codi stepped into a small side room. There was a high countertop separating part of the room and a door that exited out behind it. Bare LED strip lights illuminated beige carpet and walls. It was the polar opposite of the grandiose terminal she had come from.

The agent, in very good English, said, "Sorry, this should only take a minute."

Codi visibly relaxed until the door behind her opened and Joel stepped in followed by another agent. Something was amiss; Codi could feel it. The new agent moved around behind the countertop to join the other one and they had a two minute conversation that neither Joel nor Codi could understand. The first agent finally dismissed the other agent and looked up at Codi and Joel.

"Again, I apologize for the delay." He stamped their

passports and turned to exit the back room. "Give me a couple of seconds and you should be on your way."

As he closed the door behind him, Codi started to feel woozy. "Something's not right. We need to get out of here."

She turned to kick down the door, only to feel her body fail. It was a weird sensation, as she watched her point of view fall sideways to the carpet, just before everything went dark.

The agent reentered two minutes later to the sound of an exhaust fan clearing the room. He was followed by a couple that was remarkably similar in look and stature to Codi and Joel. The couple stripped the two comatose bodies of their clothes and redressed themselves in their outfits. They took Codi's and Joel's passports and exited back into the terminal as if nothing had occurred. After a long wait, the two imposters boarded the plane for DC, reclining comfortably in their business-class seats.

Lee leaned on the doorjamb of the address he had been given. He had staggered down a dark narrow alleyway to a green door marked by a single bare bulb. His soft knock was followed by a door opening to a small one-room clinic. The surprisingly young woman gestured for Lee to come in. She had pale skin and raven, shoulder length hair with eyes that matched almost perfectly. A medical white smock was tied around her waist. A spider web tattoo peeked above her collar along one side of her neck. She pointed to the table in the middle of the room, lit by a strong overhead lamp. Lee used his last remaining strength to scale it. The wound was only oozing now but a bright reddish color radiated on the skin around it. His breathing came in rasps. She immediately went to work cleaning his skin and listening with her stethoscope. "You have a punctured lung." She spoke in Russian, a language Lee was not fluent in.

He answered in French and the woman switched over without a missing a beat.

She finished cleaning and closing the chest wound and stitching up Lee's hand. She gave him plasma for the blood loss and a few pills for the pain. At some point along the way Lee mercifully lost consciousness.

Blackness parted as Lee cracked open his eyes. His mouth felt dry and sluggish. He was expecting a bright light in his eyes, but the room was lit with ambient lighting. He turned his head, to find a smiling face.

"I see you're back," the doctor said with a smile. She inspected Lee's pupils with a small flashlight. "You should be okay, but take it easy for a couple of weeks and finish all your medication. You don't want that infection to spread."

Lee thanked her and, with much effort, exited the premises, his tall frame stooped over with pain as he moved back down the narrow alley.

12

Red Baks — 10:14 a.m. — Subbasement, Hong Kong

Lee entered his boss's office on the first floor of the Red Baks. He was not quite himself. The surgery had gone well but the infection was slow to depart. One lung had been punctured by the fishing pole and he was still having trouble taking a full breath. General Chow Phun looked up as Lee entered his office. He let out a slow breath, resigned to the fact that his perfect weapon was no longer perfect. "I see you are healing."

"Yes," Lee rasped. His breathing was labored and a rattling sound accompanied every breath he took.

"So now the two of us are not so…" Chow searched for the right word.

"Yes, but I will heal from what ails me," said Lee, wheezing as he spoke.

Chow let the comment hang for a moment. "Perhaps." He decided to press on. "I assume there were no further leaks from Russia?"

"All evidence is up in smoke." The corners of Lee's mouth turned up at the Americanism. After spending so much time there lately, it was becoming second nature.

"And the Americans?"

"Drowned. I shoved their car into the river and waited at the water's edge more than ten minutes. Nothing."

Lee pulled a pack of cigarettes from his pocket and tapped the bottom. Remembering his condition, he put them back. "I think you can stop worrying about your leak. I have plugged it."

Chow stood from behind his desk and moved around the massive polished surface to the front. "The Americans are here."

A brief look of panic flashed across Lee's face. *"Impossible. There's no way they could have survived."*

"And yet they did."

"How?" Lee leaned forward in his chair.

Chow lowered himself into the chair next to him. "I have no heart to remove you, Lee. You have been like a son to me."

Lee's head was spinning. How could this be happening? To him, of all people.

"And you a father to me, sir," Lee replied without emotion.

Chow nodded at the truth of Lee's statement. "You have been instrumental in many of our successes. But I have a reputation that is more valuable to me than any one person. And failure, as you know…"

Lee finished his words. "Is never tolerated." Lee looked down at his feet. "I am the one who carried that message to the world for you, sir."

"Yes, I know," whispered Chow.

"And the Americans, they are truly here?"

"Yes," Chow whispered.

Lee nodded slowly, knowing he had no moves left, none he was willing to make. "Sir, if you will permit me one small kindness."

Chow looked at him, despondent.

"I would like to finish what I started. Please let me finish off the Americans. I'll find out what they know, and once that is done, let me be the one to carry out my own punishment."

Chow watched as a single tear wormed its way down Lee's cheek. He could see the truth in his enforcer's words. "So be it," he said, as he slowly stood.

He put his hand on Lee's shoulder for a moment. Then, as in a symbolic emotional severing, wiped his hands clean on his own shirt. From his pocket he handed Lee a small vial of brown liquid. Lee accepted this final gift as tears flowed uncontrollably. Chow turned and walked away, never looking back.

Codi cracked open an eye. Nothing. Darkness, no light whatsoever. She listened for a moment and then sat up, blinking her eyes into focus. She tried calling out in a hoarse whisper. "Joel?"

She listened for a response.

"Hey, Joel?"

She tried to see her environs, but the stygian darkness was void of all light. She used her fingers as probes to tell her the story. There was a small cot with a foam pad about two feet up from a smooth concrete floor. The walls were also made of concrete, as was the ceiling. There was a small sink/toilet combo thingy in the corner that she regretted touching with her hands. A locked steel door set into one wall was the only way out. No light or switch of any kind. She was in some kind of prison and the fact that there were no lights meant it probably wasn't government sponsored. She slumped back on her cot letting her mind drift.

Codi hadn't experienced this kind of darkness since a special forces team building exercise she'd been a part of two years ago. She and three other soldiers had repelled into a reverse funnel-shaped cavern. The instructor cut the ropes they had just come down on and tossed them a half-charged flashlight. He then leaned over the rim and shouted, "You have twenty-four hours to find a way out." He looked down at his watch. "Starting now."

They were a squad of four soldiers: Conrad, Suarez, Codi, and Grimes. Conrad picked up the flashlight and inspected it. It was an old school bulb-style with two D batteries inside. The way back up was impossible, as the cave walls funneled and narrowed towards the top.

Codi began coiling up the two rope ends that had been cut. It looked like they had about ninety feet in total. She threw the coiled rope onto the floor. "Okay," she said. "Everything in a pile. Let's appraise our assets."

Suarez bristled at the thought of taking orders from a woman.

A small pile formed as they emptied pockets. Half-a-pack of Camel unfiltered cigarettes, a lighter, four knives, the flashlight, eighty-six cents, and a pack of Wrigley's gum. All that was left were the clothes on their backs.

"Well, we ain't getting' out that way," Grimes said, looking back up at the afternoon daylight that streamed down from the entrance forty feet up.

Codi looked around the chamber. They were in a limestone room about the size of a round convenience store. There were three tunnels that shot off in different directions but no obvious clue as to which one to take.

"*Shh.* Listen," Conrad said.

The squad got quiet and watched as Conrad, a twenty-three-year-old African American, moved from one tunnel entrance to the next, listening. "Nothing," he said.

They huddled back up and made a plan. Conrad, Codi and Suarez would each take a tunnel and go as far as they could, based on the ambient light of the cavern. Grimes would stay put with all the gear and be ready to assist should anyone need it. They would all meet back in ten minutes.

Codi moved down her tunnel slowly, waiting for her eyes to adjust to the near total darkness. She used her hands like sensors, running them along the cave's surface to detect other openings or problems ahead. As long as she kept in touch with the wall she could find her way back. She couldn't help but think she was going to put her hand on a bat or a snake at any second, but fought hard to push that thought from her mind. She slid her feet along the floor, to prevent stepping into a sudden drop-off. Each step thrust her further into the darkening void, heading towards a blackness so dark you couldn't see your hand right in front of your face.

The further she went, the less detail she could see. Finally she reached total darkness. She pushed herself to go just a few more yards before heading back. She relied on her only remaining viable sense, touch. As she pressed around a bend in the ever-shrinking tunnel, she smelled it.

Codi stopped immediately. Her hands had hit something mushy. She held back a horrorstricken expression as she took a quick sniff of the substance on her hands—bat shit, her second-worst nightmare.

"Oh, God," she murmured. It clung to her skin like cement, but worst of all, she could hear the dry rustle of wings and faint sound of echolocation sonar from hundreds of now fully-awake bats.

Codi had no ill feelings towards most creatures, but there were a few that pushed her to the limit of her comfort zone and a few more she had an abject hatred for. Bats were right at the top of that list. She tensed in panic, as hundreds of the furry critters mobilized and took flight, right in her direction.

Their sonar bouncing around the tunnel in a jumble of chaos, like Christmas weekend in Times Square.

Waves of leather wings and claws swooped past her, some hitting her, some getting stuck in her hair. It was a nightmare of epic proportions. She lost contact with the wall and slipped and fell into what could only be described as mushy hell.

The floor was a layer cake of guano, built over time. The cake was topped off with a surface of dripping water, cockroaches, and other bugs feeding on the potent slurry. Before she could find the strength to even panic or scream, the bats had fled. Flapping out the tunnel leaving nothing behind but the stink of fresh excrement. Codi took a slow breath to calm herself, but the ammonia burned her lungs. She waited until her hands stopped shaking and then, with all her will, pushed herself out of the muck and into a sitting position. She could see nothing in any direction. And she was so turned around she had no idea which way was back. This is how people get lost and die in caves, she thought. At least she had a fifty-fifty chance of going in the right direction.

She tried to think, rather than react.

Grimes sucked on a half-finished Camel as one by one the scouts returned. He spit out a bit of tobacco as Suarez settled on the boulder next to him. "Well?" he asked Suarez.

"Nothing but blackness. Let me have a puff."

Grimes flicked the loose ash from his cigarette and passed it to Suarez. He took a deep drag and passed it back.

"Dead end."

Suarez and Grimes looked up as Conrad returned from his exploration.

Conrad looked up at the entrance hole and saw the fading

afternoon light. "Once the sun goes down, we'll never see an exit hole unless we stumble right through it."

Codi stepped into the room. Her odor preceded her. Her face and clothes were smeared with dirt and excrement. Her hair looked like an abandoned birds nest. But the overwhelming odor of ammonia in the room was almost debilitating. "I'm pretty sure I found the way out," she said, "but you're not gonna like it."

The three men shared a disgusted look.

"Lucky for you, I chased off all the bats. Now we just have to wade through a shitload of guano."

Suarez in a slightly panicked look, blurted out, "You're shittin' me, right?"

He realized what he just said and slowly but surely each man started to laugh. Even Codi found the humor in it; her white teeth shining through mud and crap-covered lips.

She led the team back down the tunnel she had explored. They pushed through the guano as best they could, using the dim flashlight to avoid a repeat of her experience. They pressed themselves through several very tight gaps. It only took an hour more before the blackness of their world began to brighten. The squad found a small exit hole about eight feet up on the side of the tunnel. With a little teamwork, they managed to escape their stone prison.

Their instructor was quite surprised at the quickness of their escape. The normal evac time was almost double theirs. He tried to hold an AAR, (After Action Report), but the smell of crap coming off the squad was so strong, his eyes burned. He finally dismissed them to the showers, and he wasn't far behind.

Joel felt like he was drifting in a lifeboat at sea. He had a burning desire to drink ocean water. He thought he must be lost at sea, and found himself saying, "Don't drink the salt water!" His eyes slowly fluttered open, and the reality of his situation began to be clear. A very different story unfolded. He remembered being gassed in the little room at the airport. Drugs explained the rocking sensation he was experiencing. He tried to move his mouth, but he was so dehydrated he had difficulty opening it. *I've been drugged!* It was a thought he shouted without words. That would explain the weird dream, he thought as his mind slowly cleared.

He was in a small industrial space. There was a glow of artificial light through the bottom of a rusty metal door. The floor was cement with a drain in the center. When he sat up his head swirled and his body rocked like a punching balloon clown. The aroma of chemicals and a recently emptied mop rack told him where he was. There was an old metal cabinet on one wall. He used the handles to help himself stand. The world spun again. He held tight to the cabinet for stability. Finally he spread his legs so he could stand on his own. The cabinet was locked, as was the exit door. He was a prisoner in a broom closet.

Chow and Jin exited the armored door to the Red Baks facility. Chow looked back at his two security guards, and said, "Make sure no one comes or leaves before I get back." He looked at the gold Audemars Piguet Royal Oak on his wrist. "I'm guessing by three tomorrow afternoon. Until then, we are on lockdown."

"Yes, sir." The guards responded.

Chow and Jin left. The guards closed the heavy exit door behind them. It clanged shut with an ominous thud. Chow led the way up to the street through the secret entrance and into a powder blue Bentley waiting curbside. They made good time to the private terminal of the airport. From there it was a three-and-a-half-hour flight to Beijing, followed by one of the most important meetings of General Chow's life.

It seemed like morning, though Codi couldn't be sure. What she was sure of was that something very bright was literally burning out her retinas through eyelids that were slammed shut. Hands grabbed her and quickly subdued her with handcuffs and ankle chains. She was dragged along a straight hallway and then deposited into a room with two metal chairs and an even brighter light. She was cuffed, both hands and legs, to a chair and left smoldering in the powerful spotlight. After what seemed like an eternity her eyes adjusted to the glare. Two days without light, food, or water had left her a little off her game. She glanced down and saw that her chair was bolted to the floor. She tried to focus her mind, but a raging headache fought back. All she could think about was how thirsty she was. Definitely off her game.

Joel lay on the floor peeking through the rusted gap on the bottom of his exit door. He had a weird bugs-eye view of a hallway on the other side. He could see beige carpet. Two steel doors were across the hallway, and a large dust bunny sat right in front of him. Joel suddenly heard a familiar voice with a few choice words coming from his emotionally-charged partner from down the hall. He shoved his left eye up close to see what he could.

Two men carried a struggling Codi past his door. He was pretty sure calling out would get them nowhere. Instead, he watched to see where they were taking her. Three doors down on the left. He sat up. He had to do something.

He stood back up and approached the locked steel cabinet. Had they emptied it or just locked it before he was stashed here. Joel found it hard to think as his brain struggled with severe dehydration. He tried the handles again. Nothing. He tried kicking at the handles. Again, nothing.

13

Washington D.C. – 9:24 a.m. – FBI Field Office – Special Projects – 3rd Floor

Brian called both Codi and Joel's cell for the fifth time and still got no answer. He hung up and drummed his fingers on his desk as he stared off into space, thinking. Was their burner phone not able to take incoming international calls? That seemed unlikely. And in light of what had happened in Russia, something was off. The FBI had protocol in place for a missing agent, but he wasn't sure they were actually missing. He had received a text from Codi before they left Russia, requesting time off when she got back to tie up some personal issues. He was glad to give it to her, but he thought she would at least check in before leaving. What was most troublesome however, was Joel. He was supposed to meet with counter intelligence and download everything.

Brian was hoping he could close out this last case so he could get started on the next one. Codi could be read in on the case once she got back. Joel was so punctual he'd be on time for his own funeral. Something was wrong. He could feel it.

By Tuesday, Brian had taken action. He engaged a task

force to find them—two agents from the regular FBI and one of his special projects agents. He set them up in a bullpen across from his office, requesting frequent updates on their progress. He made sure they were briefed on everything he knew. Something had happened to his two agents and he wanted the team scouring every lead, including searching their apartments for clues.

After at least an hour of waiting while tied to a chair, Codi slumped to the side. Her hair hung in a messy tangle and her eyes looked sunken. She had been dressed in a gray jumpsuit with a zipper down the front. A slight clicking sound signaled the opening of the door. She tilted her head up. There was a wheezing sound as the other metal chair was dragged slowly across the concrete floor and placed just behind the light, out of Codi's sight. Someone sat in the chair and continued with his noisy breathing, each breath making that wheezing sound. No words or actions, just that sound, in and out—the breathing of the damned.

Finally the man spoke. "Collette Sanders, you have been found guilty of espionage and murder. Both of these are executable offenses."

He had a slight Chinese accent. Codi gave him her best devil-may-care glare. She knew there was nothing to be gained by speaking. This was a classic lose/lose situation and she was the loser.

Lee sat there staring at the impossible sight. The woman was still alive. He had seen her go down with the car and never come up. Quite incredible, he thought.

He played with his yepian, rolling it in his fingers. It was a weapon that he had personally created and named; it meant leaf blade. It was a small, four-foot bamboo rod not much bigger in diameter than a pencil. Attached to the end was a small but very sharp perpendicular two-inch blade. The thin bamboo could be flicked like a whip, and he had become very accurate in its use. Cutting and slicing with the precision of a surgeon. He had once kept a man alive for two days as he slowly whittled him away piece by piece. He remembered how much pleasure it had given him.

"My name is Lee. You are mine to do with as I please, but I will know a few things before I am finished with you."

This just got friggn' real, Codi thought.

"But first let's have some fun."

Lee reached with the Yepian and slowly moved the blade along Codi's arm, touching it just enough to scratch a thin line of blood and nothing more. Codi watched helplessly as the curious weapon dug a small groove in her arm. She was bound tight and no matter how hard she fought she was unable to move any more than a slight lean. Lee moved the blade up to her eye and closed the distance to less than a millimeter, the point so close her eyes could not focus on the blade's edge.

She stiffened in fear as her assailant moved the sharpened blade surprisingly fast right next to her right eye. She dared not move for fear of losing her eye. Sweat started to drip from her already dehydrated cells.

The man spoke again. "How did you escape the car crash in the river?"

Codi remained unmoved.

With a whip-like motion, Lee flicked the yepian in an arc and down.

Faster than Codi's eye could register, the blade imbedded itself into her right forearm. It flicked away just as fast, leaving behind a hole and a growing trail of blood.

"You dick!" she yelled at him.

"Tell me what I want to know!"

"Screw you!" This psycho would get nothing from her.

Lee's lips danced with a smile. This would be his final chapter, but he could see this woman was going to make it very worthwhile. Perhaps he would take her up on her of-fer— screw you. The two of them could go out with a bang. Surely Chow wouldn't care if he had his way with her before completing the mission. She was not ugly, quite the contrary. This woman was lean, athletic, with strong cheekbones and a seductive figure. She had brown eyes with flecks of gold in the irises if he was not mistaken. Yes, this would be a pleasure for both of them.

He flipped out the yepian again and it snapped the zipper on the front of her overalls. Then another, and another, until the front of the jumpsuit was shredded, revealing a flat stom-ach and a pink bra.

Codi wriggled in the chair but the restraints held firm. Panic started to lay claim. She tried to force her mind to calm against the rising surge.

Beijing, which means northern capital, is one of China's most modern cities. It is home to twenty-one million people, mak-ing it the third most populous city in the world.

General Chow Phun and his top hacker, a young man who went only by the man of Jin, crossed Tiananmen Square. It was filled with a mix of working professionals and tourists as the early sunlight glinted off the morning frost. The sky was transitioning from orange to blue as they passed the guards that protected Chairman Mao's tomb. Chow gave the tomb a furtive glance. It was a layered building with multiple columns across its entrance. China, Mao's China and true communism, were in the past. Chow knew that for a fact. But there was no reason that they couldn't rebuild a better, stronger, and more feared China. A China that could take her growing capitalism and strong nationalism, along with Chow's superior technology, and grow it into the one-and-only world superpower. And that is why Chow and Jin were there today. To help start China down a path that would soon have every other nation in the world living in fear.

But that could only happen if everything went perfect. Chow had finally achieved the success he had been striving for and he was eager to share it. He was sure he had politically lubricated the right men. But politicians were a fickle lot. They could only be trusted to serve their own self-interests.

Jin almost stopped as they passed the location where Mao's tanks had infamously stopped for a single protester, a single citizen who thought he might hold back the power of the state. He had been a fool. Nothing marked the man's act. No one knew whom he was or if he was even still living. It was a moment that lived only in memories.

At the far end of the square stood a gigantic building. Chow and Jin climbed the wide band of triple-tiered steps that passed through looming marble pillars. This was the Great Hall of the People. It was over a thousand feet in width and six-hundred feet from front to back, making it larger than any capital building the west had to offer. Chow was dressed in a fine hand-tailored suit made by a friend in Hong Kong. Jin wore a white turtleneck under a two-piece tweed suit. Their polished shoes clicked in unison on the marble floor as they entered the lobby. Once through security, they would take one of the many red carpet runners that led to the executive elevators.

"Let me do most of the talking," Chow said. "If they have any technical questions, you handle that."

Jin nodded. It was show time.

Agent Tony Kwuo and Chelsea Keener of the recently formed FBI task force had made themselves comfortable in the bull-pen. Each had established a work area and was busy on their phones and computers finding and following leads. Special Agent Gordon Reyas had moved all of his equipment down from his cubicle to join them. The room had a small round table in the middle surrounded by metal chairs and a row of tables with office chairs along two walls. The front was all glass and the people who worked there had nicknamed it The Fishbowl. It was bare bones and there was no place to hide, but as a work environment it was functional.

Gordon had acquired the last known footage of Codi and Joel as they were processed through customs on their return trip from China at the Ronald Reagan Airport in DC. He brought it up on the big screen mounted on the wall. The image angle was dodgy, as it was slightly from behind, but you could see a tall and lanky man in a tracksuit and a lithe brunette in black slacks and a white blouse.

"There they are." Tony pointed them out.

"What is he wearing?" Chelsea leaned in to take a closer look.

"Russian gangster chic," Tony said.

"Are his tennis shoes *gold?*" she asked.

"That's the fashion of a case gone bad, or a lot of drinking on the job," Brian said. "Okay, so they landed here in DC, and then what?"

"Customs said they cleared at 3:27 p.m.," Tony said.

"That matches the time stamp on the video as well," Chelsea said.

"See if you can get any hits on a camera outside the air-port," Brian said. "Maybe we can piece a trail together."

Tony started hammering on his keyboard. "Ok, give me some time."

147

The three agents worked to piece together a clearer picture of where Joel and Codi went after arriving in DC. Delivery pizza arrived and went cold; most of it lay forgotten on the table.

Joel mechanically kicked at the steel cabinet with his left foot. His right foot had gone numb about twenty minutes ago. He was making little progress, but knew they were in a desperate situation. His mind seemed to go in and out of focus as his body fought the lack of fluids in his system. He stopped briefly and leaned his head against the cabinet staring down at his beleaguered feet. He had reached the end, and there was no going forward. His vision was blurring in and out and he was sure he now had three feet, no, make that four. As he looked closer, he realized it wasn't a foot but one of the cabinet handles. He had succeeded in knocking one off. He dropped to his knees and held the chrome piece of metal in his hands. It took a full minute for him to realize its significance. He shook his head and reached up and pulled at the other twisted handle. The doors popped opened.

He stood motionless in shock. A distant scream, muffled through the door, penetrated his brain fog. *Codi!* She was in danger.

Joel stood back and surveyed his smorgasbord. Every shelf was full. The top shelf had medical supplies, including a six-pack of 200 ml Nongfu spring water. He immediately guzzled two bottles and felt as if the world just might continue to rotate. The second shelf had cleaning supplies, like bleach and soap. There were a few odds and ends like aluminum foil and clothespins, and in the back corner was a butter knife. The bottom shelf had paper products like toilet paper and paper towels. Joel mentally dug through his newfound inventory and came up blank.

He sat back on the floor and tried to noodle a solution as he sipped on his third water bottle. He could start a fire possibly but that would just bring the bad guys to him. A chemical concoction of some sort, again, would just affect him unless he could get it out into the hallway somehow. But the effects would be limited at best. He forced himself to focus.

"Come on Joel, you got this," he told himself.

Then, all those nights of watching random YouTube videos clicked. *Thermite.* You could make thermite out of aluminum foil and iron oxide—rust. He'd seen it done. It melted right through steel plate.

He grabbed the roll of aluminum foil and the butter knife. He then began to scrape the rust from the bottom of the door and from a spot just inside the cabinet. He wasn't sure of the proportions needed but felt reasonably sure it was something like three-to-one. His confidence grew as a small pile of rust amassed on the foil. He laid the foil flat on the floor and spread the rust evenly across it. He began folding the foil on top of itself in one-inch-wide strips. He then smashed it and folded it until he had a band about the size of a school ruler. He used the butter knife to cut it in two and then proceeded to wrap the exit door's two steel hinges with the combo. Now he just needed to find an igniter. Joel searched through the cabinet again.

"Seriously?" He came up short and collapsed back down in bitter disappointment.

Codi did her best to stay defiant, but the reality of her situation was bleak. Her clothes were shredded and her underwear clung in place by a thread. Both her arms were bleeding as was a spot on her left cheek. But the cut that worried her most was the side of her neck. She could feel the warm blood running down her neck and with it, the last of her energy. She prayed that her jugular had not been pierced.

She decided to take another tack. "I'm sure you're aware that I am not a spy but a duly appointed federal agent for the United States government."

The words came slowly to her, as severe dehydration, blood loss and intense stress combined together. She concentrated with all her capacity. "I am in the act of closing out a cold case and there is no information I have that I can't share."

The silence after her speech made Codi think he had not heard her. She decided to call it out louder, but before she could, the man spoke.

"But how did you escape the car crash?" he asked.

"That's the bug up your ass?"

She told her torturer how she and Joel had escaped, how they had used the trapped air in the rental car's curved roof and then swam underwater to the far side of the passing barge. The man seemed to hesitate as silence filled the room.

"What do you know of Operation Blind Pig," he asked, "and who else knows of it?"

Codi looked up slowly and deliberately. "Everything. It is being declassified as we speak. Check the Internet and see for yourself. The conspiracy nuts are having a field day with it already."

"Liar!"

A sudden excruciating pain followed as the Yepian tore a chunk out of her thigh.

Codi had played her last hand and it had been for naught.

Her head dropped in despair. Now all she had left was hope. A thin chance, at best.

The carved rosewood walls were just visible through the smoke-filled haze in the room. General Chow Phun and Jin took their appointed seats, and the meeting began. The round conference room was purposefully set in the center of the capital, and was shielded by a barrier wall that prevented eavesdropping. There was a series of high-tech screens along one wall with a control station attached to it. Sitting at the large circular table in the middle of the room were eight of China's junior elite assistants. Not quite the power brokers Chow had hoped for. But they were all looking for a path up the ladder. Maybe Chow could provide them one, or at the very least, get them to pass his message up the chain of command.

After brief introductions, Chow began. He told them of a Russian operation from the fifties that had developed a technology they called CCI that could blind the enemy to approaching bombers. Jin explained that they had used an electrical leach planted in the enemy's radar installations. The leach would filter out a very specific frequency from all others. The radar system would appear to work as normal and any regular incoming aircraft would be identified and tracked. But if a bomber were adapted with hardware to transmit this specific frequency, it would be invisible to their radar.

Chow then told them how they had stolen the Russian technology and the scientists behind it in a clever twist that the Russians never thought possible. For a while, China had the ability to breach any major government's airspace.

Chow looked around the room as he spoke. The men seemed interested in his story, but like any good up-and-coming politician or poker player, they looked unfazed.

The man from the Central Secretariat said, "Chow, who cares? This was so many years ago. Why do you waste our time with a history lesson?"

The man from the State Council agreed and soon others

joined in. Chow motioned with his arms for patience. "Please, just hear us out. It will all make sense momentarily, I promise."

Chow continued. "We have modernized this technology."

This statement seemed to dull the murmur. "I now have…" He let that statement hang in the air for just a moment. "We now have the ability to send a missile right into Washington DC without them being able to see it, or detect it. In fact, the first they will know of it is when they hear it screeching down on their heads."

The room went silent. Even the hanging cigarette fog seamed to clear.

"Jin." Chow prodded him to take them through the basics.

"That's right," Jin said. "We have implanted a transparent code within NORAD that will make everything seem to work as usual, except it will be blind to one very specific frequency. And if we broadcast this frequency from, say, a missile as it cruises, that missile will effectively be invisible to their detection equipment."

Jin interlocked his fingers and sat back down, satisfied with his simple and direct explanation.

That started a choir of voices, all clambering to be heard, some very excited, some very fearful.

"China is not at war with the US."

"We depend on them for a large part of our GNP."

Chow had expected this. He adjusted his suit and stood for emphasis. "That kind of thinking has made us weak." Some spittle flew from his rubbery lips as he spoke. "We used to be powerful and feared. Now we make toys and TV's, and we panic when sales drop."

The room quieted, as no one knew what to say.

"Perhaps if you would authorize a test," Chow said. "Say, a medium-sized rocket, no bomb, just a rocket, launched into America's heartland and left for them to see our ability. They would know that they couldn't stop us from doing it for real. Now, imagine the next time you go the bargaining table. What would the war-fearing Americans do? They would think twice before taking Japan's or South Korea's side in a trade dispute, that's for sure. We would call the shots for a change. We would dominate the east *and* the west, as others lived in fear, fear of the great red dragon. I implore you to talk with your superiors to help them understand. We would be happy to give them a test of the technology."

An argument flared between members of his audience again. With that, Chow gave a slight bow and said, "I await your decision."

He and Jin exited the room amid a parade of petty arguments, each underling opinionated but essentially powerless.

14

Washington D.C. – 4:32 p.m. – FBI Field Office – Special Projects – Fish Bowl

"Cab!" Gordon called out.

The other two agents turned.

"Got Joel entering a cab." Gordon cast the image up to the big screen.

Tony stepped closer for a better look at the man entering a cab. "Weird," he said. "It's like he's aware of the cameras. We keep getting these glancing views from him."

Chelsea asked, "Where's that cab off to?"

"I'll contact the company and see if they have a record."

Throughout what was left of the day, they followed the trail, slowly piecing it together.

"Got him!" Gordon pointed to an image of Joel exiting the cab and, finally, it was a straight-on view that he'd acquired from an ATM camera just ten feet away. "He's coming out of the cab on Dalworth Street."

"Who the hell is that?"

The three agents turned to see Special Agent in Charge Brian Fescue standing behind them. They looked back to the screen.

"Increase the resolution, Gordon," Tony requested.

They all moved closer to the screen as Gordon fulfilled the demand.

A better quality picture appeared. It was not Joel. It was someone who looked like him, but it was not him. Four mouths sagged in unison.

Joel looked at the slice on his thumb. It was still seeping blood. He had sliced it open on the rusty bottom of the door while scrapping it. Initially, the cut had been a minor nuisance, but now it was beginning to throb. Maybe tetanus from the rusty edge, he thought, worried. He grabbed a first aid kit from the cabinet. He popped it open. Inside was an impressive collection. He found a Band-Aid and some antiseptic. Luckily, most items were labeled in both English and Chinese. He picked through the kit and lifted a small jar of glycerin. Its high viscosity made it move like syrup in the glass container. It was an emollient used to treat skin irritations.

Gaping at the slow moving fluid, a memory kicked in. He dug through the kit until he found what he was looking for—Potassium Permanganate, used as an antifungal. He had his igniter. He had seen an exothermic reaction take place when it was mixed with glycerin. *Thank you, YouTube!*

Joel placed the dark purple crystals in a bowl shape he formed from the foil, on top of each hinge. He then retrieved the glycerin bottle. He held his breath as he poured about one teaspoon of the viscous liquid over each pile of the Potassium Permanganate. Almost immediately there was a reaction. First smoke, then flames. The exothermic reaction was hot enough to ignite the homemade thermite. The thermite, once ignited, burned at just over four-thousand degrees, melting the hinges like they were butter.

Smoke filled the small space, and shards of liquid metal fountained out from the conflagration.

Joel took cover in the corner until the thermite completed its mission. He then kicked at the melted hinges and the door gave way. He was free.

Smoke started to fill the hallway. Time was limited. Someone would soon notice.

Chow and Jin had been quiet for most of the trip back to Hong Kong. As the G550 flared and lowered its flaps on approach to Shek Kong Airfield, Jin could feel his boss's gears turning. The man was a genius and never suffered fools.

Chow was disgusted by how the meeting had gone. Friends that had been loyal to him during his stint in the military seemed to shun him lately. Was it his age or the disease that left him looking like a severe stroke victim? He might never know. But as of today he needed to take the reins. It was time for his plans to be unleashed, and he knew exactly what to do.

"Our country's youth." He shook his head with antipathy.

Jin looked over as his boss dabbed at his chin.

"They speak boldly but have no spine when it comes to action. I fear that smart phones and memory-foam mattresses have made them soft and lazy."

Jin slid his smart phone out of sight.

Chow sighed softly as he put on his seatbelt for landing. He looked over at Jin with a fire burning in his eyes. "This was unfortunate, but not entirely unexpected. It is time to take matters into our own hands, Jin."

Jin nodded. He feared for those whom his boss's wrath was now focused on. The jet bobbled in the air and the wheels locked in place. Jin turned and looked out the window at the fast approaching runway, unsure what would come next.

Joel ran down to the door he'd seen them drag Codi through. He carefully turned the knob. He slipped in and, completely silent, closed the door behind him. He gripped the butter knife so hard he was losing feeling in his trembling fingers.

A few feet in front of him was a tall lanky bald man sitting in a chair facing Codi. There was a large bright spotlight illuminating her bloody and battered condition. The man was whipping a bamboo-looking pole at Codi, while he degraded her verbally, telling her what he was about to do to her and how she was powerless to stop him. The jumpsuit she was wearing had been shredded, and her bra was held together by a thread.

For probably the first time in his life, Joel didn't hesitate. He moved silently towards the man and jabbed the dull knife into the side of his neck with all his might. The man spun on Joel faster than Joel could have imagined with a look of surprise and anger. But somehow, Joel brought down both his fists in a sweeping tomahawk motion and dropped the man to the floor. He was out cold.

He dug through the man's pockets and fished out a set of keys to the handcuffs, a cellphone, and a handgun that was holstered in the back of the man's pants. He quickly released Codi and helped her to stand.

"We've got to get out of here now."

A confused Codi looked up to the man standing next to her. "Joel?"

Joel could see she was in a bad way. He sat her back in the chair and ran, calling over his shoulder, "Wait here."

He dashed to the storage room and grabbed the first aid kit and the remaining waters. He dashed back down the hall, as the fire alarm initiated a soft beeping. Codi had staggered out of the room and was leaning against the doorjamb, holding a bamboo rod. On closer inspection, he could see a blade was attached to the end of the pole. *WTF?*

He grabbed Codi's arm and the two moved along the hallway to a door down the hall. He pointed the confiscated pistol and pushed the door open.

It was a server room. A small console was manned by a young man with heavy black-framed glasses. He had started to go bald prematurely and had embraced the comb-over. Joel pointed his gun at the man and gestured for him to get on the floor. The timid man obeyed with a wild look of fear, not fully understanding the words coming from Joel's mouth. Joel grabbed Codi and pulled her inside. He kept an eye on the man while he had Codi drink as much water as she could. He quickly wrapped her neck wound and all of the deeper cuts. She had lost some blood and was going into shock, but otherwise she was in fair condition.

It was amazing what water can do under the right conditions. After finishing her second bottle, Codi looked right in Joel's eyes and said, "Thanks."

He nodded in his classic self-deprecating way but he was so glad to see her.

"So, how did you escape?" Codi asked in a raspy voice.

"Never lock a YouTuber in a supply closet—too many possibilities."

Codi raised one eyebrow at Joel, who tried to be tough and stoic, but the corners of his mouth betrayed him.

"You okay?" Codi asked.

"Yeah, I just sliced my thumb, trying to..." He realized the stupidity of his statement and stopped mid-sentence. "I'm good."

"So what's next?"

He checked the clip of his stolen pistol. Full. "We reach out and try to touch someone."

Codi pointed her bamboo weapon to the man on the ground and pantomimed taking off his pants. He looked more scared of Codi's weapon than he was of Joel's gun. He tossed his pants to Codi. She put them on and quickly tied what was left of her coveralls into a fashion-statement blouse only a Parisian could love.

The Fishbowl was silent as the four agents tried to process their failure. Codi and Joel had simply disappeared, and in this modern world of surveillance, that was nearly impossible.

"Okay let's try this again," Brian said. Something was not right and things were now getting very serious. Where and what had happened to his two agents?

"Go back to the beginning," he said. "Recheck everything, starting with them leaving Moscow. I want to know if this is the man who cleared customs as Special Agent Joel Strickman or did we screw the pooch trying to track him."

Three heads nodded.

"For all we know, they could be in serious harm's way. So let's get to it now, people."

Gordon turned back to his console, typing furiously.

Brian left The Fishbowl, his mind swirling.

Lee opened his eyes to a throbbing at the back of his skull. He sat up, and a shooting pain in his neck added to that pain. He reached up and found the handle of some sort of table knife protruding from his neck. He yanked it out without a second thought. Blood poured from the wound, but he could tell nothing vital had been severed. His fingers moved over his front pocket and found that the poison vial given to him by Chow had broken with his fall. He processed this fact for a moment and then came to a conclusion. He no longer had the luxury of an honorable death. Chow would have to wait.

It was time to clean up a mess, time for vengeance. He would sweep the world of these two Americans, but not before they groveled and pleaded for death.

He stood with effort and staggered out the door. Smoke and a fire alarm filled the hall. He reached for his gun, gone; his cell phone, also missing. He turned and moved quickly towards security, blood leaking down his neck onto his shirt. Time to take control of the Red Baks.

Joel, hoping to get a message out, looked at the keyboard covered with Chinese characters. It was an impossible task. He closed his eyes and typed regularly as if he had an English keyboard. The words on the screen were gibberish. He looked over to Codi with a shake of his head.

Codi held up the stolen phone to make her point. "No cell service here either."

"Yeah, wherever *here* is."

"I guess it's time for Plan C," she said.

"I didn't know we had a plan A."

"Trust me, there's always a plan A."

"So what's plan C?"

"I say we burn this place to the ground."

Codi held up a lighter she had taken from their prisoner. Joel couldn't agree more. He worked quickly to take down the server. He yanked wires and pulled and smashed equipment. Codi collected as much flammable material as possible and put it in a pile. She took a moment to break the bamboo weapon she had been tortured with and laid it on top. She removed the blade and put it in her pocket. The water she drank was starting to work through her system; even her brain was firing again.

She kept an eye on the IT man they were guarding and

noticed that he had peed himself out of fear. She was happy to have copped his pants before that happened. She almost found herself feeling sorry for him, but after her last forty-eight hours, her compassion was on empty.

Codi did a quick check of the room for any possible assets but found nothing useful. She opened a small closet door and noticed, thanks to a bilingual sign, the fire control shut-off valve. She quickly spun the valve closed. They started a fire and escorted the IT man out of the room in front of them.

Using the IT man as a human shield, the two agents moved down the hallway at a brisk pace. The smoke from Joel's earlier experiment had mostly dissipated, but a black, tar-like, toxic cloud from the fire Codi had started billowed out from behind them.

Codi suddenly stopped. The door next to her had a lightning bolt symbol on it along with some unreadable Chinese characters. She tried the handle but it was locked. It took Joel two bullets to change that. She wasted no time pulling all the breaker levers down and shutting off all power to the building. The fire alarm turned off and the battery backup lights flickered to life through the sudden darkness, doing a poor job of illuminating a small area every twenty feet with a pale red glow.

The security station was at the end of the first floor hallway. It led into the only exit tunnel. The sealed armored door could only be unlocked from the inside and was secured with both electronic and manual dead bolts. There was a small station for the guards to work from and an airport-style screener to process employees, both coming and going. The two security guards looked spooked. They had been tasked with keeping the place locked down, but the fire alarm and faint smell of smoke had them on edge. Then a complete power outage killed the electronic locks on the door and left the area in partial darkness.

They were ready to shoot at shadows when Lee ran up to them and assuaged their fears. No one had come or gone since the boss had left—good.

"Sir, you are bleeding," one of the guards said.

"Get me a bandage," Lee snapped with a wheeze.

The guard attended to Lee's neck wound, while Lee armed himself.

"Come with me," Lee told one of the guards, and they started back into the heart of the facility. They would clear it one room at a time until he had his prisoners back.

A sudden flow of humanity heading towards the exit forced them back to the security station. Lee held his AK-74 into the air and shouted, "The next person to take a step forward will be shot."

The mob stopped in their tracks.

Codi was hoping that between the fire and the power outage the workers would evacuate the building so she and Joel could slip out unnoticed in the confusion. As employees started to head for the exits, it looked like her plan might be working. They had released their captive and he had scampered off with the escaping hoard, like panicked rats before flames. Codi and Joel followed. The hallway split into four directions like an intersection. The two agents watched as the evacuees turned down one direction—the exit. They discreetly followed a group up two flights of stairs and down a short hallway that split to the right.

Codi stopped dead in her tracks at the sight ahead.

A mob of about thirty employees was yelling at three

heavily armed men that were preventing them from leaving. Codi and Joel moved back and peeked around the corner. There was shouting and yelling. But the image was clear to Codi. The place was locked down and no one was getting out. She could just glimpse the man who had nearly gotten the best of her. He was armed, standing with the guards and shouting something at the employees. She fought back the urge to charge directly at him and take her revenge. Another place, another time, but soon.

She spun back to Joel and whispered, "The guards look a little busy. Time to take things up a notch. Come on."

Codi pulled Joel with her as they set about igniting more fires throughout the facility. The area was filling with toxic fumes and smoke. She improvised two wet towels she'd found into rudimentary gas masks. They stayed low as they moved, just to be safe. Smoke inhalation was no joke, it killed long before flames did.

With hurried caution, she popped open a door that led into a large room filled with cubicle offices. The room was empty save a larger glass-enclosed room on the left. Inside, an old man with a short bowl cut looked up from a desk. He pushed up his thick black glasses on his nose as he took in the new arrivals. He hurriedly kept typing on his computer. The man was not Chinese, but rather had more of an Eastern European look to him, and he looked to be well into his eighties. Codi moved quickly through his open office door. He looked down at the gun in Joel's hand and dropped to his knees, almost crying, and blubbering in Russian.

Codi and Joel did not respond.

He tried again in rough English. "Please help me." That, they understood.

"I am Doctor Shura Mosin from the Russian science and

technical division," he said. "I have been kept here many years against my will. Please take me with you. I beg you."

Joel held the gun on him while Codi did a quick frisk.

"He's clean."

She grabbed him by the arm and helped him to his feet.

"How do we get out of here and where is here?"

"There is only one exit. You are in China." He looked perplexed. "How is it you do not know this?"

"Up until ten minutes ago we were prisoners as well," Codi said. "Come on, Doc, let's get out of this dump." She gestured for the man to follow.

Shura looked back at his screen. He seemed pleased that whatever he was doing on his computer was completed. He followed Joel and Codi as they continued lighting fires. They led the doctor out of the room as flames billowed behind them. The hallway was empty, but a layer of smoke was growing by the second.

Lee had the crowd starting to calm down. The fire alarm had stopped and the emergency lights were doing their job. The problem was the smoke. It was getting worse. They had no choice but to evacuate. The question was how Lee was going to do it so that he could get the employees out, lock the place back up, and hunt them down. He took the exit key and moved towards the heavy door, instructing the frightened employees on how he would allow them to leave—one by one.

Shura looked over Codi's shoulder at the heavily compacted crowd gathered at the exit door and spilling into the hallway.

"Joel, gun," she hissed.

He tossed it to her, and she handed him her knife.

"Find something to get this crowd moving faster. Doc, see if you can help him."

Joel and Shura Mosin ran off, while Codi kept watch on the exit hallway.

In the bathroom down the hall, Joel found a steel soap canister and yanked it off the wall. He handed it to the doctor and told him to empty it out.

The doctor poured the powdered soap on the floor and then held the canister while Joel refilled it with his remaining Potassium Permanganate and a wad of paper towels.

"Here hold this." Joel handed the canister to Shura and fished the glycerin bottle from his pocket. He set it on the sink. He took the small blade from the stick weapon Codi had given him and poked a few small slits in the canister. He handed Shura his knife as he grabbed the canister and turned to reach for the glycerin on the sink.

"Hold it right there, doctor!"

Joel looked back in shock to see Shura frozen, ready to stab him in the back. Codi was standing in the doorway pointing the pistol at him.

"Thought you might try something," she said to the doctor. "Now put the knife down very slowly."

Shura lowered his hands and started to place the knife on the floor.

"You will never get out of here alive," Shura said with a sudden new-found strength. He spun, unexpectedly flinging the blade at Codi while diving to the left. She never took her eyes off him. She didn't hesitate, and pulled the trigger while feinting to the left to avoid the flying blade. The bullet punched through Shura's C5 cervical vertebra, knocking him to the ground. His black glasses skittered across the floor. Codi stood over her him, gun raised.

Joel had frozen at the sudden noise of gunshot in the bathroom. The cordite stung his eyes and his ears were ringing. He blinked the abrupt tears away and tried to take in what had just happened. Codi bent down to Shura and inspected his wound. He was paralyzed from the neck down.

"Looks like you were only half right doctor. *You* are the one never getting out of here alive."

Shura's eyes bulged. He desperately tried to speak, but only his mind, heart, and lungs were functioning. He could hear and see, but nothing more.

"What, no witty reply? Shame."

Joel finally found his voice. "How...how did you know?"

"Didn't. Just wasn't taking any chances. Now, are you ready with your little toy there?"

Joel looked at the canister in his hands. "I think I can cause enough of a panic to get us out of here. Come on."

Codi knelt down next to Shura. She placed the glasses back on his face. "Wouldn't want you to miss the end."

Doctor Shura Mosin watched with tilted strained eyes as the two left him behind.

Once back at the corner, Joel poured the glycerin into the container and quickly replaced the lid. The exothermic reaction spewed flames and smoke at a high velocity out the slits and seams of the canister making a loud fizzing sound. He rolled it down the hallway to the now partially subdued group that was starting to exit one at a time under Lee's watchful eyes.

Fearing it was a bomb, the panic level spiked to an instant ten. The fear of being blown up quickly overcame the fear of being shot. Like frightened lemmings, the hoard pushed for the doorway, shouting. Shots were fired but there was no stopping them now. Codi and Joel pressed into the crowd, flowing with them. There were shrieks from the wounded and then screams from the guards as the tables turned. Bodies flowed like a raging river out the exit door, chased by smoke and heat as the Red Baks slowly died behind them.

Codi and Joel shoved through and over a pile of bodies as they pressed through the passage. She could see a tunnel ahead. A thin veil of hope began to surge.

15

Washington D.C. – 4:32 p.m. – FBI Field Office – Special Projects – 3rd Floor

The phone on SSA Brian Fescue's desk rang. He grabbed it without looking. "Fescue."

Brian's eyes practically popped out of his head when he recognized the voice on the other end. "Codi, Joel? Where the hell are you two?"

"Our best guess is somewhere in Hong Kong." Joel's voice sounded flat and digital.

"China? How are you in China?"

They started to debrief him on everything that had happened, when he said, "Hang on a sec."

Brian dashed over to The Fishbowl and put the call on speaker. "Okay, go ahead."

Codi and Joel went through their harrowing last few days. As Brian listened to the unbelievable story, a giant weight was lifted from his shoulders. His agents were okay. Battered and bruised, but okay.

Once finished, Codi and Joel signed off with the promise to check back in after they ditched their stolen cellphone for fear of being tracked, and got another one.

It was time to bring his people back and work this case from the safety of the USA. Brian punched for a new line and dialed up his friend at counter intelligence by memory. He had his friend's team arrange for the American embassy to send a man with a valid government credit card and new phones to meet Codi and Joel. He was to stay by their side until they were delivered to safety.

For Codi and Joel, it was time to do some shopping—food, clothes, and a shower, all on the FBI's dime.

Brian hung up and turned to look at his team. They had been searching the D.C. area without much luck and he'd been worried sick. But worst of all, they hadn't even been close to the truth. Something much bigger than they could have imagined was in play, and he was going to get to the bottom of it. He turned to the two temporarily assigned agents.

"Looks like you can pack up now that our agents are found. I want to thank you for your assistance."

Special Agent Tony Kwuo and Chelsea Keener nodded as they shook his hand.

"Glad things worked out," they said. They turned and started packing up their things.

"Gordon," Brian said, "I want to see you in my office when you have a sec."

The last thing Lee remembered was a mass of humanity mashing its way past him. He had opened the exit door to allow an orderly evac of the premises, but the crowd had suddenly rabbited. He remembered shooting a couple of runners, and then there was a blinding flash as something shoved him into the metal doorframe. He untangled himself from two corpses and stood.

With his head already compromised from being

cold-cocked earlier, he felt groggier than he should. Plus, his neck was throbbing. First his side, now his neck. The smoke was thick and caustic. Lee knew he would not last long in these conditions. He closed the large metal door behind him and stayed low as he staggered down the exit tunnel. There was a rumbling sound. The infrastructure of the facility started to compromise. He had escaped just in time.

Inside the bathroom on the first floor, Shura Mosin was right where he'd been left. An old, wounded man who could do no more than watch, as tons of concrete and rebar gave way making a direct path for his skull. He thought of his homeland, the one he had betrayed, and then he thought of nothing ever again.

Lee gasped at the fresh air of the city as he stepped into the street. A giant dust cloud followed the collapse of Red Baks, sending pedestrians running and screaming. He was now a man without home or country. It was time to access his old underground contacts and call in a few markers. He had but one desire in his blackened heart—to find and execute the two American agents.

The nine-story glass and steel police station was laid out like any other. An entrance that controlled the flow in and out, restricted access to the main offices, with holding cells and interrogation rooms in the back. After an incredible meal and a change of clothes, Codi and Joel had been taken to the Yau Ma Tei Police Station by their babysitter. The embassy man seemed more than happy to be rid of his delivered charges as he sped away. From DC, Brian had pushed his hardest to get things moving along, but red tape and political negotiations forced him to work a deal with the Chinese police. Codi and Joel would tell the police everything they knew about their kidnapping and ultimate escape. In exchange, the Chinese would safely escort them to the airport and facilitate their return. It was a political win, a win for both sides, but Brian just wanted to get his agent's asses back on US soil ASAP.

The FBI had no jurisdiction in China, and he didn't want things to get blown into a public and political fiasco. He knew that politics would trump expediency and even life if things went south, so he would just have to be patient.

Brian had arranged for Codi and Joel to meet with Inspector Ang, a man who had come very highly recommended from their assets at the US embassy. As with most political hot potatoes, a representative of the US embassy and the Chinese politburo would be joining the meeting. Brian prayed it would grow no further and that, in a few hours, his agents would be on a plane home.

Inspector Ang seemed like a level-headed down-to-earth policeman. Codi could tell right away that the man had earned his position, not been given it. There was none of the pretentiousness that goes along with that. Ang was dressed in a nice silk suit that fit his five-foot-ten frame perfectly. His jet-black hair was short and well groomed. Codi and Joel had taken time to purchase practical clothes for the trip home. She wore a plum-colored pair of Lululemon studio pants and a gray loose-fitting long-sleeve tee. They were probably knock-offs, but they were comfortable. She had her hair up in a ponytail and had purchased a small black backpack to hold a few personal items. Her neck had been properly bandaged, and the other cuts were covered as well. Joel had charcoal checked slacks and a white collared shirt. He had rolled up the sleeves and had found a replacement pair of glasses that worked well enough. His thumb had a Band-Aid on it. A small duffle held his phone, hand sanitizer, and a toothbrush.

Codi and Joel had been advised to share everything with the Chinese police, so they did, starting with handing over the gun they had taken from the tall unknown suspect.

They then proceeded to spend four hours cooped up in a small overheated interrogation room where question after question was asked and answered. Codi had initially given a direct and honest statement. But the Chinese political officer dismissed her story. He told her that if they hadn't been FBI agents, he would assume they were making the whole thing up. There was no evidence and no suspects other than a tall, mean Chinese guy. This did little to pacify Codi's rising anger against the man.

"What do you call this?" she said, pointing to her many bandages.

After another thirty minutes of essentially calling them liars, Codi was done. "Look," she said, "if you don't want to believe the truth, I'm done trying to explain it to you."

The officer bristled at the woman's bold words. An intense silence followed as the two gave each other the stare-down.

Joel cleared his throat in an attempt to cut the tension. "Maybe you could check the hospitals," he said. "He had a butter knife imbedded in his neck." Joel demonstrated with his finger on his neck. "Or, run the gun we brought in, or go to the building and see for yourself." Even Joel was getting frustrated.

"It's called *police work,*" Codi added in disgust.

In the end, the political officer from the politburo simply said thank you for your time in broken English and left. Inspector Ang apologized for the man's behavior and then closed out the meeting.

Once outside the building, the political officer took out his phone and texted a brief message. He re-pocketed his phone, got in the back of a black sedan, and it sped off.

Inspector Ang had Joel and Codi sign multiple layers of paperwork and then walked them to the exit. The US representative shook hands with Codi and Joel. He then hurried back to his office to make his report.

Paperwork was the backbone of every government.

As the three left the building, dusk had settled over the city. The change in light hit Joel like a kick to the skull, reminding him just how exhausted he was. A uniformed police officer stood next to his vehicle, lights on the roof bar flashing. He saluted Inspector Ang. The Inspector introduced his officer as the man who would be taking them to the airport. He said his goodbyes to Codi and Joel and they got in the back of the vehicle.

Inspector Ang closed the door and watched as it drove away.

Chow and Jin turned left on Fuk Wa Street. They could see smoke in the distance. A fire truck thrust past them in a hurry to its destination. Chow seemed lost in thought, oblivious to the blare of the siren. "When we get back," he said, "I want to meet with you and Shura. I have a little something I need you to get started on."

"Sure."

"This is going to be an eventful week," Chow said, rubbing his unfeeling hands together.

As they approached the abandoned abattoir where his beloved Red Baks was housed, Chow paused, looking at the smoke and flames rising from below. Part of the old building had collapsed into the offices below ground, and the fire brigade was doing their best to stop it from spreading. It was a total loss.

Chow found himself unable to speak for the first time in years. His love and passion was gone. He had built it, he had grown it, and he had ruled it. What could have happened? He had no idea, but someone would pay.

Jin leaned to their driver and said, "Don't stop. Take us back to the airport."

Special Agent Gordon Reyas tapped on his boss's door as he entered Brian's office. Special Agent Tom Calloway, also with the special projects division, was sitting in one of the seats across from his boss. At forty-eight, Tom was the oldest agent in the office. His hair was long since gone, along with a sense of humor. He gave Reyas a simple nod and then folded his arms across his chest.

Reyas took the empty seat. Brian was on the phone, and it sounded serious, but hearing only half the conversation made it difficult to piece together. Finally, Brian hung up. He drummed his fingers on his organized desktop.

"You wanted to see me, sir?" Reyas asked.

"Yes. Something's going on in China and I want to get ahead of this thing before it bites us in the ass." He paused to stare off for a moment, thinking. Reyas and Calloway shared an awkward glance.

Then Brian outlined what he wanted from them. "I want you two to stop what you're doing and put all your efforts on this and this alone. Understand?"

"Yes, sir," Reyas said.

"I'm having you interface with Agent Callan over in Counterterrorism. And I need you all up to speed *yesterday*."

The police vehicle pulled up behind a white van stopped at a red light a few blocks from the police station.

Codi and Joel were spent. They had suffered a complete overload during the last three days. Joel allowed himself a half-smile. It was finally over. They were going home. He stared out the passenger side window, numb to the sights and sounds of the electric city.

Hong Kong at night was a sight to behold. It made the lights of Vegas look like amateur hour in comparison. Locals and tourists roamed the sidewalks as neon and backlit signs vied for their attention promising a good deal, a good meal, or a good time.

An old black sedan pulled up and stopped along their passenger side. It was unusually close, but hey, this was China. Joel thought nothing of it. Codi was still pissed from a wasteful interrogation that she was powerless to do anything about. She was having trouble letting go and wanted to let loose a string of expletives. It didn't help that the political officer was a sexist pig who'd kept eyeballing her during the briefing. She'd been close to calling him on it, but held back in an effort to just make it all go away. Besides, it would change nothing. But maybe she would be feeling better right now. She noticed the driver in the black sedan next to them climb over and exit through the passenger side of the vehicle.

"Something's wrong," she said, reaching for her door handle.

Before Joel could react, the police officer driving them killed the engine and turned with a gun pointed at Joel and Codi.

"This is my stop," he said.

He exited the vehicle holding his gun level and true. He kicked his door closed and backed away. A propane truck with a single tank on the back pulled up close along the driver's side, blocking them inside the police car. Their driver turned and ran.

Lee exited the truck and pulled the pin on an incendiary grenade he was carrying. He set it next to the tank in full view of Codi and Joel. He gave them a smile meant only for the damned, and sprinted away.

"Shit!" Joel cried. He did his best not to crap his pants as reality hit.

Codi jarred him out of his panic. "We got about ten seconds before that incendiary device burns through the steel of that tank and we go up like a roman candle."

Inspector Ang was happy to be done with the two FBI Agents. His job was hard enough without dealing with international and political ramifications. He turned and headed back towards his office, taking the entry steps two at a time. As he opened the glass door that led to the lobby, a sonic boom assaulted him. Three blocks away he saw a large flame-ringed mushroom cloud moving skyward.

Without hesitation Ang spun and ran towards the source.

As he came around the corner, he stopped, frozen with disbelief. It was a mess—flames, car parts, and pieces of bodies filled the intersection. He recognized a few pieces that were left of the squad car that was holding three police officers, two of them American. He mourned the dead, but mostly mourned for himself. This was just the first explosion. This whole mess was off and he feared it would all land in his lap.

16

Chung Kong Road – 5:18 p.m. – Hong Kong

Joel quickly tried to open his door but it was a police car and the back doors could only be opened from the outside. Plus, the two vehicles on either side were so close it would be impossible to exit even if they could open them.

"We're trapped," he said, glancing at the fuse still burning on the grenade.

Codi didn't hesitate. She removed the headrest from the seat in front of her. It had two ten-inch metal rods that allowed for height adjustments. She gripped and swung it towards Joel's side window with all her might. Even hopped up on adrenaline, it took three hits for the window to crack and a fourth for it to shatter.

The incendiary grenade was housed in a soda can-like container, much like a smoke grenade the police use. It has a five-second fuse, and once pulled, starts a chemical reaction that lasts over thirty seconds. During that time, it burns through even the most heavily armored of steel, creating a small ball of extreme heat. Incendiary grenades are typically used to destroy unused or unexploded ordinance but can be effective against tanks as well, as they will melt right through the heavy armor and cook everyone inside.

The grenade ignited in a small unimpressive flash. It quickly grew into a cauldron of burning magma as the phosphorous and benzene reacted. It burned at over five thousand degrees, melting through the steel propane tank.

Joel was first out the window, and Cody didn't wait. Her shoulder shoved his butt and legs out of the car as if he'd been shot from a canon. She quickly followed, and they rolled across the black sedan's roof. Codi dropped to the gutter next to Joel, as the propane tank ignited, initially shooting flames out of the burned hole like a flame thrower. People all around screamed and ran for their lives. The gutter at the intersection had a steel grate cover that accessed the sewer below. Codi used the rod from the headrest she was still holding and lifted and yanked the cover aside. As the flames reached the inside of the tank, it could no longer maintain its integrity. The tank blew. A giant fireball expanded out and up. Steel and rubber vaporized.

Codi followed Joel as they dove into the flowing sludge ten feet below. The massive explosion sent flames and a concussive force after them, slamming them to the bottom.

Lee watched from a safe vantage point three blocks away. He saw the grenade burn through the steel tank and ignite the gas inside, creating a giant flamethrower. He watched as, remarkably, Codi and Joel escaped the police car and rolled over the roof of the car next to them. He almost started chasing after them, until he realized the danger. Lee watched them drop down to the gutter and never get back up, as the ignited gas moved into the tank, changing the flamethrower into a powerful bomb. The explosion was so intense that Lee was knocked on his ass with his ears ringing. The fifty-foot area around the truck held nothing but a few vehicle parts and scorched earth. No one could have survived.

Inspector Ang surveyed the burning mess. He was at a loss for an answer. Accident or deliberate, it was unclear. But as a cop, he found it too convenient. Maybe Codi and Joel's story had merit and someone really did want them dead. His training kicked in and he searched for a bystander that seemed out of place. Most bombers stick around to watch the fallout they had caused. Perhaps he could, at least, spot the culprit.

Nothing.

Too many unanswered questions and not enough evidence to go on.

Codi was the first to push from the sticky murk. The sewer was lit by burning rubble a few feet from her. Joel still laid face-down in the brown soupy flow. She pulled him from the sludge, put her arms around his chest, clasped her fingers together, and yanked. Brown goop shot from his mouth and he started coughing. He followed it up with several retches and finally blinked his way back into cognizance. It took him a few moments to realize he was sitting in a river of flowing crap.

"God, it stinks in here," he yelled over his ringing ears.

He turned and vomited once more. Codi looked like she'd been dipped and coated, but the whites of her eyes still shined in the dim light. Joel looked puzzled at her slight smile.

"What?" he said.

"I'm glad that worked."

"What?"

Codi shouted louder to be heard. "I'm glad that worked.

For a minute there, I thought I might have to give you mouth-to-mouth."

"Oh, yeah."

"Well your mouth was full of..." She pointed to the brown sludge that flowed past them.

"So, what, you would've just let me die rather than get a little poop in your mouth?"

"No," she lied. "I'm just glad it worked."

Joel nodded slowly, then turned and vomited again.

They made their way downstream, looking for the next exit ladder. The experience was overwhelming beyond their ability to handle, their intellects mercifully shutting off some of the details and dulling their senses.

Inspector Ang had moved closer to the flames as they subsided. Emergency response was on the way and other police officers had joined the disaster, everyone trying to get a handle on the situation and help as many people as possible. As he stepped onto the curb, Ang noticed that the sewer grate had been removed. It didn't seem all that out of place, given the situation, but it did deserve checking out.

Cody pulled her way up the ladder of the next exit grate. She used her back as leverage to dislodge and move it aside. A glow of neon and traffic noise filled the sewer pipe. She reached for the lip to pull herself up, but a hand reached down and grabbed her. She resisted instinctively. But then a familiar voice cut through.

"Agent Sanders, let me help you."

It was Inspector Ang. He helped them out of the sewer, and quickly moved them off the street into a back warehouse of a small shop next to the street.

He managed to borrow two blankets from the proprietor after flashing his badge. Ang asked them to wait while he got his car. Cody wasted no time dropping her soiled clothes. She ripped a chunk off the blanket to use to wipe her face, and wrapped the remainder around her body. Joel followed suit.

"Damn it," she said. "This is the second time something like this has happened to me."

"You've landed in crap before?" Joel asked.

"Guano, and I'm not sure which is worse."

"At least you can check that off your list," Joel said without mirth.

"Funny."

Joel looked around. There were stacks of boxes and other inventory surrounding them. A half-coconut shell full of old cigarette butts was on a small shelf. Codi sat next to it on a tree stump that had blackened with time and dirt. Joel sat on a large wooden crate with smudged red Chinese writing on the side. He looked forlorn as he awkwardly tried to place his hands somewhere without touching anything.

"Joel, you gotta just go with it," Codi said.

"I'm sure I have yellow fever, typhoid, and several other deadly diseases. Maybe even the H1N1 virus was down there."

"I know of one you got for sure," Codi said.

He looked up at his partner's words, still uncomfortable in his skin. "What one?"

"Shibreth."

Joel looked baffled. "Shibreth? Is that a Chinese virus, a waterborne pathogen? What is it?"

"Your breath smells like shit—Shibreth." Codi's lips parted in an uncontrollable smile as a slow chuckle escaped.

Joel started to snicker at the absurdity of it all, which made Codi laugh even more. Soon they were both giggling like school kids.

Inspector Ang entered the warehouse in time to hear two adults cackling like children. He was puzzled, but hey, they were Americans.

Lee watched as the police and rescue vehicles began to swarm the area. His work was done. He turned and began the ten-block walk back to a parking lot where he had left his car when he picked up the propane truck. *Finally,* he thought with a rare smile. Now to plan for what came next. His future with Chow was over, but fate had dealt him another chance. Lee needed to disappear or end Chow if he was to go forward from here. Much to consider.

He pulled out in his white coupe Shuanghuan Noble, heading for a well-deserved drink and perhaps some female companionship. The car was a three-door hatchback made by Shuanghuan Motors for China and Canada, as innocuous as any car in Hong Kong. And for the moment, it fit his needs perfectly.

Lee had never been good at relationships with the opposite sex, and the current male to female ratio in China did him no favors. It wasn't because he was unusually tall or that he looked like a feral cat hunting a trapped mouse. It was his job. He was a solitary hunter/killer, not a team player, and not especially nice by nature. But luckily for Lee, money could get you almost anything you desired.

As he turned left at the intersection of Heung Yip Road, he just about drove off the street. Sitting in the car in the opposite lane was one very much alive female American agent.

Impossible.

Lee waited for them to pass by and then spun around to follow them at a discreet distance.

They rode in Ang's car, a white four-door Citroen Fukang, back to his place. Joel was laying down in the back seat moaning like he'd been poisoned. Codi took the time to brief Ang on the recent attempt on their lives. He was furious at the betrayal of his officer. It was a problem in modern China, a government rife with corruption doled out at the highest level. The officer was no doubt one of the many plants that the Tong and other groups use as information conduits.

Inspector Ang found himself breathing out of his mouth as the smell that clung to the two agents became overpowering. He opened the car windows and finally pulled his shirt over his nose as he drove, seeing through tear-filled eyes and suppressing his gag reflex. Ang finally pulled to a red curb along Kwun Tong Harbor. He placed a police placard in the windshield and walked Codi and Joel towards the water. They crossed several floating walkways made of old wooden planks and crowded with tethered boats of every size and condition. Most were made from leftover materials, seeming to defy the laws of physics by staying above water. The air was ripe with burned cooking oil, old fish, and diesel. Families lived and died here. The sounds of children laughing reminded Codi that perception often dictates one's happiness. Ang stopped at a fifty-foot Chinese junk floating along a section of dock.

The junk evolved during the Song dynasty in 960 AD. This one was a teak, two-mast boat with full red sails and a back-up diesel engine. It had the classic high stern and projected bow. A wooden plank ramp angled up eight feet to the deck above.

He invited Joel and Codi to board with a wave of his hand. "Welcome to my home. All aboard."

Lee parked dockside just in time to see Ang close the cabin door of a junk. He turned off the engine of his vehicle and settled in to wait. He considered the extreme possibilities that could have allowed the female to survive the explosion.

Codi and Joel wasted no time hitting the showers. After buffing every cell of skin on his body, Joel exited the bathroom in borrowed clothes.

He tapped discretely on Codi's bathroom door. She opened it to see Joel's face twisted up and moving side to side. He was trying to follow his nose to a source of odor only he could smell. Codi was wrapped in a towel with glistening wet hair flowing over her shoulders, the gold flecks in her brown eyes sparkling.

"Something still smells," Joel said.

"You know, it's possible your sense of smell is just off."

"I don't think so."

"And that's my problem, how?"

Turning and sniffing in every direction, he looked pathetic as he tried in vain to source the smell on his person.

Codi took pity on him. "Fine, come in."

She pulled Joel inside and inspected him with a sniff. "Oh, God."

"You found it already. What is it?" Joel asked.

"It's your aftershave."

Joel lifted his hands in defeat. "I didn't have a choice, so I tried to drown the smell with some brand of Chinese cologne I found in the medicine cabinet."

"You should have chosen differently. This is twice as bad. It has my eyes burning."

She grabbed a couple of cotton swabs and took his jaw with one hand to cock his head to the side. "Hold still." She inspected his head, hair, and ears.

"Ah."

"Ah, what?"

"Stop moving," she commanded. Codi started to clean

his left ear. "This must be the first time you've had to clean excrement off your person."

Joel could only mumble an answer with Codi's vice-grip on his jaw.

"There." She let go and came away with two very brown-tipped swabs.

"Thank you. That was driving me crazy. I couldn't figure out where the smell was coming from."

"You're welcome. Here, these are yours. Now scoot."

Joel carefully took the soiled swabs and slowly headed back to his own bathroom, but not before glancing over his shoulder at the beautiful towel-clad woman who'd just saved his ears.

Ang served a round of Baijiu, a rice-based liquor. Codi held her shot into the air. *"Ganbei,"* she exclaimed as the others repeated the toast and followed her lead. As a warm sensation spread through her body she began to feel human again. Joel swished his mouth before swallowing, just in case there was remaining bacteria.

They sat in the teak-walled salon in silence. Codi took in her surroundings. The room was warm and inviting with an intricately-patterned wood floor, leather seating, and a white-paneled ceiling. The salon flowed into a spacious galley accented by a large through-hull mast beam and three port-holes on the starboard side.

"Your boat is lovely," she said. "Thank you for your aid."

"It was my father's pride and joy," Ang said. "And now, with houses going for over a hundred million dollars here in Hong Kong, it is my home."

Ang nodded towards a prominent picture of a gray-haired gentleman with a look of confidence. "Living here keeps me close to him, even though he is no longer with us."

"I'm sorry."

Ang just nodded. The casual banter eventually turned to the events of the last forty-eight hours. The mood went somber.

"So what next?" Ang asked. "I assume you will head back to the states."

"Yes. I'm sure we're past due at the office and there's most likely a task force being put together to find us," Codi said, *"again."*

Joel stood up. "I'd really like to get this guy who, three times now, has tried to kill us,"

"And, thank goodness, failed," Codi said with little emotion.

Joel's anger was elevating. He started pacing. "Nobody blasts me into a river of shit and gets away with it. Plus, he tried to rape and kill you. And who knows how many people died in that explosion? This man is still out there. He doesn't get a pass, and I want him *bad.*"

He looked almost deranged as he said these words. It was a side of him Codi hadn't seen before. Honestly, she felt the same way. It was time to change from defense to offense. No more being a target.

"As far as anyone knows, the two of you are dead," said Ang. "Blown to bits in that explosion. This is a rare chance to make a play for the people who are behind this without them seeing it coming. For all you know, there could be a leak coming from your side of things."

Joel and Codi contemplated his words. If they were honest with themselves, he was right, they didn't know.

"Maybe it is better if we stay dead for now," Codi said thoughtfully.

Ang looked down in contemplation, clasping his hands together. The room grew suddenly quiet.

He raised an eyebrow and followed with, "Perhaps we can

help each other." He looked up and made eye contact with the two Americans. "As I see it, we can get you false papers that will get you on a plane tomorrow morning and out of China. Or, I could use a couple of rogue American agents bent on revenge and completely disregarding their authority and orders, to help crack this whole thing open." He smiled at the thought.

Codi and Joel shared a glace, well aware what going forward might mean—forced leave, fired, even jail. But they were not going back home without their pound of flesh. It just wasn't going to happen.

Joel looked away thoughtfully. "It's time to burn the boats," he said.

"What?" Codi asked.

He turned back, more sure of himself. "1519. Capitan Hernan Cortez. When he arrived in Veracruz, he burned all his boats in a desperate move to motivate his soldiers. They ultimately conquered Mexico."

Codi nodded. "No going back."

"Exactly."

Ang interrupted their thought. "We might not need to be so desperate. The British were very good at monitoring and collecting information while in control of Hong Kong. My father worked with them as part of a division of MI6. And…" Ang contemplated his next words. "I do a little something for them now and then."

Codi and Joel perked at this revelation.

"Obviously, it would not go well for my current employer to know this."

"Obviously," Joel said.

Codi and Joel followed Ang over to a built-in mahogany desk set against the back bulkhead. Ang pressed a hidden button and a wood panel slid open to reveal an advanced electronic display. "Action will be required to put an end to this," Ang mumbled as he waited for the system to boot up.

Codi had always been a woman defined by her actions, but perhaps she had just irreversibly overstretched. Still, going back without some satisfaction was not going to happen.

Ang pressed several keys and the large screen came to life with a login. He entered his password, and a blank page popped up with a single search bar. "Okay," he said to them, "tell me everything you can remember about this man."

"His name is Lee," Joel said. "I heard a guard call him that."

Ang cocked his chin and narrowed his eyes at Joel. "Lee?"

"Yes."

He took an incredulous breath and entered it into the search bar. "That narrows it down to half-a-billion people. What else?"

Codi and Joel gave Ang a detailed description of the man. With each detail, the list of suspects narrowed.

Ang said, "The fact that he was able to get inside information and put together the ambush in the street, tells me he's probably connected to a triad or black market group. These men share information and favors when it suits their needs. But it must have taken some serious horsepower to burn a mole at the station just to get to you."

Ang entered some additional data and a list of about two hundred names, complete with pictures popped up. "Looks like there are less Chinese assassins over six-feet-tall then I thought. This list is quite manageable." Ang looked pleased.

Joel and Codi scrolled through the pictures until they came to number 157. The picture was grainy and old, but there was no mistaking the predatory expression of their assailant. Joel leaned in and read the English words next to the Chinese characters below the photo.

"Chun Lee, alias Kwai Chang Caine, Kwi Gon Jinn, and Kato. That's funny."

"What is?" Ang asked.

Joel pointed to the names. "The alias names, they're all TV and movie character names."

"I guess he has a sense of humor."

"Not that I've seen," Codi said.

Ang leaned closer. "Looks like he's ex-military special forces. Hmm, he was on death row for a while and was then recruited for a special mission."

"By whom?"

Ang clicked his tongue absently as he searched for the information. "Just a sec."

He drilled deeper into the E-file. "Doesn't say. It also doesn't say why he was on death row. Looks like some high level redaction has taken place."

Ang read on. "He is suspected of ties to the Green Dragon Triad and the Chu Lon Fue, a nasty black market group that operates mostly in southern mainland China."

Ang continued to glean all he could from the file, but most of the rest was his physical description, something they already had. Codi stifled a yawn. Her eyes were bloodshot and she was feeling the effects of the drink.

"Red Baks," Ang said.

"What's that?" Joel asked.

"It's just a notation here at the bottom."

"Sounds like hemorrhoid cream," Codi said.

Joel tried not to smile by biting down hard on his lips. His body jerked several times suppressing a laugh until he found some control.

The late hour, lack of sleep, and crazy recent events were making them punchy. Ang looked up at Joel who was now beet red and trying to control himself.

"If you got a case of Red Baks," Joel said, "you'll wanna shut that down."

He and Codi both started laughing.

"Maybe we should get some rest and pick this up in the morning," Ang said.

"Perhaps," Codi said with a giggle.

Ang hid a smile of his own and showed the two laughing agents to their rooms.

Americans, he said to himself. He would never understand them.

Lee watched from his car as the lights on the junk winked out. The five Advil he had taken were doing their job on his pain, and he still felt alert. He checked the time on his phone and started his car. He had gone through every possible scenario in his head, but for the life of him, could not figure out how Codi had survived. Seeing her drive off with that man from the police station nearly made Lee drive his car right into theirs, but that was not how he operated. This would be done on his terms and tonight. He marveled at the ridiculousness of it all. First the river, then the Red Baks, and now an explosion that had obliterated most of a city block. It was unimaginable to him. He let the anger in his body grow and flow. His thoughts turned to the task ahead and his own mortality. It had become a mission he must complete.

He briefly reviewed the kaleidoscope of his life's memories. He had been a good soldier and a great assassin. These were the things he could take with him when he was gone, things he could be proud of.

He put his car into drive and pulled away.

Soon, he thought.

17

Washington D.C. – 4:32 p.m. – FBI Field Office – Special Projects – 3rd Floor

The message left little doubt. Agent Sanders and Strickman were dead. They had been involved in an unfortunate gas explosion that decimated an entire block on the east side of Hong Kong. The investigation was still underway, but a detailed report would be filed through the proper channels. An FBI representative had been assigned from the Hong Kong office, and he would keep Brian updated on his findings. Brian hated politics but he knew that there was no way around them. Learning how to play the game was critical to one's success, especially in DC.

His superiors were compassionate but unyielding to Brian's plea to be part of the investigation. They had even denied his request to send agents from his office to China to support the effort. They wanted no part of this Hong Kong hot potato. Brian informed Agents Calloway and Reyas to stand down for the moment. He paced his office, feeling helpless. The space had never seemed smaller. It was time for him to change his perspective. He grabbed his coat and left the office before five o'clock for the first time in over a year.

Agent Fescue opened the front door to his beautiful wife Leila and their youngest child Abigale sitting at the kitchen island. It was a white kitchen with a dark granite-topped island with seating for four. They were surprised to see Brian home so early.

"Hi, guys." He gave his wife and child a kiss. "Where's Tristan?"

Tristan was their energetic five-year-old son, a wavy-haired boy with the same mocha colored eyes as his dad.

"Backyard playing, why?" said Leila. "What's wrong? Is everything okay at the office?"

Brian let loose a smile that filled the room. "Tristan come on in here," he called out the back door.

To Leila, he said, "I just needed to realign some priorities, and there is nothing more important than this." He gestured to his family.

Tristan ran into the room yelling, "Daddy, Daddy!"

He hugged his dad.

"Come on, go get cleaned up," Brian said. "We're going to Chuck E. Cheese's for dinner."

Tristan did his celebration dance. They were going to his favorite restaurant.

Leila stepped close to her husband, gave him another kiss, and whispered, "You hate that place."

"I know."

Ang leaned back from the computer screen and checked his watch. It was 3:07 a.m. He stretched and decided he was done for the night. He felt and heard a creak from someone moving on his boat. Ang reached stealthily under his desk and came away with a Glock 23, a present from his part-time employer.

He spun to the source of the movement, gun leveled and ready to fire.

"Easy, Ang."

Ang recognized Codi's voice, as she stepped into the salon and the glow of his monitor.

"Sorry."

She yawned between words. "I crashed like the dead, but I just couldn't quite keep it all turned off."

"Same here," Ang said, as he put his gun down on the desk. He reached over and flicked a small light on next to him. "While I was up, I did more digging, even reached out to a couple of contacts about Red Baks. Turns out it's not hemorrhoid medicine but a think tank run by an old-school red communist general named Chow Phun."

Codi moved next to Ang and looked at the face on the screen. It was a very unique face captured as he was exiting a limo. She guessed the man was in his late sixties. He had black intelligent eyes that seemed to pierce right through you. The right side of his face hung like a wet tee shirt while the left side seemed normal.

"He stepped down from his position to head several off-book projects for the politburo," Ang said. "I'm sorry to say he is very connected."

"Looks like he has some kind of ailment, maybe a stroke," Codi said.

"Yes. That might be why he stepped down when he did. The thing is, the Red Baks is the complex you and Joel destroyed."

This information galvanized Codi almost instantly. "So he's the one behind all this. But to what end?"

"With the Red Baks gone, we no longer have a lead as to his plans or whereabouts."

Codi sat in the chair next to Ang. "So what, we don't know where he is and we can't go after him?"

Ang spun his chair to face her. "No. We just have to be very careful how we do it. Luckily for me, I have you two to blame if anything goes wrong."

"I was thinking the same about you, Inspector." Codi held the inspector's stare with equal intensity.

"Perfect." Ang smiled. "Let me show you something."

He pulled up what he had found.

It had taken Lee fifteen minutes to silently move the gas cans into position on the bow of the docked junk. He attached a remote igniter to the closest can and then checked the matching remote in his hand. The green micro LED on the roll-of-dimes-sized device meant it was primed and ready. He pressed his left thumb down and held it there.

He headed for the nearest hatch, pulling a pistol from his waist as he moved. The chrome door handle was well maintained and turned without a sound as Lee slipped inside. Muted voices came from the salon ahead. He moved like a wraith, following the voices.

He waited for the perfect moment before stepping into the room. "Good evening."

Codi and Ang spun with equal speed and disbelief. Lee's pistol remained leveled at them, ready to fire.

"Drop it on the floor, carefully," Lee commanded. He pointed to the gun resting next to Ang's keyboard.

Codi raised her hands and turned slowly. Ang judiciously picked up his Glock by the barrel and dropped it to the floor.

"Now kick it away."

Ang kicked his pistol hard in the direction of Lee. Lee stepped over the sliding gun as it skittered across the polished wood floor beyond, his aim never faltering. "Foolish man. Now both of you put your hands on your heads."

Ang and Codi complied.

"Slowly." Lee cautioned.

Lee moved closer to his seated victims, trying to process the perfectly healthy woman in front of him. "I have tried to kill you and your partner three times, but apparently the cosmos are not in favor of this happening. This is difficult for me to accept. But I feel as though it is no longer in my hands."

Codi and Ang shared a brief glance in confusion.

While keeping the gun on Codi and Ang, Lee moved to sit on the small couch across from them. "Two days ago," he said, "I failed my protector when you survived the river. I have therefore forfeited my life. He allowed me a second chance. This was a most generous act, as it has never been allowed before, and I was not going to spurn it."

Codi stared daggers at the man who had tortured her and planned to rape her.

"But after the two of you escaped, I took another approach and dedicated myself to your demise at all costs, no longer under the protection of my boss. It was personal."

Codi practically rolled her eyes trying to will the man to get to the point. It was bad enough to be killed by him, but she was in no mood to be forced to listen to his life story first. Please just shoot me now, she thought.

"I now find myself at odds. Three times you have proven yourself incapable of being killed—*three times.*" He stopped, looked at his gun, and then back up.

"I have faced my own mortality. That changes you. The things I've done, the people I've hurt. And looking at you now…"

A moment of silence followed before he continued. "I had planned to go out in a blaze of glory, taking you all with me as a final grand performance. But now, as I sit here, I am moved in a different direction, a change of heart, if you will."

Codi decided it would be worth the risk to dive at the man's gun. She'd take a bullet, but maybe Ang would overpower the assassin and have a chance to live. She leaned forward ever so slightly onto the balls of her feet, ready to spring.

"In fact, I find myself unable to continue as planned. There could still be more for me, even a second chance to do things I have never allowed myself. So maybe you are not supposed to die quite yet and there will be some type of redemption for me."

What? Codi was sure she misheard.

"Therefore, I have decided to help you."

Lee lowered his head and weapon in complete submission. He sat in the love seat across from them and slumped. Codi and Ang both tried to process the information, but nothing was adding up. It was so far out of their box at the moment.

Lee looked as though, perhaps for the first time in his life, he didn't know what to do next. He wanted to just be a regular person but had no clue how to get there.

Codi finally leaped at the opportunity. "You say you want to help us?"

Lee looked up, distraught, and slowly nodded his head.

"Then who ordered you to kill us?"

"General Chow Phun."

"And that's who had us taken at the airport?"

"Correct."

"Do you know where is he right now?"

The assassin hesitated.

"Lee, redemption comes at a cost," she said.

"Probably at his second base of operations in Fenghuang. He has a house there."

Ang caught on to Codi's plan, quickly realizing this moment might not last. "Maybe we should hold the gun." He gestured.

Lee looked to the gun now lying by his side and nodded.

"Why does he want us dead?" Codi asked.

Lee stood and held his pistol out for Ang to take.

"You were getting too close to a technology they were preparing to test on–"

Two quick shots deafened the room as blood spouted from Lee's torso. The once-assassin-turned-ally crumpled to the floor. He wheezed as he turned to see his executioner. "You? You are supposed to be dead."

Lee's life poured out onto the floor and his head dropped, along with a final statement: "Use caution when trusting your enemy."

Joel stepped through the cordite smoke holding the Glock.

He had awakened to voices and carefully moved to investigate. Seeing a Glock 23 on the floor, he picked it up just in time to see Lee point his weapon in the direction of his colleagues. Joel wasted no time in ending the man who had plagued him since Russia.

Joel was ecstatic. He had saved the day.

Codi was pissed. Joel had killed their best chance of getting to the bottom of things.

Ang was confused about the small device with a black button and a small flashing red light that had just rolled out of Lee's other hand.

"What did he mean by 'use caution when trusting your enemy?'" Joel asked, confused.

A sudden beeping sound coming from the small device on the floor was followed by an explosion. It rocked the bow of the junk so violently that it nearly broke in half. Flames grabbed at the wooden vessel, quickly engulfing the bow and forward cabins. The bulkhead turned into a spray of wooden daggers as the entire ship bucked with the concussion. Codi was the first to dive for cover. Joel, who was standing closest, was knocked across the room. Ang caught a large sliver of teak in his abdomen and was spun to the floor.

Codi crawled to Ang and helped him to his feet. She pushed him to the exit hatch and ran back for Joel, calling his name through blown-out eardrums. With the hull of the ship breached, black sea water rushed to find equilibrium. Codi had been on a sinking boat before and it had nearly cost her her life. There was no chance that was going to happen again. She shook Joel awake and helped him to the exit. By the time they reached the top of the floundering junk, they had to step up to reach the dock.

Ang collapsed on the dock, and Codi stepped over to investigate. A wood spike the size of a dagger was imbedded in his side. She wasted no time and pulled it out before he could brace for the pain. A low moan escaped him.

"You'll be okay," she said. "It looks like it just punctured muscle."

"She hates hospitals," Joel added needlessly.

They wrapped his wound with part of Joel's shirt and plodded off for Ang's car.

The last of the flames sizzled out as the junk slipped below the water.

General Chow Phun abruptly stood, slamming his hand down on the solid wood table. He felt no sting or pain in his numb hands, only heard the sound they made. He had been irritable and angry ever since seeing his precious Red Baks destroyed. And his incessant pacing had continued to wind up his black mood. He had gone through two handkerchiefs dabbing the constant drool from the corner of his mouth, and the persistent rash was bright red.

Jin had been living on pins and needles, not sure when or

if the general's angst would be turned his way. They had flown the jet to a small strip where a four-door olive green Beijing BJ212, a cheap knock-off of the old Jeep Wrangler, was waiting. The thirty-minute drive through the countryside was breathtaking. Lush forest, streams, and hills made way for a narrow winding road. There were a few terraced rice fields among the hills, and an earthy smell filled the journey. The people who lived here were the real heart of China, Jin thought to himself. A quaint town came into view as they rounded a verdant hill. Fenghuang was an incredible sight. A slow moving river cut through a town that seemed time had forgotten. Chow had taken them to his home there, a place he called Chongde Hall.

It was a four-story structure built by the wealthiest man in town over three-hundred years ago. Chow purchased it from his estate eleven months back. The design was classic box-style Chinese architecture with a front portico and a tier shape. It was made of teak covered in many layers of finish that had gone dark with the passing years. The wood was set off by two stone lions guarding either side of the entrance. Inside, polished wood floors supported beams that curved up, meeting in the center of a domed ceiling in a spoke pattern, and supported by a large central stone column. The rounded design continued throughout the home giving it a hobbit-like feel, but for grown-ups. A wide, curved staircase granted entry to the upper levels. It was made of carved rosewood with two dragons intricately wound through the banisters. Carved wood lintels and a collection of antiques adorned every room.

Chow finally sat down and took a calming breath.

"Jin, I want to thank you for your loyalty. It is the most important thing to me."

Jin simply nodded.

"I am a man with a finite expiration. It is not far off. But before then, there is much good we can do for our country. If you will help me finish my mission, I will make it worth your while."

Jin leaned in towards his boss. "Boss, I am humbled by your offer and I will give my best to your needs."

Jin kept his real feelings to himself. He said the words his boss needed to hear, but in truth, he was trying to find an exit strategy that didn't involve his demise.

"How was I supposed to know he was on our side? The man was a killer. Or that he was holding a dead-man's switch? I thought I saved your life. He killed nineteen people and injured dozens of others, just to get to us. Surely, I did the right thing."

Codi was driving Ang's Citroen Fukang with Joel yammering in the copilot's seat. She absently scratched at one of her wounds that was actually starting to heal. Ang was resting in the backseat, his abdomen throbbing in pain. Truthfully, Codi was glad that Joel had killed Lee, although she wished he had done it after they had gotten what they needed from him. Of course, she would never tell him that. It was way more fun listening to him postulate.

Joel continued. "I mean, what kind of FBI agent kills a man, then leaves the scene of the crime to do God knows what next, probably more crime? This is going to come back on me big time."

The road trip to Fenghuang was nine hours and required two pit stops and a refueling. Joel had talked non-stop for the first three hours. Finally his adrenaline wore off, along with the emotions that followed the killing of another human, and he lapsed into slumber.

Fenghuang, or Phoenix Ancient Town, is one of the most idyllic well-preserved ancient settlements in all of China. Once a frontier town built in 1704 and a center for trade and cultural exchange, Fenghuang was now a breathtaking riverside town with narrow winding alleys, temples, and rickety stilt houses built along the Tuo River. The town borders the lazy river that ran through a spectacular mountainous tree-filled region. It was exceptionally tranquil and a full step back in time.

Codi pulled their vehicle to a stop in an outlying parking lot. "Looks like we walk from here," she said.

Matt Campbell sat back in his wheeled office chair and rubbed his eyes. It was late. Selecting the herd had taken much longer than expected. They had placed thirty bovines in a pen erected in the back warehouse, each carefully selected for its condition. BRDC, or Bovine Respiratory Disease Complex, had been diagnosed in each cow. Most had clear mucus running from their nostrils and some coughed incessantly. They were a veterinarian's nightmare.

Matt stood and went to the viewing window as technicians prepped the FCBT (Focusable Cellular Beam Technology). It was the acronym given to his invention that was once called SkyStorm by the man who had stolen it and caused an international incident. It was an invention that had nearly infected half of London with a deadly illness, and nearly killed Matt in the process. Since getting it back, the military had taken charge. They had given the device the odd acronym. Matt suspected they'd done so without consulting anyone from marketing.

The lab where he now worked was on heavy lockdown with what Matt thought to be ridiculously over-the-top security. He was monitored and second-guessed at every step. But things were still developing, and Matt found himself just happy enough to keep moving forward one foot in front of the other.

"Sequence nominal, all systems operational," someone said from behind Matt.

"Initiate sequence and fire on my mark," Matt's boss called out.

They watched as the FCBT was pointed at the herd. There was a brief hum and then a small snapping noise. That was followed by a winding-down sound as the system transitioned back to its standby mode.

"We have a successful firing," someone yelled.

Matt watched as the cows continued to move around the pen as if nothing had taken place. But he knew differently. In an instant, all thirty cows had been vaccinated by the FCBT. It had sent the vaccine through the air at a cellular level, penetrating and inoculating their every single cell at once. The improvement in the bovines' health would be remarkable by morning.

With the test completed, Matt's mind started to wonder. He found himself thinking about Codi. He had sent her an apology email and a first class ticket to Boston in an attempt to make up for his inability to host her the previous weekend. So far, he'd heard nothing since then. Was she mad? Did she even get the email? When it came to women, he was no expert, but other than his love for his work, she was it for him.

Maybe he should try calling Brian or Joel to get the real story. He looked at the time and picked up his phone.

18

CHONGDE HALL — 5:02 P.M. — FENGHUANG, CHINA

The sound of a door bursting open broke Jin from his thoughts.

"Finally," Chow shouted.

Jin looked up to see eight very serious looking men enter the home. *Mercenaries,* he thought. Each carried a large duffle and seemed to follow the command of one, a salt-and-pepper shoulder-length-haired man with a ridiculous Fu Manchu and the eyes of a predator—Poh. He looked like he had seen and done horrible things. The squad was followed by two studious looking men who clearly were struggling to fit in.

Chow greeted the man, Poh, and welcomed him to his home with a traditional slight bow. He made no other introductions and asked them all to join him for a cup of tea. The group sat around the large table that could seat twelve and made small talk. An old gray-haired woman with a stoop entered the room carrying a tray of tea and rice cakes for all. She had a wizened no-nonsense look and a slight tremor that caused the pot to shake, nearly spilling the tea. Each time she poured, the men watched in rapt attention. Would she spill the tea or not? It was a strange ritual and Jin almost laughed out loud at the absurdity of it. He studied her for a moment, thinking she looked more Malaysian or Nepalese, but they were in the south of China, so who could really tell.

After tea, Chow took the time to introduce everyone and personally thank them for being part of the new China they would all help create. "Each one of you is an integral part of our success or failure. And I ask that you give me your best during the next twenty-four hours." Chow looked around. Each and every person nodded or replied to his request.

They were ready.

From the parking lot, Codi and her team crossed the Hong Bridge. Its three arches and pagoda-topped pass-through spanned the slow moving river, providing wind and rain protection for residents and tourists alike.

Codi looked slack-jawed at her surroundings. The town was a study in duality. Most residents preferred to live their lives the old way, including their dress. But because Fenghuang was a must-see tourist destination, there were people from all over the world mingling with the locals, each with their smart phones and modern ways. It was only a matter of time before the local holdouts gave way to the crushing advance of modernization. But in the meantime, it was truly magical.

Using Ang's contacts, they checked into a private guesthouse across the river. It was a funky place with a central courtyard decorated in a hodgepodge of modern and time-worn. Codi crossed the garden's stone steps that led to her room where a white birdcage chair hung from the ceiling. The room was lit by an ornate stained glass window, and next to it was a small bed with a green lotus-patterned comforter. She sat with a plop, trying hard not to just lie back and give in to sleep after the long drive.

Ten minutes later, the three met back in a small common

area just off the kitchen. With a detailed map spread out on the table, they started to make a plan. The first step was to locate Chow's historic home and survey the area.

The team mingled with the scores of tourists as they slowly made their way to Chongde Hall. Codi dipped her feet in the river as she scoped out the historic building, pretending to take pictures of the area. There were two heavily armed guards that were alert and patrolling. Joel and Ang chatted as they worked their way down the alley behind it. Ang was still hurting from his stab wound but did his best not to show it. He glimpsed to the security cameras and the locked steel gate covering the back door. This was the place.

The group met back at the Miss Yang Restaurant for a local dish called River Fish. It was surprisingly tasty even though Joel was sure it was full of heavy metals.

"So here is the situation." Ang proceeded between bites. "We can only assume that Chow Phun is there. Without hard evidence, there is no way I can make a raid on Chongde Hall. It would be the end of my career, and whatever the general is up to would still transpire. Thoughts?"

Codi didn't wait for Joel to answer. "I didn't come all this way to start playing by the rules."

"I didn't think you had, Agent Sanders," Ang replied.

"Good. Please call me Codi. As I see it, one of us could slip in over the rooftops at night, find whatever hard evidence is needed, and then slip back out." She used her fingers to make quote marks around the term *hard evidence.*

Joel added, "You call in the authorities, and *bam,* the whole stinking thing is behind us. Most of it legal and by the book."

Codi's lips arched upward. "Or we could just go in with guns blazing."

Ang said, "Since the only guns we have are two back-up pistols from the trunk of my car, I suggest Plan A."

He had shown them his trunk before leaving Hong Kong. It was meticulously organized and well stocked, with lift-out drawers and a host of supplies, including climbing gear, emergency water jugs, extra clothing, and even tactical gear.

He must have been a boy scout in a previous life, Joel thought at the time.

"The problem is," Ang said, "I'm the only one who speaks Chinese, but I am not in any condition to do much climbing." Ang pointed to the wound on his side. "So you will have to see, not hear or read, something worthy of hard evidence."

Codi briefly focused on a distant point with a half-nod. The task had just gotten that much harder.

"Fescue." Brian said as he picked up his phone.

"Brian."

It took a moment for Brian to recognize the voice. "Matt. What's going on?"

Brian put down the file he was perusing and focused on the call. The two friends covered the small talk territory quickly and got to the heart of the matter—Codi. Brian was not about to tell Matt the official version so he watered it down. He hadn't heard from her and was worried.

"That makes two of us," Matt said.

Since her mission to Russia was not covert, Brian had no qualms about giving Matt some particulars. The hard part was how she had gone missing in China, resurfaced, and was now presumed dead. All very strange and troubling. But until he had absolute proof, he would keep that information to himself.

"Look, Matt, I can't tell you everything, but you know Codi as well as I do. She's probably kicking butt and taking names."

Brian lied, knowing that the prognosis was bleak. "I promise I'll call the minute I know anything."

This seemed to appease Matt and the two hung up.

Matt turned hopeful. Maybe Codi had been too busy to reply, or maybe she didn't see his email. She might not be mad at him after all.

But then again, how hard was it to send a text.

The arrival of the men had completely changed Chow's disposition. He was now actively engaged, and Jin could feel the darkness lift from the room.

"Ok, down to business."

Everyone at the table stopped talking and looked to Chow.

"I am afraid our leaders have grown soft suckling on the wealth of the west. It is now up to us to bring about the change our people and our country needs. A path is now open to return to our true communist roots, more important now than ever. Soon, others will fear not just our billion-man army but our technology as well. Soon, we will show them what is possible, and it will leave the rest of the world in dread. They will know we can strike at them anywhere, anytime, and they are powerless to stop us."

This started a small wave of excitement among the men.

Chow laid out his plan, and the squad got to work. Poh interjected a few times with concerns and ideas. Ultimately all agreed, and each went their own way, setting the plan in motion. Jin found a quiet corner to set up his computers as the squad busied themselves preparing a cache of weapons, grenades, and other paraphernalia. The two studious men moved to the third floor where an open work area was established. They worked on a prototype that was nearly complete. It looked like a small radar dish attached with cables to a toaster-sized box. They double-checked everything, including Chow's plan. It was only a matter of time before all would be ready

Codi pulled herself up onto the roof of a clothing store three buildings over from her target. Joel and Ang watched from the alley below. The town had gone to sleep, save for a few wandering tourists. The moon had peeked over the mountain and was casting a cold distorted reflection on the river's surface. She was dressed all in black, some from Ang's trunk and some from a local shop. The tiled roof made for treacherous going, but she kept three points of contact at all times, looking like a giant spider moving across the skyline.

As with most cities in China the space between buildings is often very narrow or nonexistent. She scaled up to the edge of Chongde Hall, where she jumped and pulled herself onto its roof. She moved slowly and carefully. This was not a race. The top of Chow's home allowed for a spectacular view of the river, as lit homes and shops along its bank reflected a myriad of colors across the water. The peak of the portico held two small windows. Codi lowered herself down and checked the lock on one. It was old and flimsy. She used her knife to quietly force it open, and lowered herself inside.

The room was dark and smelled of dust and mold. The glow from the small window illuminated several bodies standing in the room. Codi drew her pistol instinctively and dropped behind a wooden chest. She peeked out to see that the bodies were made of stone. She felt stupid. On closer inspection she realized they were not stone but terracotta warriors. In the dim glow they looked very realistic.

She had always wanted to see the display in northwestern China. More than eight-thousand warriors, one-hundred-and-thirty chariots, and over five-hundred horses were built to protect the first emperor of China in the afterlife. She ran her fingers along the plated armor. The detail was incredible. Too bad she didn't have time for a selfie.

Codi turned the door handle and moved down an empty hallway. It appeared that this section of the house had seen little use lately. She peeked down from the top of worn stairs that led to the floors below. She could hear voices in the distance. If only she had the gear to plant a bug. She could be on her way back out the window right now. Instead, she moved down the stairs one step at a time staying close to the edge to prevent any creaking as she moved.

The room below opened into a large open space. There were two fifteen-foot rows of tables, approximately six feet apart. They were covered with equipment, testing electronics, even a satellite dish that looked like it was for receiving cable TV. Codi had had some experience with rogue technology in the past, but everything here looked innocuous. And without knowing its purpose she had no real evidence to initiate a raid on the general. She pulled out the phone Ang had given her and started recording. Using the digital zoom, she captured tight shots of the gear littering the worktables. She hoped the audio would come through and that Ang could make something of the conversation that was taking place.

A door to the room suddenly opened. Two men struggled to carry in a crate and place it at the head of the table to the right. Codi leaned down to get a better view. There were Chinese characters on the box, but nothing that would help her ID the contents. Luckily, one of the men in a lab coat, picked up a crowbar and started to crack open the crate. The wood panels fell away to reveal a black cone-shaped object. She snapped two quick pictures. She recognized it right away—a guidance nosecone for an intercontinental ballistic missile. *Shit.*

Joel and Ang waited in the darkness of the alley. Ang was on his third cigarette, his mind filled with worry, the wound in his side throbbing. Suddenly, he smashed his cigarette out and pulled Joel back further into the shadows. A pair of guards appeared moving along the alleyway. They had not expected security to make such a wide sweep. Ang held their one re-maining pistol in his hand, as he and Joel crouched behind a wooden trough used to catch rainwater. They held their breaths as the two guards surveyed their surroundings, being careful not to miss anything suspicious.

The cool evening air had little effect on Joel. He started to perspire. He could hear the guards speaking softly to each other but had no clue what they were saying. Ang hunkered lower as the two guards moved in their direction. The glow from a hand rolled cigarette illuminated the face of the man on the left as he drew in a restricted breath. He placed his hand on his partner's arm to stop their walk.

They both pulled AKS-74U machine pistols from their shoulders and readied themselves for action. The AKS-74U, a slightly more modern and compact version of the AK-47, fired a slightly smaller bullet but at a faster rate.

The man on the left flicked his cigarette away. He was all business now. Something had their attention and they were looking right at the trough that hid Joel and Ang. The guards started to investigate. Ang quietly cocked his gun, using the palm of his hand to hide the noise. He was coiled like a tight spring ready to leap. As the two men stepped up to the trough, a laugh caught their attention.

They turned to its origin, a group of three German tour-ists laughing and staggering down the alley. They started sing-ing a bit too loudly, obviously drunk. The two guards put their guns down and watched as the group moved past. The guards then followed behind them at a respectable distance, but not before the guard on the left retrieved his tossed cigarette and sucked it back to life.

Joel and Ang let out a collective sigh as a distant sneeze caught their attention. It was followed by a rattling noise, a muffled cry, and then a giant splash that doused them with the trough's water.

Codi breeched the surface, sputtering and flicking the soaked hair out of her face. She coughed up some of the water from her lungs. Joel and Ang looked like matching drowned rats. They stared in shock at their partner as she climbed out of the trough.

"Sorry," Codi said in a forced whisper. "I was holding onto a roof tile while you two were playing hide the weenie with those two guards. There's a bird nest up there and I must be allergic to something in it. That sneeze came out of nowhere, the tile broke off and, *voila,* swan dive."

"Well I give you a ten on your entry," Ang said, with a slight smile as he brushed the water off of his clothes.

"It might be bird flu," Joel added, in obvious concern.

"No bird flu here," Ang said, unaware of Joel's tendency towards germaphobia. "It started several hundred miles to the north."

"Did you see Chow?" Joel asked Codi.

"No. Come on let's get out of here." She was already leaving as she spoke.

Joel hurried after her calling in a loud whisper, "What did you find out?"

Codi held up the smart phone. "I found out that this phone is not waterproof."

"Intercontinental ballistic missile guidance nosecone? Are you sure?" Ang asked Codi.

"Ninety-five percent. I was stationed at Kaneohe Bay in Hawaii for a time and there was a missile display with several Chinese and Russian mock-ups."

Ang nodded his head in understanding. "Okay. I can't think of anything good you could use one for. I'll make some calls on the landline, since our only cell phone is dead."

Ang stood from the yellow Formica table at their guest-house and moved to the old rotary phone in the living area.

Joel placed their soggy smart phone in a bag full of rice, saying, "At least it's easy to find rice around here."

Codi moved to the refrigerator to see what she could manage for a snack after her high-calorie-burning adventure.

Ang walked back in a moment later. "I contacted a friend of mine in the Ministry of State Security. We have to assume that the local police are in Chow's pocket and unable to handle this anyway."

"Good call," Joel said.

"They're sending a squad of two trucks and twelve men."

"That's great news. When will they get here?" Joel asked.

Ang hesitated. "Tomorrow noon."

Codi let out a short breath. She should have known. Bureaucracy moved slowly in every government.

Joel looked at his watch. "Twelve more hours."

"It could be all over by then." Codi looked like a lioness in a cage as she paced, knowing there was nothing she could do but wait. She tried the power on the drying cell phone. Still dead. "We should at least stake the place out and make sure no one leaves Chow's home. I'll take the first watch."

It was a sound idea and Joel volunteered for the second watch, with Ang taking the last.

Chow watched as his men loaded the canvas-backed truck under the glare of several work lights. They had converted the vehicle to look like a military FAW MV3 4X4, complete with a red star on both doors. He was wearing his old PAL general's uniform adorned with his many medals. Two of his men were dressed like military aides to match. Chow looked down at his phone expectantly. No new messages. The one working corner of his mouth dropped mechanically.

"Trouble sir?" Jin had seen the general's reaction and was feeling the tension of pre-mission jitters himself.

"No. Just waiting on an important text." He pocketed his phone and gestured to Jin with a swish of his hand. "Get on board, son."

Once the truck was loaded they pulled out through the cover of a heavy mist that buried the town in mystery. The trip to the silo would take twenty minutes, giving them another two hours before sunrise.

19

GUEST HOUSE – 5:48 A.M. – FENGHUANG, CHINA

After a fitful sleep, Codi breathed in the aroma of freshly brewed coffee. It drew her from her bed to the small kitchen.

"Where did you find this?"

"There's a hotel down the street that caters to tourists." Joel beamed, as his coffee ritual was finally back.

Ang entered the room. "Something's up. About fifteen minutes ago the two guards went back inside and then the lights in the whole house went out. I crept up to a window and saw no activity. They were very focused during their shift and now they're gone."

"Anyone enter or exit since?"

"Not a soul," Ang replied.

"Could they be sleeping?"

"Maybe, but they were definitely on a schedule last night. Things were very busy. It seems improbable that they would work through the night, allow the guards to take a break, and what, they just all go to sleep? I double-checked the back door, and nothing. It's like they disappeared into the fog."

Joel set his beloved coffee down and stood holding the phone in the rice bag. "It's working."

The cellphone powered up. The text message was unreadable to him. He handed it to Ang.

"Problems," Ang said. "The road from Wuhan has been washed out. They are having to reroute and the new ETA is more like three p.m."

"Damn," Joel said.

"This just keeps getting better and better," Codi muttered.

"We should check out the house," said Joel.

The morning mist clung to the town like a mud facial, leaving visibility at less than ten feet. Codi and Ang moved through the Hong Bridge across the Tuo River. The sleepy fog-enshrouded town was awe inspiring, but they had no time for sightseeing.

Joel was assigned a different path, approaching the house from the other side. Two-hundred yards up was a stepping-stone path across the river. Each step was a stone column two feet in diameter and placed two feet apart. They spanned the river but were not recommended for anyone who'd been drinking, as you had to stride or jump from stone to stone. The mist was so thick that Joel couldn't see even halfway across the river. He took a deep breath and started to make his way across, half-hopping and half-stepping as he went, keeping his arms out at his side for balance. About halfway, he came to a sudden stop. A young woman materialized out of the fog, coming the other way. She was holding a baby, and there was no way to pass. Joel forced a smile and started back.

After she reached the bank, Joel started over again, hopping and stepping his way across. This time Joel ran into a man carrying a small bundle of firewood. Joel had made it more than three-quarters of the way and was not willing to go back again. He gestured for the man to back up, but the man refused and stepped on the stone directly in front of Joel. Joel gestured again, but the man gave him the universal sign for not a chance; you back up. This was getting old fast and Codi and Ang were counting on him. Joel did the only thing he could think of at the time. He shoved the man into the water. "Sorry," he said, "but I got a thing."

Joel continued moving to the other side, glancing over his shoulder to make sure the poor soul could swim. Just the opposite was true. The man had lost his firewood and was struggling to keep his head above water.

Joel stopped.

"You gotta be kidding me."

Once they reached Chongde Hall, Codi and Ang dropped low and surveyed the building. All was quiet, just as Ang had said. There were no guards stationed at the front door.

"Thoughts?" Codi asked Ang.

"I have been instructed to wait for our reinforcements," he said.

"Right. How long are you planning to hide behind us?"

"My hands are tied. But if you were to storm the front door, I would have to follow and try to intercede."

Codi slunk over to the entrance. The argument had been short. Codi and Joel would take the blame if anything went wrong, and Ang could live with that.

The front door was an ancient affair with bronze rivets and thick wooden beams. In place of the old lock was a modern deadbolt. Ang quickly worked to unlock it.

Once inside, the beauty of the large domed ceiling set in dark wood was lost on Codi. She and Ang moved to clear the home one room at a time. The problem was, they had only one gun between them. Codi had a mostly sharp kitchen knife, hoping to pick up a weapon along the way.

They worked in tandem, professionally clearing each

room. Soon the first floor was done—empty. The second floor was mostly bedrooms. They crept carefully from room to room, and the message was becoming clear. The home was empty. At the top of the stairs was the third floor, the open room Codi had seen the night before. But other than a few parts, the room and tables were empty. No hard evidence, no intercontinental ballistic missile nosecone. With practiced efficiency they finished their search but both knew the answer: they were too late.

As Codi and Ang returned down the carved wooden staircase to the first floor, they each processed the trouble that was coming their way, both political and legal.

They were discussing quickly exiting the building and denying ever having set foot in it, when Joel burst through the back door.

"FBI, nobody move!" His gun was drawn, ready to shoot. His clothes were soaked and he dripped all over the wood floor.

"You're late. And wet." Codi said.

Joel sheepishly put his gun away. "Sorry, got hung up."

He hooked a thumb over his shoulder. "Back door was open so I popped in. There's no sign of anyone out there."

"Same in here. It looks like they left sometime early this morning," Ang said.

"The question is how."

A grating sound from the back wall caught their attention. A large wall panel was rising upward, revealing a passageway illuminated with bare bulbs strung along the ceiling. Two armed guards were chatting as they made their way back into the home.

Ang yelled out, "Police! Freeze or I'll fire."

This caught the two men by surprise and they panicked, diving in opposite directions. Ang fired a shot into the space where the man on the right had just been standing. A quick reply of 5.45 mm full-auto lead sprayed back in Ang's direction, shredding the staircase. Codi, who didn't have a gun, wasted no time diving for cover behind the banister. Ang ducked and fired blindly, as bullets chewed up the space surrounding him.

Joel, who had not been detected by the two hostiles, dropped to the floor and emptied his clip in their direction. The man on the right twitched and died, his finger falling from the trigger harmlessly. The other man dove behind a large jade dragon. He reset his sites on the man who had just killed his partner. The temporary reprieve of bullets aimed in Ang's direction allowed him to jump over the railing and seek cover behind the stairs.

Joel rolled for a yellow upholstered sofa, leaving a snail trail of water behind him. He hid behind it as a full assault of gunfire dissected the couch and the wall behind it. Joel continued to scramble, and dove out from behind the far side of the couch, followed closely by hot lead. The only amnesty was when the assailant's clip ran dry. Joel had nowhere left to hide. It was a good fifteen feet to a warrior statue in the corner.

The guard quickly reloaded another clip and leaned out to reacquire the soggy man across the room. Joel had no more ammunition. He was now nothing more than a moving target.

Ang had anticipated the guard's move and had wormed his way into position for a shot. As soon as the man leaned out to reacquire Joel, Ang fired two quick bursts. The first one hit the man in the neck and the second in his temple. It ended the man's life but not before reflexes caused his finger to clamp onto the trigger. A wild spray of bullets flew everywhere, like a loose garden hose turned on full. It ended with a giant chandelier crashing to the floor, sending crystal shards everywhere.

The room was a mess, but Codi, Ang and Joel had somehow survived. The three moved to the center of the room to survey the damage. Codi took the occasion to arm herself with the dead man's weapon. Joel bent over to examine a bullet hole in his heel of his shoe. "That was close," he said.

Codi looked over to Ang who was brushing the dust out of his hair. "You got a little something on your shirt," she said.

Ang looked down to see three bullet holes stitched under his right armpit. "Whoa."

Abruptly, the back door opened and an older, hunched-over woman shuffled in, carrying groceries. She stiffened at the sight of the carnage. She looked over to see three strangers aiming weapons at her. A sudden scream escaped her, followed by groceries crashing to the floor.

The glow of two pole-mounted lights revealed Sheng Luo PLA missile silo 089. It was disguised as a fermentation house in the middle of an orchard. From a distance, it blended into the agriculture of the area and would be right at home in Napa Valley. It had a red-tiled roof and beige stucco walls with arched windows and a fermentation tank rising from the ground next to it.

The military-looking truck came to a brief stop, and half of Chow's team jumped out and moved off on foot. One of them started climbing a nearby telephone pole. Another, carrying a sniper rifle, jogged into the nearby orchard.

The driver let out the brake and continued on to the silo a half-mile ahead.

Jin triggered the jammer that would prevent any communications in the area. The truck pulled to a stop next to the building. A large wooden door opened to reveal two heavily armed guards who took the unexpected arrival seriously. They squinted through the headlights' glare of the truck. General Chow stepped down from the passenger's side and walked slowly and deliberately over to them. The two guards stiffened even more at the sight of the backlit general.

Chow called out, "At ease, gentlemen."

They disregarded the order.

"General Chow Phun of the People's Liberation Army southern division under the direct orders of the Vice Chairman." Chow pulled out an official looking document that had all the needed details, as far as a lowly guard would know.

"I am making surprise inspections to twelve PLA Missile Silos today."

"I will have to check this out sir," said one of the guards. "We don't get generals just stopping by, especially at night."

"Of course, but please hurry. I have a full day ahead of me."

The driver of the truck stepped down casually and lit a cigarette. One guard eyed him suspiciously, while the other went back inside to confirm the general's orders. Chow paced around, looking put out. He went over to his driver to join him for a smoke.

The operations room for the silo was a large rectangle. It was state-of-the art electronic sophistication with human and analog redundancy for everything. There were two matching control consoles that looked like a cockpit for a computer geek. On the desk-like surface was a sophisticated terminal with an extended keyboard. The rest of the room held various electronics and communication devices. The floor panels had the ability to lift up so you could access the electronics and wiring running throughout. On the back wall was a set of elevator doors. On the opposite wall was an armored exit door leading to the security room and then the outside.

In one of the cockpits, technician Wei flicked his lighter

for the tenth time and swore. The fluid was empty. "Got a light?" he asked his co-worker.

Zhang stepped over and pulled his Bik lighter out. He watched as the flame ignited the tip of Wei's smoke.

Wei inhaled to complete the action and nodded his thanks. The twelve-hour shift they worked was far from over, but nicotine helped him stay calm in a room with no windows. His claustrophobia was just strong enough to be a constant reminder that he worked in a space that was more dungeon than office. Luckily, the military had never discovered his secret and his career as a military tech was showing promise. Just last week he had interviewed with his superiors to potentially oversee the technical operations on the entire southern missile defense network, a job that would get him outside from time to time and put a few more Yuan in his pocket every month. He drew another puff into his lungs and let the tension go, as he contemplated his future.

Ang turned to Joel and Codi.

"She says her name is Tenzin. She works and lives here but she speaks a southern dialect of Mandarin that is really hard to understand, so I could be completely wrong."

They were gathered at the kitchen table. Codi had given her a glass of water and Ang was trying to kindly interrogate her. They went back and forth speaking rapid fire Chinese. Ang did his best to keep things calm and level-headed. Joel had followed the secret passage to an empty street exit three buildings over. He returned, carrying the fallen groceries.

"They definitely left through the passage, and there is no sign of anyone, just the two dead guards," Joel said as he entered the room.

"Nice shooting, by the way," Codi said to him.

Joel just nodded. He never liked to take a man's life and the weight of it was often unbearable. In fact, had he given it some thought, he'd realize that he'd never even shot at another human being before he met Codi.

Ang summed up their situation. "We got nothing here but two stiffs, an old woman, and no evidence."

"Looks like Chow is in the wind and able to finish whatever it is he has planned," Joel said.

The utter failure was hard to take, especially after all they'd been through. His body language screamed defeat as Joel sat next to his partners.

"Okay, let me sum things up." Joel ticked off his fingers as he went through the past several days. "Something we discovered from a Russian special ops mission in the Arctic during the fifties called Operation Blind Pig, is making a retired General Chow Phun very nervous. So nervous, in fact, that he arranged to have us killed, kidnapped–"

"At an international airport, which is no small feat," Codi added. "Oh, and replaced with lookalikes to throw off our office."

"Right." Joel continued his summary of the last few days. When he got to his third finger on his second hand, he stopped. "Electrical leach."

"What?" Codi asked.

"Electrical leach. That was the term Andrei Tatter used, the fishing guy. What if Chow has a modern day equivalent?"

"But we don't know what it does or if it even exists," Codi said.

Joel took on a faraway stare, as his fingers absently tapped on the table. "Maybe, but back in the fifties it was attached to the DEW Line system, an early warning radar-based structure. What if they used the leach to bypass the system somehow?"

Joel looked around the room. "Now we have a missile

guidance nosecone and possibly a way to make it untrack able."

"An intercontinental ballistic missile that is untrack able. That can't be good," Codi said. She rubbed the back of her skull trying to thwart an oncoming headache. "We gotta find and stop Chow."

"Easier said than done," Ang said, with a look of defeat.

They sat in silence, no one suggesting their next move.

"You want to stop Mr. Chow Phun?" All three agents looked at the old woman who had just spoken English. Each looked like they had just bit into a lemon.

"You speak English?" Joel could scarcely say the words.

"Who are you?" Codi dared to ask.

The old woman stood, no longer hunched over. She looked at the group with sharp appraising eyes. This was not the frail housekeeper they had thought she was.

"My name is Tenzin. I work for a group called The People for Tibetan Freedom. We monitor various people and facilities throughout southern China with many such as I. In Tibet, we have no military to push China from our borders, but infor- mation can be a different type of weapon, and we wield it with all our might. What little autonomy we now enjoy as a people was hard fought, using blackmail and information leaks."

Joel's mouth dropped open in disbelief. "Incredible."

"Yes, but I'm afraid you might be too late to stop Mr. Chow Phun."

"What do you mean?" Ang asked.

"Yes, tell us everything you know," Codi said.

"One moment, please," Tenzin said.

The very short woman with thick gray hair moved like a cat out of the room. Codi peeked out the door just to make sure she didn't run off.

Tenzin returned and set an old leather-bound book on the

table. She flipped it opened. Inside was a carved out section filled with handwritten notes and drawings.

"I do what I can to spy, and copy anything that happens in this house. Mr. Chow Phun has been busy building some kind of radar or satellite blocking system for ground-based missiles."

She pulled out a piece of paper showing a very detailed drawing of a rocket nosecone with a satellite dish built into the front. It was covered over by a clear dome to maintain its aerodynamics.

"I saw something like this last night," Codi said.

Tenzin pointed with two fingers to the document. "Here. This is what they took to Sheng Luo."

"Sheng Luo?" Joel asked.

"A rocket silo."

The three agents were trying to catch up but her words were processing too slowly in their brains.

"Don't tell me you don't know what he's up to?" Tenzin said. "How were you planning to stop the unknown?"

Codi was the first to respond. "We may not totally know everything but we are determined to stop him. Where is this silo?"

Tenzin told them everything she knew about Chow Phun's plans, which turned out to be nothing more than a location and a plan to attack and take over the silo. As far as his designs and use of the nosecone, nobody knew for sure. But it seemed very clear to all that Chow and a mystery rocket nosecone, along with access to a working ICBM, was really bad news for both their countries.

20

PLA Missile Silo 089 – 4:58 a.m. – Sheng Luo, China

The console buzzed in the operations room. Zhang grabbed the headset. Wei listened to his partner's one-sided conversation.

"Hang on a sec."

Zhang told Wei about the issues outside.

There was nothing worse than a pissed-off general looking for payback. Wei quickly dialed his superior—nothing. He tried the hard line—dead. Then the radio, then the keyboard. Nothing was getting out. Wei had been through communication failures in the past, but never all four backups failing at once.

"Protocol six," he told his partner.

This signaled a complete lockdown of the facility.

"Tell the general we are sorry," Wei said. "Protocol six is in effect and we are locked down."

Wei hung up the receiver and started flipping switches that were part of the lockdown procedure. Wei pulled out the operations manual and severed the chain that anchored it to the desk. He noticed his hands were starting to shake.

The first guard came back out of the building looking a little concerned. "Communications are down, sir," he said to Chow. "Even the hard line is not working. That means we are going on lockdown. I'm afraid I can't let you in."

"I understand your orders, but I have mine as well," Chow said. "And I'll be dammed if a rice-slurping private is going to turn me away. Do you know the hurt I can lay on you and your family for this?" Chow said the last part with real venom in his voice.

"Yes sir, but my superior can do the same, so no matter what I choose, I'm screwed. Therefore, I'm following protocol as dictated by my direct superior. Sorry, sir."

The two guards backed towards the entrance watching the truck and the general carefully. Just before they got to the door, a shot from the nearby grove rang out.

One of the guards dropped face-first to the ground, a piece of his skull missing. The general and his aides quickly overpowered the other guard before he could react. They held him face-down in the dirt while they zip-tied his hands and feet.

"It's about time. Come on," Chow said.

The driver gave a whistle and bodies quickly swarmed, emptying all of the truck's contents. They efficiently hauled everything into the security room.

"Five minutes before the next satellite passes," Jin called as he watched the proceedings. "Get that truck out of here, I want everything to look normal for the next flyover."

The last of the gear and men hustled inside the building, as the truck moved away.

The security room was small, and with all the men and gear they were literally crammed inside like sardines. There was a guard desk with two chairs and a steel blast door that was secured on the back wall. The desk had a half-completed

Mahjong game and a small terminal with a keyboard. A large monitor showed a view of six cameras covering a 360-degree view of the surroundings. A shelf on the sidewall held a hot plate with a kettle and tea supplies.

Poh grabbed the guard that was still alive and shoved him against a wall. "What is the code for entering the armored door?" he asked the man.

The guard shook his head in fear, not uttering a word. He had seen his friend shot right beside him and had no doubt the same awaited him, even if he talked. Poh pulled his knife and placed it next to the man's right eye. The guard forced his eyes shut not wanting to see the danger.

Poh asked him again, and when the guard continued to refuse to answer, he flicked the blade, puncturing the man's eye. A gelatinous ooze spilled out to the sound of a mournful cry. The pain was intense but short lived as the guard's right vision dimmed and his eye died.

"What is the code!"

The guard whimpered through tears and blood. "Protocol six, the door can't be opened."

"We know there is an override code. What is it?" Poh countered.

He moved the knife to the guard's genitals.

"Last chance. How about one ball to go with one eyeball." He chuckled at his joke. "Or I could just make a clean sweep of everything down there. Wouldn't take much. What is the override code!"

The guard was so traumatized that he was blubbering incomprehensibly. The knife pressed higher and the words suddenly became more panicked but now understandable.

Jin wasted no time imputing the code into the terminal on the guard's desk. He glanced over at the game of mahjong that was spread across the desk. Several red tong and green dragons in evidence on the discard pile. A loud click followed, turning every head in the room. The steel blast door started to open.

Inside the operations room, Wei heard the click that signified the opening of the blast door. He grabbed the operations manual and hit the alarm button. A claxon and red flashing lights filled the room. He ran for the elevator, screaming to his subordinate, "Hold them off!"

Wei punched a code in the keypad next to it. The elevator doors started to open and he dashed through, hitting the down button repeatedly. As the doors slowly closed he could just make out Zhang all alone, armed with his pistol, standing his ground. He was ready to stop the intruders.

Two of the general's armed men crashed low through the large door's opening gap, their silenced guns drawn and ready. From inside the elevator, Wei heard two quick muffled pops followed by a thud. As the car slowly descended, ridiculous music played a happy folk tune.

The general's team moved quickly into the operations area. It was nearly three times the size of the security room. There were two large control consoles touting a collection of indicator lights, switches, and keyboards. Crumpled on the floor with an unused pistol was a blood-soaked operator, Zhang.

"The room is secure sir, but there is no sign of the lead tech."

Jin held up the severed chain attached to the console. "Operations manual is missing."

"Get me that tech before he destroys the manual," Poh ordered. "He couldn't have gone far. Go."

Poh ran to the elevator doors and listened. A decreasing whir told him what he needed to know. With a couple of hand gestures, his men used steel bars to pry the elevator doors apart. They hurriedly attached two rappelling ropes, and two of his men dropped into the shaft chasing the receding car to its final destination.

Wei knew he was out of time and opened the operations manual. He grabbed his lighter and flicked it. He prayed for a flame so he could burn the book to ash and with it the ability to operate the missile silo. A small flame burst on the wick but it died as quickly as it was born. He tried again—nothing. Wei flicked and flicked until his thumb was raw. It was no use.

Finally, the car came to a stop at the bottom. Wei started to shred the first page by hand as a pair of combat boots crashed through the access panel on the car's roof. Wei reached for his pistol but was struck in the face as his assailant dropped to the floor. Wei spun with the impact, just as the elevator doors opened to the subbasement level. He reacquired his aim before the soldier could drop his rappelling rope and bring his gun to bear.

Four shots echoed in the tight space. Wei watched as his combatant slumped to the floor, dead. He then looked up at a second man holding his smoking weapon through the access panel. It was pointed in his direction. The man was struggling to get through hole. Wei looked down to see two red dots on his chest bloom with color. The gun in his hand dropped to the floor as his legs started to wobble. He grabbed the book and exited the elevator.

The room was a large tube-shaped area with a ninety-eight-foot-tall ICBM standing in the middle. It was painted olive green and had its model name, DF-5B, stamped on the side. Black metal scaffolding held it aloft and gave technicians access to the rocket. In the middle of the floor was a black hole that allowed for exhaust.

Wei wobbled like a raging drunk for the rocket, his plan desperate and poorly thought out. He hoped to throw the manual into the abyss of the missile's exhaust tube. His vision was dimming as he staggered forward. The railing to the exhaust exit was just ahead. But his feet failed him and Wei dropped to the floor, scattering the book out of reach. He tried to crawl to it. Just a little further...

The assailant in the elevator's access panel had fired two shots down into the lead tech almost at the same time as the tech had fired at his partner. He then had to re-holster his weapon and untangle his rappelling rope to get down into the car. But the rope caught on an attachment bolt to the elevator. He saw the tech stumble out of the elevator with the operations manual. He flicked out a knife, cut himself free, and dropped into the car. He ran after the tech.

Inside the main silo, the soldier paused. There was a dead man, the tech, his fingers touching the operations manual. It was just inches from a deep exit tube built directly below the rocket to vent the flames.

The soldier dropped to the floor and picked up the book. He looked up at the giant ICBM, one of man's greatest military powers. He stood and started back to the elevator.

Jin placed the blood-spattered manual on the console and opened it up. He pieced the torn first page back together and began the startup process. The first thing on his list was to get the silo out of lockdown and turn off that obnoxious alarm.

The Southern Great Wall is a shorter version of its famous brother to the north. It is often overlooked, but was at one point 150 kilometers in length. Though most of it is now destroyed, there are several sections that stretch across the lush southern landscape, a reminder of a long forgotten hatred between the Mio and Chinese people. Codi looked out the passenger window of their car as it paralleled the Southern

Great Wall for several hundred meters. It was a marvel of engineering, housing over five-thousand soldiers at its apex.

Ang finally had some good news. Their back-up had re-routed and was now only fifteen minutes behind them. All that was left was to find Chow and point them in the right direction.

They pulled off the road onto a dirt trail that stopped just before the peak of a hill. Their backseat driver, Tenzin, had been a chatterbox for most of the way, pointing and gesticulating her directions. She exited the car and hustled up to the top of the hill, not waiting for the others, and lay down on the ground.

Codi followed to lay beside her, impressed with the old woman's fortitude. Ang and Joel followed. Tenzin pointed to a quaint building in the tranquil valley below. There was a red tile roof set on a rectangular building covered in flowering vines. A small domed fermenting tank was attached on the left side with a matching roof.

There were a few arched windows, a large wooden door and stone pavers encompassing the foundation. The building was surrounded on all sides by an orchard of peach trees. The smell was intoxicating with ripe peaches hanging from every tree.

"It looks like a fermentation building at a vineyard," Codi said.

"Yes, for making peach wine, but that is what they want you to think. It is Sheng Luo PLA Missile Silo 089," Tenzin replied.

Codi looked skeptical and borrowed Ang's binoculars. On closer inspection there was some seriously heavy-duty conduit piping on one wall. The roof had several small aerial antennas and a satellite dish partially hidden by the roof's peak.

Tenzin pointed to the side building that looked like a small tower. "The dome opens up for launch."

Codi panned her view to the smaller round tower. Its domed roof had visible seams, and the ground held three large exhaust vents, angled away from the building. "That is definitely *not* what it appears to be," Codi said, as she handed the binoculars back to Ang.

The group pulled back down the hill. Tenzin looked up at Ang. "Well, good then. My work here is done."

"What?" Codi said.

"Wait. We might still need you for–" Joel started.

"For what, to point my accusatory finger in another direction?"

"We don't even know if General Phun is in there," Ang countered.

"I can guarantee you, *that* is Mr. Chow Phun's target. I am but an old woman, I can be of no further use to you now."

Tenzin turned and started to walk back down the dirt road calling over her shoulder. "Just remember, Mr. Chow Phun is a very smart and clever man."

Ang stared for a moment and then turned back to Codi and Joel. "Smart woman."

Joel looked worried. "Yeah. She may be the only one who gets out alive."

Tenzin called out from a distance. "Try not to get your-selves killed."

"And she's a mind reader too," Joel added.

21

PLA MISSILE SILO 089 – 8:22 A.M. – SHENG LUO, CHINA

The dead were dumped unceremoniously in a stack on the silo's concrete floor. The two scientists, with the help of one soldier, moved the replacement nosecone down to the sub-basement. From there the scientists took their tools and began to climb the scaffolding to the missile's top. The soldier used a gantry crane to attach and lift the new nosecone up for installation.

The alarm stopped. It was as if a great weight had been lifted from Jin's chest. *"Finally,"* he mumbled.

Chow stepped over next to him and looked at the screen.

"I'm into the system," Jin said, "and there are a lot of things I can do, including launching the rocket. But without an authorization code, the nuclear portion will be inert."

"Start by filling the rocket," Chow ordered.

Jin's fingers flew over the extended keyboard, and with a flick of the enter key, hydrazine along with liquid hydrogen and oxygen began to fill the individual tanks in the lower stages of the rocket.

It took time to remove the original nosecone and replace it with their prototype. That was followed by several electronic dry runs to confirm everything was operational. Chow spent most of the time pacing and watching Poh double-check security on the perimeter.

Ang pulled out their cellphone to check on their reinforcements' progress. He pushed send several times without luck. "I got no signal."

"Is it still wet?" Codi asked.

"No, it's working. It just won't go through."

"They're probably jamming the area," Joel said, while looking around for a source.

Codi felt useless just waiting there for backup to arrive. In principle she was not really a backup kind of girl, preferring instead to forge ahead no matter the cost, pulling the troops along with her. But they were not in Kansas anymore and the last thing she needed to be was the focus of an international incident. She would wait a bit longer.

"That means the general is most likely already in there," Joel added.

"And doing God knows what while we all sit around talking about it," Codi said.

A rumble punctuated Codi's comment, as two smaller troop transports came to a stop next to Ang's car. A small but sturdy colonel stepped from the passenger's seat of the lead vehicle and approached. He shook Ang's hand, as Ang introduced Codi and Joel. The colonel eyed them with disdain and refocused on Ang almost immediately.

"This better not be a waste of my time," he said to Ang. "Getting here was a real bitch. You said there might be a breach in one of our silos?"

"Yes. Sheng Luo PLA missile silo 089. It's just over the hill."

Codi and Joel felt helpless listening to the two men speaking Chinese.

the sheer

The colonel pulled out a map and located the silo. It was indeed just over the hill next to them. "I should take look. You three wait here," he said in broken English.

He climbed to the top of the hill and peered down at the lone building in the middle of a peach grove.

Codi walked over to Ang and spoke quietly to him. "This is bullshit."

"What would you have me do?"

Codi knew he was right, but the slow, uncaring quality of their new leader was driving her crazy.

The colonel stomped back down the hill. "All is quiet."

Codi could not hide her disappointment. The colonel seemed unaffected.

"I don't like it."

She turned to look back at him. Had she heard right?

He switched back to Chinese and spoke to Ang. "We'll go in and investigate. Once we have secured the facility we will come back for you."

"If the general's in there, they may be expecting trouble," Ang said.

"*If* the general's in there, I will buy the first and second rounds tonight for all, but I doubt this is the case. But don't worry, my men are highly trained and ready for anything."

The colonel switched back to English and addressed the Americans. "You focus on staying here. I don't want to throw you in jail for interfering."

Codi had to bite the bottom of her lip to stay calm.

With that said he turned and left.

"Corporal Ling!" the colonel called out.

A young man with a buzz cut and a can-do attitude hustled up to the colonel and gave him a terse salute.

"Let operations know our position."

He nodded and ran off to the truck.

Ang interrupted, holding his smart phone up as a demo. "They are jamming the signals here."

"Interesting. We use a specialized military signal, so not to worry." He said the words with a heavy patronizing measure.

Ang knew when to attack and when to retreat and now was the time for playing nice. "I'm sure you are right."

Ang moved to stand beside his two American cohorts.

"What was that all about," Joel asked, not understanding what had been said.

"A simple case of might makes right."

Codi and Joel both knew instantly what Ang meant.

"Great," Codi whispered.

The three watched as the energetic Corporal Ling ran back from his truck and saluted the corporal. "Sir, there is no signal getting in or out."

Codi leaned over to Ang, whispering through nearly closed lips. "Let me guess, they're being jammed."

Ang slowly but purposely nodded his head.

"Take the radio and go as far away from here as you need to get a signal. Let them know that we are being jammed and are going to investigate."

Ling ran off with his orders.

The colonel turned his attention back to Ang. "Inspector, do I have to leave a few of my men here to babysit?"

"No, we will do what you ask. Just be damn careful, please."

"I intend to."

The colonel called his men together to form a plan. They loaded up in the vehicles and roared off towards the silo.

The scientists scrambled out of the subbasement, their task complete. The ICBM looked just like it always had, except the green tip had been replaced with a clear Lexan tip, complete with radar dish and some very specific equipment housed inside.

"We got activity outside," one of the men called.

"What? How?" Chow hurried to Poh's side to see the security feed. "I'm counting on you to make this go away."

"Of course," Poh said. "It is what we do." The squad leader called out brisk orders and his men readied for a fight.

Codi waited until the trucks were out of sight, and ran to the hilltop to watch the fallout. Joel tried to catch up.

"*Codi.* We were supposed to wait here. I gave them my word."

Ang, exasperated flung his arms in the air and ran after them.

From their vantage point they watched as the two vehicles approached the silo. They paused for a second and several soldiers exited the back of the truck. They followed behind the truck, using the sheet metal as cover.

Codi watched. Sitting on the sidelines was hard, but if they could watch the man who'd caused them so much strife go down, it would have to suffice.

As the truck and the men neared the building the arched front door opened slightly.

"Get out of there," Codi mouthed to herself.

Poh hinged open the door and stood to the side as two of his men aimed their Type-98 recoilless rifles at the two troop transports. Nicknamed the Queen Bee, they shot a 120 mm projectile from a handheld fiberglass tube. The multipurpose warhead rocketed to its target in less than ten seconds from the pull of the trigger. It was capable of penetrating up to 800 mm of armor-piercing steel and then fragmenting the pieces throughout the vehicle, killing all of its occupants.

Target acquired," the two men said.

"Fire on my mark," Poh said. "Three, two, one, *mark.*"

Two rocket-aided projectiles shot from the building. The drivers of the trucks instinctually parted company in different directions at the sight of the streaming fireballs. But the guided explosives tracked their movements. Before they could get ten feet, both vehicles exploded in balls of flame and flying steel.

Several of the soldiers who were on the ground returned fire and a brief but intense firefight ensued. As the last bullet flew, the picture was clear—two down on the general's team and none left on the assault team.

Chow's remaining men pulled back into the silo, and Poh reported, "All of the attacking force has been put down, General. They appear to be regular PLA army."

"I am at a loss as to how regular army could have gotten wind of our plan and acted on it so quickly," Chow said, pondering.

"General, before you start pointing fingers within your own organization, let me say they were not in an attack formation."

The general looked at him with a new curiosity.

"It was more like a routine approach. They were most likely only here to check on something."

Chow paced, ready to explode at any moment. But he took the time to re-center himself and get back to the business at hand. How they got there was no longer his concern. Keeping focused on the mission was. "Get a team out there right away and clean up the evidence," Chow ordered.

"Yes, sir."

"Jin!"

Jin hammered a few strokes on his keyboard. "We have… thirteen minutes till the next pass, sir."

"We are on it." Poh said, and left, barking orders to his men.

Codi turned from the carnage, sickened by the careless waste of life. Joel and Ang watched as three soldiers moved through the battlefield dispatching anyone who was still breathing, occasionally bending over to rob the dead.

"They're playing for keeps," Joel said. "I can't imagine we have a chance at success here." He sounded despondent, half-shaking as he spoke.

Codi sat back up. "I've been thinking, Joel, it's time for you to get back in the game."

"What?"

"Back in the game," Codi repeated.

Joel looked confused.

"I know you really loved Annie. We were all lucky to have been a part of her life."

Agent Annie Waters was one of the original team members. During a case, she and Joel became very close and found love at a time and place that would normally make it impossible. They say love will find a way, and it did. But Joel had to witness Annie's death at the hands of a traitor, and was helpless to stop it. As she died in his arms the flame that the two had built winked out, leaving Joel battered, enraged, and lost.

"And now is the time to talk about this?" Joel asked.

"Why not? You get one chance to go through life. Every day is a gift, and you, my friend, have a lot to give. If I don't make it past today I would never forgive myself for not bringing it up."

"Please tell me you're not going to do what I think you are," Joel said.

"Well, first of all, I'm not telling, I'm doing."

Codi stood. "You two stay here. I'm going to make this whack job go away."

She started to move down the hill towards the building.

"Codi, wait! I think I have a better plan," Ang called.

Cody paused and turned back to Ang.

"Look," he said.

Codi turned to see several men exiting the building into the cleared area around the building. She ducked down and moved quickly back to the cover of the hill.

"And for the record," Ang said to Joel, "Codi's right. You should get back in the game."

"Seriously, you too?" Joel felt surrounded.

"Inaction leaves a regret you can't forget," Ang said.

"Sounds like a fortune cookie, but I agree," Codi said.

"Believe me, I have made that mistake, but never again," said Ang.

Ang and Codi shared a knowing look.

They watched as six men, two in regular clothes and four in uniform, quickly spread out and went to work. Two men put out the fires that were once troop transports filled with men, and the rest moved the bodies and debris over to the ruined vehicles and began stacking them in a pile.

"What the hell?"

After all the flame and smoke was gone they tugged two large bags out of the building.

"Camo netting," Joel said.

"They're hiding the evidence of the battle," Ang added.

"But why?" Joel asked.

Codi pointed up with her finger, as a smile grew on her face. "Satellite."

"Of course, Chow's hiding it from the satellites," Ang said.

"And they're running low on soldiers," Joel said.

"What makes you say that?" asked Ang.

Joel pointed for emphasis. "Two of those guys are not in uniform. I'm betting they got pulled off the tech side of the operation to help out."

"They're working really fast," Ang said while looking up in the sky. "The next pass must be coming soon."

Codi stood and motioned with her hand. "Come on, I have an idea."

Ang and Joel followed her back down the hill to Ang's car. They grabbed the three 3.5 liter jugs of water that Ang kept in his trunk kit and emptied them out. Ang went through his kit and pulled a few things together: a first aid kit, climbing gear, and a bulletproof vest size Small. It would fit only him.

Codi grabbed her kitchen knife and went to the hood.

She cut the heater hose from the engine, and Joel used it to syphon gas from the car's tank into the empty water jugs.

"Hey."

Joel jumped a mile at the sudden comment from an unknown source, spilling gas on his shoes. Corporal Ling, holding his radio, stood nearby watching.

"Jeez, you scared the crap outa me," Joel stammered.

"Hey." Ling smiled showing crooked tea-stained teeth. He wiped his free hand through his disheveled hair.

Ang popped his head up from the trunk and Codi from the hood at the surprise visitor. It was clear that Corporal Ling spoke only one word of English, *hey.*

Ang filled him in on what happened and all were surprised how well he took the complete elimination of all his comrades. He fell to the ground for a few moments, letting the information course through him. After a brief moment he looked up and asked Ang what he should do next.

"Did you get a signal through?"

"Yes," he said proudly."

"What did they say?"

"They said they'd make a note of it and run it by his commander once he returned."

Ang translated.

"Typical," Codi said, familiar with the standing military policy around the world of do nothing until you see the enemy with your own eyes.

"Ang, translate this for me, would you?" Codi said. "We are not waiting for backup that may or may not arrive. We are going in there and we are going to stop Chow. You can either come with us, or you can hike back to where you had a signal and try to convince someone to send immediate help. But if you come with us you'll be taking orders from us, understand?"

Ang translated and the two went back and forth a few times.

"He says he wants to come with us."

"Okay, so, where's his gun?" Codi asked.

Ang asked the question.

"He left it in the truck when he ran off to use the radio."

"Perfect, four against the world, one unarmed. I have…" she opened the curved banana clip on the AKS-74U she'd taken from the dead soldier at Chow's house, "half a clip. Joel?"

Joel opened his pistol's clip and looked. "Three bullets."

"Ang?"

"One mostly-full clip."

"Well, there you have it, that and some climbing gear. How can we lose?"

Codi grabbed a jug and started for the hill.

Joel handed his jug to Ling and pantomimed for him to carry it. Ling grabbed the jug happily and somehow his crooked yellow smile got even bigger. "Hey!"

"Yeah, hey,' Joel deadpanned as he turned to follow Codi.

They carried the jugs up the hill and waited. There was no

sign of any movement outside the silo. The four moved stealth-ily through the peach trees towards the edge of the clearing where the silo sat. Codi had laid out her plans in advance so no talking was required.

They kept the camo netting between them and the silo, as they crept low carrying their improvised gas containers. Joel collected his jug back from Ling.

"Hey!"

"Hey." Joel smiled at the blithesome Ling. He held his hand up to signal *wait here*. But as he started to leave, Ling followed anyway.

Each used their jug to make as big of a letter as possi-ble. Three jugs, three letters. Ang had assured Codi that the Chinese would recognize the international call for help—SOS.

They strategically placed their gas letters next to the camo netting hoping to get a two for one. Ang used his lighter to ignite the letters and the four ran back to the cover of the peach grove.

Joel spoke with excitement. "That should get their satel-lite's attention."

"An SOS in flames next to a nuclear missile silo? You would think," Codi added.

From the cover of the trees, they split into two groups. Ang and Ling went counterclockwise and Codi and Joel went clockwise, working their way to the backside of the building. Ang's wound was bothering him and he had a slightly stooped style to his run. Codi and Joel moved as quickly as possible without making any noise. It was going to be close.

22

PLA Missile Silo 089 – 9:13 a.m. – Sheng Luo, China

"Looks like the fire didn't stay out," said one of the guards in the outer guardroom, while looking at the security monitors.

The screen clearly showed a view of smoke and flames building up just beyond their camouflaged netting.

The other guard went to the exit door and looked back at his partner before opening. "You see any movement?"

"Nothing out there is still alive. But we better get those flames out before the general has a coronary."

"Hey, we get the same pay whether he lives or dies." He laughed at his perceived joke as he opened the main door and moved out into the courtyard with a fire extinguisher. The second guard left the monitor and pushed to the doorway to watch the proceedings. He kept his rifle pointed in the direction of the reborn flames.

Codi and Joel had sprinted through the groves and dashed for the back of the building at a dead run. They stayed under cover of the trees and waited. As soon as Codi saw the guard with the fire extinguisher, she ran to the side of the building. Joel kept at her heels as they moved to the front of the building, with their backs against the wall. Codi held her gun ready for battle.

They had hoped that the fire would provide the needed distraction for them to cross the clearing from the orchard to the back of the building without being noticed. They were ten feet from the door on the hinge side, unable to see if it was clear or not.

After reassuring himself that there were no threats, the guard relaxed and decided it was safe to have a smoke.

Codi heard the telltale sound of a lighter click and used the distraction to her advantage. She used her left arm to pin Joel to the wall out of the way. With gun raised, she pulled the kitchen knife she'd taken from the guesthouse out of her belt. She swapped guns with Joel taking his pistol for close quarters combat. Joel tried to look less awkward than normal, holding the assault rifle. She stepped carefully to the open door, which provided a small modicum of protection. She could feel the soldier on the other side of the door breathing, as he watched his partner disappear behind the netting to put out the flames. A puff of smoke cleared the door as he exhaled. Codi took a slow breath and pounced. She held the knife low to her torso and thrust it up and away as she twisted around the door towards the man.

The guard caught movement from the corner of his eye and reacted by moving away from the source. Codi extended her elbow to the limit catching the man mid rib. The blade scraped across protective bone and found the soft tissue between. It pushed through his lung tissue and just clipped his left ventricle before all forward thrust was lost. Codi pulled the blade from the man, causing a sucking sound, and cocked her arm for another thrust. But it wasn't needed. The soldier slumped to the floor, his left foot twitching to the beat of an unheard song. She quickly looked in the room for more targets and was relieved to find it empty.

As he rounded the camo netting, the guard noticed that

the fire was in the shape of three large letters. Immediately, he knew something was wrong. He turned and ran for the cover of the building, calling out a warning to his comrade.

Codi heard the man yelling in Chinese. She turned in time to see the other soldier running back to the silo waving and yelling. When he realized Codi was not his partner, he dropped the fire extinguisher. He drew a bead on this new threat. Codi quickly took aim as the running man lifted his weapon to fire in her direction, but before she could pull the trigger, two quick bursts from beside the building ended the man's progression. Joel walked out from behind the door, the barrel of his gun smoking.

Codi pulled the dead man out of the entrance and relieved him of all weapons and ammunition.

"He must have realized that someone was still out here when he saw the fires," Joel said, practically hyperventilating as he spoke.

"Well, don't just stand there, Joel. Go get his gun and ammo."

Codi almost rolled her eyes as the admonished Joel ran off to the man he'd just shot. The fire had spread to the netting and the whole battlefield would soon be exposed again.

Hopefully, the satellite would catch it.

Ang and Ling came running around the other corner of the building, out of breath.

"I heard shooting, are you two okay?"

A quick nod and the toss of the dead man's gun to Ling was his answer.

Things were looking up. They had a way inside the silo and were significantly better armed. Codi moved into the doorway and stepped into the room. Her first instinct was to shoot out the security camera mounted on the sidewall. A rattling caught her attention. She looked over as two grenades rolled across the floor. She saw a large steel blast door at the far end of the room closing behind them.

"Grenade!" Codi screeched as she dove out of the room between the standing forms of Ang and Ling.

She hit the ground and immediately rolled right. Ang and Ling followed quickly behind as a percussive wave from the blast killed everything within a thirty-foot radius.

Poh waited on the other side of the now closed blast door with two of his men. He counted down the grenade's fuse and then hit the button to open the automated door, once the two muffled blasts sounded. With guns blazing his men surged through the opening, sending bullets around the now blackened security room. As they reloaded, Poh covered his men from the doorway. A dust-covered shape from outside the room rolled into view and fired, cutting one of the guards nearly in half. The other guard was forced to dive behind what was left of the security desk.

Codi inched to the edge of the doorjamb using it for cover as bullets pinged just above her head. Joel ran back from his kill and crouched on the other side of the doorpost, splitting the shooter's attention. Codi glanced back in time to see Ang and Ling. They had taken the worst of the blast. Ang was dazed and trying to sit up.

"Stay down!" Codi called to him. She turned back and exchanged shots with the soldier inside.

"Seal this door now!" General Chow Phun screamed, sputum flying from his drooping lips. He was waving his hands in the air, his face flushed and angered.

"Hold! I still have a man out there." Poh fired off a burst to keep the two intruders at the front door from entering.

"Move it," Poh called to his man as he laid down cover fire again.

But the general didn't wait. He pushed the button on the wall that activated the armored door.

Codi saw the man behind the desk make a dash for the steel door. She held her barrel around the corner and fired blindly at the man. A bullet to the thigh spun him to the floor. He crawled as fast as he could to the closing door, reaching for his leader to pull him through. Poh was forced to pull back with the closing door. The man willed himself to move, half crawling, half stumbling. He finally leapt forward the last few feet. But his leg gave out and he fell half-in, half-out of the jamb.

The steel blast door hardly noticed the screams and cracking bones as it reset itself to the closed position.

Codi turned, unwilling to allow the visual to enter her memory. Joel walked into the room just as the man was bisected. His eyes grew large as saucers as steel severed flesh and spine right down the middle. He froze momentarily and ran outside to puke.

Poh turned in disgust as the top half of his men died right in front of him. He wanted to scream and shoot Chow for closing the door too soon, but knew it would change nothing. Instead, he ordered the door welded shut. He would not have this sacrifice wasted.

Jin watched as a stick welder fired to life, binding door to jamb, sealing him inside the operations room. A note of finality suddenly struck him as he now knew for certain he was on a one-way journey. This was not in accordance with his plans.

An internal struggle of epic proportions ensued. As he saw it, his options were now extremely limited, and only one hundred percent success would give him any hope of getting out of this place alive.

So be it. Luckily, this was one of his specialties. He had always been a one-hundred-percenter.

Codi and her team entered the decimated security room. They looked at the sealed blast door at the end of the space. There was no getting through it. Every control panel was blown or shot to bits. They now controlled the outside and one room inside the silo, but had no way to get inside.

She inspected the blast door that led into the rest of the facility. She could feel the warmth generated by the stick welder on the other side.

"We need about a hundred pounds of Semtex to get past this door," she said.

Joel tried to lighten their situation. "Sorry, left it in my other trousers."

He had a pale glow about him as he looked through the burned and melted computers on the bullet-ridden security desk. He poked around, hoping to revive one. "Total bust here too," he finally said.

Ang returned with Ling from their inspection of the outside. They were shaken but still going. "No other entrances," Ang said. "The windows are for show only. It's solid concrete behind them. We did manage to take down the rest of the cameras so at least they are blind."

"Desperate men locked inside a missile silo. That's a recipe for fun and games," Codi said.

Ling was making some strange gestures across his face.

"What's he doing?" Joel asked.

"Oh, he walked right through a huge spider web out there," Ang said.

Joel checked the floor to make sure the spider hadn't made its way inside as well.

Ling noticed they were talking about him and stopped wiping to look up. "Hey," he said with a grin.

Joel, was starting to like this guy. "Hey, back," he said.

Ang, turned their attention back to the matter at hand. "Okay, so no entrances means they can't get out either."

"Yes, but the fact that they welded this door shut might be significant," Codi said.

"What, like a one-way mission?" Ang asked her.

"That's what I'm thinking."

"Damn."

Codi turned to Joel. "Looks like the only way in is through the sewer."

"I'd rather die."

"Careful, you might get your wish."

Joel nodded, suddenly more wary of their situation.

Inside the control room, Jin wiped a bead of sweat from his brow as he finished up the sequence that would launch the rocket. All that was left was to insert the code. That would activate the trigger system on the nuclear warhead, making it operational. He would feel some joy, retaliating at the country that had killed his friend Park Je Kwan. Plus, with a successful launch, he felt sure they would be allowed to leave.

He and Park had spent many nights together before Park left for his mission in America. They had grown close, and a unique friendship and bond had formed. They had talked of plans and dreams for when he would return as the conquering hero. But his unexpected death by a drunk driver had taken all of that away. America would now pay.

General Chow Phun felt a vibration in his pocket. He pulled out a small black box. It was tuned to a special frequency that allowed it to work around the jammer. There was a brief text starting with, "You're welcome." It was followed by two twenty-seven-digit passwords. His lips quivered with a small crooked smile. This was it. "Jin!"

Chow set the box down on the console and watched as his computer genius opened the nuclear activation page and entered the GO codes. A green "accepted" prompt returned and Chow knew his contact had been worth every Yuan. He dabbed at a line of drool that was headed for his uniform with numb, scarcely responsive fingers. He knew his mortality was short, but he would make sure to leave lasting prosperity and power for the country he loved. He placed a fatherly hand on Jin and waited for the young man to turn to him. He looked into his eyes and in a soft and kindly voice, said, "It's time."

Jin nodded solemnly at his boss, turned, and went to work. After a few moments of flashing keystrokes, Jin hit the last key with a flare.

He announced, "Ten minutes until ignition."

A low electronic alarm with flashing yellow lights confirmed his statement. A digital display started counting down from 09:59.

The announcement echoed in the small security room. Codi and Joel did not understand the words but the message was clear. "Times about up," Codi said.

Ang added, "Ten minutes until the rocket blasts."

"We need a way inside, and now," she said.

The four-person team churned with energy that would not focus. They needed a viable plan, and nothing was obvious.

Joel sank to the ground. His adrenaline rush had run its course.

"Wow, you four really screwed things up without me around." Four heads turned in unison to the source.

"Hey?" Ling asked, unsure if the new arrival was friend or foe.

Tenzin walked into the blown-out security room like she was strolling through a park.

"I thought you said you were too old to help out." Joel seemed genuinely confused.

"I'm also too old to sit by and watch Mr. Chow Phun play you for fools."

There was no witty retort. The journey to this ultimate failure had taken its toll.

Joel pantomimed morosely as he stared at the blackened floor in front of him.

"The only access door is welded shut," Codi said, "and we are fresh out of explosives. We don't have a way to cut through the steel mesh on the outside vents. We have a few bullets and some rope, but no way to stop the launch."

"Exactly," Tenzin said. "As I see it you have everything we need for the perfect plan."

23

PLA Missile Silo 089 – 9:41 a.m. – Sheng Luo, China

Jin was feeling the tension as a single drop of sweat ran down his cheek. He had always been a hacker, and as a hacker, or sometimes called a black hat, he had always worked remotely, several steps removed from the actual damage he caused. This was different. The moment Chow had their exit welded shut, death was looking more and more likely as his only escape. He began to doubt his decision to stay on. Ever since their operation in the Red Baks was destroyed, Chow had become reckless and desperate. And now, staring at the potential loss of thousands of lives, maybe they had gone too far. But Jin could think of no way out.

"Sir."

Chow stepped over to Jin and put a reassuring hand on his shoulder. "Yes?" he asked.

"Once the rocket crosses into America, our work is done here," he said. "How are we supposed to get out?"

"Poh!" Chow called out.

The Squad Leader stepped over to Jin holding a small canvas case. He reached inside. Jin flinched, assuming it was a gun. But Poh pulled out a battery-powered grinder.

"I have the key." Poh smiled like a shark.

Jin nodded uneasily and slowly went back to work.

Chow and Poh shared a laugh and moved away.

The two scientists fiddled with their temporary equipment. It was designed to initiate the specific signal transmission that would render the missile invisible to America's defenses. Once engaged, the electronics in the nosecone would continue to broadcast until obliterated by the nuclear detonation. "All dry runs nominal, switching to automatic," one of them said.

Chow watched as the man pressed the keys that would make the signal autonomous.

"The rocket is now in control, sir."

"Excellent work, gentlemen. Poh they are all yours!"

The two scientists both stood in a panic as the menacing and heavily-armed Poh moved in their direction. The one remaining soldier joined him. He pointed his rifle at the scientists.

"You both have had military training, am I right?" Poh asked.

They nodded fearfully.

"Good. I am a little low on men," Poh said.

He handed each man a weapon, saying, "The only way inside here is that door." Poh pointed as he spoke. "We don't know the size or capabilities of the force out there, since they took out our cameras. We think it's a few of the PLA regulars left over from our skirmish."

Poh finished with his pep talk and stationed them in positions to help thwart any attack through the door.

Jin looked back and forth over his shoulder, listening to the instructions. They were down to one soldier, Chow, himself, plus Poh and his two new recruits. It was less than optimal, in his mind. He would need to be very careful from now on if he was to survive his current predicament.

"Mr. Chow Phun is sick. His days on earth are numbered. I don't think he's planning to survive this operation," Tenzin said.

"So, you're thinking they'll stay locked up in that room, all safe and sound, till the missile hits its target?" Joel asked.

"Precisely."

"How does that help us? Joel asked.

"It gives us about five more minutes. I say we sit and relax before that missile fires off."

Codi immediately knew what Tenzin was proposing. "She's right. We've been so focused on the direct approach, that once it failed, so did we. There is nothing we can do to stop this thing from launching." She finished speaking and sat down next to Tenzin. She crossed her legs and leaned her head back.

Joel looked apoplectic. But soon, Ang and Ling followed until he was the only one pacing back and forth.

"Hey, do you mind closing the door while you're up? I don't want to get cooked when that missile goes off," Codi said.

Joel slammed the door. "Anything else?"

He stared at his four team members, all sitting on the floor relaxing. He could barely breathe.

The domed roof on the faux fermenting tower opened like the petals of a flower, allowing plenty of egress room for the ICBM. The pre-ignition sequence started, and the first vapors shot out of the two thrust chambers. It mixed with the fuel, and the booster engines enflamed, completing the ignition sequence. The center sustainer engine followed suit, and the resulting combustion forced through the thrust chamber created more than fifty-thousand pounds of lift, enough to push the missile from its perch.

"We have ignition." Jin smiled. He had always wanted to say that.

Flames shot through the vents on the side of the tower, scorching anything in its path. The flowering vines along the wall that gave the building much of its charm were atomized. The missile gradually lifted from the launch pad, its support scaffolding withdrawing as it ascended.

Chow screamed, "I can't see anything!"

"We're blind, General," Jin called out. "They shot out all our cameras. Give it time, there is one they missed on the roof."

Sure enough, the clear tip of the ICBM appeared on the rooftop camera, purposefully pointing to the sky. It was followed by the olive-green cylindrical shape of the missile, with each stage growing in size. Chow watched, rapt, as the final stage entered the screen, its distinct fins flared out for stabilization.

The half-smile that he could muster on the good side of his face nearly reached his ear. The room rattled with the immense controlled explosion of the rocket's ignition. It increased in magnitude until it finally cleared the silo and moved up into the air. Chow watched as the fearsome weapon continued upward into the morning sky. It was a glorious sight.

The burnt-out security room became very quiet. As the rumble in the room intensified, Codi and Tenzin quickly laid out their plan to the team.

Tenzin found a large steel caster that had blown off the security desk, and thought to herself, this should do nicely.

Codi ran from the room to the tower. The roof was opened like a lotus blossom. They had mere moments until it would close back up. She threw the rope, lasso style, up over one of the triangular pieces of roof, pulled the ends together, and began to climb the double rope up to the gaping hole. Soon, Ang and Joel followed.

"Hey!" Joel called and waved his hand for Ling to do likewise. The man was part monkey, and scampered to the roof in a blink.

"Hey." He smiled, looking at Joel.

Ang tested the temperature of the steel roof supports. They were still hot from the rocket. He wrapped his coat around the metal and then tied the rope around the coat. The coat started to smoke. They needed to hurry. He dropped the loose end of the rope down a hundred and twenty feet inside to the silo floor.

Ling was the first to slide down. Codi wasted no time. She sent Joel and then Ang down before Ling had exited at the bottom. As she turned to join them, the roof mechanism engaged and started to close. The sudden movement caught her off guard and she fell from the roof.

"The roof is closed and all systems are nominal," Jin said.

Chow was pleased. He stood to pace for the third time in a few minutes. If only he could make things go faster.

"We got action on the other side of this door," one of Poh's new recruits called.

Poh went over to investigate. He put his ear to the steel and listened. There was a distinct scraping sound moving across the door. Everyone in the room watched as he listened. *Bam!* A sudden rap of steel on steel rang through the room. Poh jumped back.

"I think they are preparing to blow the door," the soldier said.

The banging continued about every two seconds.

256

"What are they doing?" Jin asked.

"They'll knock holes in the seams, and then force a plastic explosive like C-4 in the gaps," Poh said. "The resulting explosion will open this door, welded or not,".

"Best guess?" Chow asked

"Twenty minutes, maybe thirty."

"Then we'd better use the time wisely."

The room bustled with activity as they fortified positions to combat the coming threat.

Poh was the only one left who knew how to fire the Type-98 recoilless rifle, so he would man it.

"Time to target, Jin?" Chow called.

Jin looked at the digital map that showed an icon for the ICBM and its American target of Chicago. The counter showed thirty-nine minutes, twelve seconds. He called it out.

Chow nodded his head slowly in anticipation. It would be close.

Codi grabbed blindly as she fell, hooking her left hand on a beam of the roof's infrastructure. Her hand gripped the metal piping like a vice, as her body jolted to a sudden stop. The jerk threatened to pull her hand free and drop her to a sure death. She managed to hang on, swaying by her fingertips for a beat, before she swung over and grabbed the rope. She wrapped her feet around the rope and took a second to recompose. That's when she noticed the seared flesh on her hand from the metal piping. She sucked it up and slid down to her waiting team. Once on the ground, Codi put hands to knees as she tried to catch her breath. Her hand throbbed but it could wait.

The bottom of the silo had a fresh coat of burn on everything. It was circular in design to match the ICBM's shape and devoid of any material that might burn with the rocket's launch. The scaffolding was blackened and retracted. Ling stared in wonder at the sight of the large underground space. There was a small black mound that used to be human on the floor.

Codi moved to the burn cover on the elevator control panel. It was set back away from the main blast zone. She lifted the panel to find only a single black button. "I guess no security is needed from this side. Thoughts?"

"If we push that button, they'll be waiting to blast us the moment those doors open up to a room we know nothing about," Ang said.

"And if we take the time to climb the shaft, we might be too late," Codi countered.

"What if we were to…" Joel started.

Codi pushed the button before Joel could finish his thought. He let out a short sigh. "So, shoot first and talk later?"

Codi smiled. The training of her partner was finally working.

They all took defensive positions to cover the elevator doors the moment they opened.

Ling leaned on his trigger, ready to pull, as the two doors split apart. The car was empty. Codi released a breath she didn't realize she'd been holding, and stepped out from behind a large pipe. She led the way into the car. Ling, smiling, followed next. It was all a grand adventure for him. Codi worried that he was unaware of the danger that might lie ahead.

Once loaded, she leaned over and hit the Up button.

"Going up?" Joel asked with a jumpy grin.

24

PLA MISSILE SILO 089 — 10:30 A.M. — SHENG LUO, CHINA

The constant tapping on the armored door was getting to all of them. It started as a scraping sound, which then transitioned to banging. When would it stop, and did it signify a forthcoming explosion? Chow dabbed at his chin as a drop of nervous sweat trailed down his temple. The missile had launched. Now all they had to do was stay fortified here until they were past the failsafe point.

Jin felt the most vulnerable with his back to the door. Everyone else was bunkered in a defendable position, each anticipating a firefight that was ticking down with each bang on the wall. Suddenly the tapping stopped. The room tensed. Jin grabbed his keyboard and pulled it with him as he hunkered down under his console.

General Chow said, "Jin, can you lock-out the missile so it no longer takes commands?"

Jin shook the nervous tension from his hands. "We are not past the failsafe point yet, General."

"How much longer?"

Jin glanced out from his spot under the console at the screen. "Three minutes and twenty-eight seconds, sir."

"Okay. At three minutes and twenty-nine seconds I want the missile locked-out."

Jin started the process that would close out his side of the rocket's control so no one could stop it. He peeked with one eye over his desk again so he could confirm the operation as he typed. Once complete, the missile would no longer receive data, making it impossible to abort or cancel its mission. He watched as the time ticked down, his finger hovering over the return key that would send the code.

The ridiculous Chinese folk tune that played in the elevator must have been put there as a joke, Codi thought. But it continued on its happy merry way as the car slowly rose to the operations room. She looked over at Ling who was humming quietly along with the song. This day couldn't get any weirder, and if today was her day to die, weird wasn't the worst way to go. The team split into two per side of the car, one low and one high, using the door gap for cover. The car slowed to a stop. It paused for what seemed like an eternity, before a ding was followed by opening doors.

The tapping suddenly started back up again, only much faster.

"They're getting desperate," Poh called out in false hope. The prolonged tapping was even getting to him as he dried his hands on his shirt.

A soft ping from the back of the room was hardly audible over the room's tension and the now fervent knocking. Jin looked over his shoulder. The elevator doors opened to an empty car.

"Hey, what's with the eleva–"

Gun barrels, followed by bullets, answered his query.

Cody went high and Joel low as they swept the right side of the room. A mirror action followed with Ling and Ang from the other side. The room had been so focused on the blast door that they were caught off guard. The rear attack took the lives of three soldiers almost instantly, two of them recent recruits.

Poh and Chow had been bunkered further back and were able to get to safety. Jin ducked further under his console taking his keyboard with him. He then did his best impersonation of the ostrich defense and buried his head between his legs. But he kept a mental count of the time left before he could lock out the missile.

It quickly became a stalemate, with both parties pinned down, and bullets pinging back and forth without finding a target.

Poh saw the Type-98 recoilless rifle that was just out of his reach lying on the floor. He reached out a leg and started to slide it towards him. A bullet pinged off his anklebone, shattering it. He pulled his leg back without a sound and fired a few rounds back at the elevator while gritting his teeth. He reached out and grabbed the weapon and pulled it back to safety, furious at the lucky shot that had undoubtedly maimed him. He quickly loaded it and pointed it at the elevator.

Chow held his hand up to stop Poh from firing, an action that would mean the deaths of everyone in the room. He called out to the force occupying the elevator. "Come out with your hands up. You have nowhere to go."

Codi looked to Ang and held up her finger to her lips. Though she had no idea what the man had called out in Chinese she could easily interpret the message. She answered Chow in English. "What do you want?"

Chow's mind raced, as he struggled to understand the situation. "Am…Americans?"

"Not just Americans. The ones you kidnapped and tried to kill!" Codi called out.

His head started spinning. This made no sense. *"You!"*

Codi remained silent waiting for Chow to make the next move.

"You are too late to stop the missile. Your precious Chicago will be uninhabitable for the next thirty years."

Joel and Codi shared a look at this revelation—*Chicago.*

"What about all the innocent people," Joel called out. "Civilians that have done nothing to you or your country."

Codi held up both her hands to get Joel to stop. She could tell they were just spinning their wheels. The clock was ticking and a prolonged conversation with a psycho would do them no good. They needed a plan to get them out of the elevator. Maybe she could goad Chow into making a mistake.

"Too bad about your lab in Hong Kong," she said. "Red Baks, I believe it was called right before we burned it to the ground."

This solicited a string of swear words and bullets all aimed in their direction. But the general maintained his hidden position.

Joel tapped his watch. They were out of time.

"Enough stalling, General," Codi said. "It's over. Come out with your hands raised."

"No, you come out with your hands raised," Chow relied. "We have a very large weapon pointed in your direction ready to fire. If so much as one more bullet comes out of that car, I will obliterate you."

This was not what the team wanted to hear. Was he crazy enough to blow everyone up, along with himself?

"Jin," the General called out, "how much time!"

"Ten seconds," he replied.

"You have ten seconds to comply," Chow said with confidence.

Ling waved at Joel. He didn't understand the words being spoken but he knew his duty.

"Hey," Ling pointed to himself.

Joel looked perplexed at his gesture. Then it hit him. "Hey, no you don't!" he said.

But Ling gave him a short bow and ran out of the elevator, rifle blasting.

Codi used the distraction and followed behind, shooting at the muzzle flash of Ling's attackers. As they zeroed in on the moving target, Ling, there was a short but sustained engagement. And then it was over.

Codi ran to the fallen general and kicked the gun from his hand. She noticed a man with a Fu Manchu holding a rocket launcher. He was staring at the ceiling with only one eye. The other eye was now an entrance wound from a 7.62 mm bullet.

Joel ran to his friend Ling. He was lying on the floor with a few rounds stitched across his torso. He knelt down and looked at the man who had sacrificed himself for them. He placed his arm under Ling's neck and held him up.

"Hey," he said weakly, as he looked into Joel's eyes.

"Hang in there, Ling. You're gonna be okay," Joel lied.

"Hey," Ling said, even weaker, this time with a half-smile set against blood-stained teeth.

"Hey," Joel answered as tears filled his eyes. Ling's smile grew from ear to ear, and then his eyes fluttered and closed.

Ang surveyed the mess, trying to decide where to begin. He heard knocking on the other side of the door. Movement caught his eye as a man slid across the floor and snatched up a fallen pistol from one of the scientists.

Jin had felt trapped like a rat in a cage as a firefight roared all around him, bullets pinging off the various steel surfaces. He was hoping to just wait things out until he could surrender. But suddenly their attackers were speaking English. Americans—here. How was that possible? A rage built in his soul, just thinking about how they had been responsible for the death of his friend Park. It was at that moment when Jin realized Park was not a friend but something more. He had loved Park. He had loved him like no one else he had ever known, and America had taken that away. He spied a pistol lying on the floor a few feet away. He hit the enter button on the keyboard and locked out the missile. He dove for the gun. He grabbed it and pulled the trigger until it stopped firing.

The woman turned from her position next to the general and without hesitation, fired a quick three-round burst. His body bucked with the impacts and he dropped his empty gun. He staggered and fell to his knees.

He tried to make sense of his life as he gaped at the floor in front of him. His lips tried to speak but only for a brief moment, like a fish out of water. He died a confused and conflicted man who had never been able to act on his feelings. In the end, Jin had been nothing more than a pawn to a mad man.

Codi turned her attention and her weapon back to the general, not giving him any quarter. She called out, never taking her eyes off Chow. "Ang, what's the damage!" she yelled.

Ang looked around and then down. "Two down, Ling… and me."

There was a fresh hole in his shoulder. He slid down the wall leaving a red smear behind. Codi was conflicted with which path to take. Save the general or save her friend.

"If I had more time, I'd ask you a few questions or maybe take you to the authorities," she said to Chow. She could tell by the man's look he would never talk in time. And frankly, after all she'd been through, she didn't care.

Chow leaned up on one elbow, coughing up blood from his wound. "How is it you are even here? I must know." The general sneered at her with hateful eyes, blood and spittle drooling down one side of his twisted face as he spoke.

"Prepare for disappointment," Codi said. With that, she pulled the trigger and ended the man who had only taken from her.

Codi turned to see Joel sobbing over Ling's body. "Joel, snap out of it! We've got to find a way to stop that missile!"

Joel nodded though his tears and found his second wind. He quickly wiped the tears from his eyes and surveyed the room, taking in all the technology. Some was shot up with bullets, some seemed to be working just fine. A unit about the size of a toaster with an antenna was sitting on the top shelf. He powered it down. "Jammer's off," he announced.

Codi stuffed a rag in Ang's shoulder to staunch the bleeding. "You're gonna be fine," she said, "maybe even get a medal. Now help us stop this missile."

Ang nodded and stood on wobbly legs. He joined Joel at the terminal to help translate.

Codi took Ang's phone and dialed. She stared at the screen, willing it to work.

"Director Fescue."

"Working late?"

"Codi! Where the hell–"

"Shut it. Now listen very carefully. I got about…" she looked at the phone's screen. "…one bar on my battery, and Joel, how much time?"

Joel looked at the map showing the ICBM icon and the

United States coming into view as it streaked across the northern Pacific.

"Fifteen minutes."

She said to Brian, "And you've got fifteen minutes until a nuclear-tipped ICBM hits Chicago."

"Shit."

"Tell me about it."

Codi quickly filled her boss in on the last forty-eight hours, skipping everything that was not related to the next fifteen minutes.

"It's eight p.m. here, and seven p.m. in Chicago. Stay on the line. I'll be right back," Brian said.

Joel hit the abort button on the console several times. Nothing happened. With the help of Ang they tried to recall the missile through the keyboard.

"Can you stop it?" Codi asked.

Joel took a deep breath as the reality hit him. "Not from here. The missile's been locked-out. There's no way to abort it."

"No recall or self-destruct?" Codi added.

"All locked out."

"I could contact authorities here in China but it might take more than fifteen minutes just to get them on the line," Ang said.

"Fourteen minutes," Joel announced.

The tapping on the blast door was getting quieter. They all shared a solemn moment. Had they come this far just to fail?

"Wait a minute!" Joel brought up the map. "We can't stop it, but I might be able to track it." He quickly laid a grid over the missile's path and with Ang's help calculated the trajectory and coordinates that it would follow. He patched it into a webpage and sent the address to Fescue's email.

Codi watched over their shoulders, and the second it was

sent interrupted her boss. "Check your email, the one labeled 911."

Agent in Charge Brian Fescue was in a panic. The path to action in a bureaucracy was overgrown and circuitous. Two hurried calls, no answers. First to his boss and then to the director of the FBI. Time was ticking. Finally, he got through to the vice chairman of the joint chiefs of staff's assistant. The assistant gave him a number they used for emergencies like this. It had cost precious time. Their ability to scramble and intercept was almost gone.

He pulled up the site and could see the missile was just crossing over the west coast.

To say the call was challenging was a gross understatement. General Dilworth was extremely skeptical. Brian had finally gotten the general to open the webpage.

"This looks Chinese," he murmured.

"That's what I've been telling you, *Chinese* ICBM." Brian was trying to keep calm as he knew it would do no good to get angry.

"How did you get this number?" the general asked.

"Sir, we haven't much time, *please.*" Brian decided to beg.

"Just a second. Hold your horses, son."

The general made a quick call to his contact at NORAD.

Brian was a wreck with the slowness of everything. NORAD did a check and recheck, but no missile appeared to be headed for Chicago, let alone, anywhere else.

The general was not about to scramble emergency fighters without proof. Besides, if it was good enough for NORAD, it was good enough for General Dilworth. But just to be on the safe side maybe I'll…

Brian had had it with this man. He decided to push a little

harder. "General, if you don't listen to me right now, you're gonna have a five-megaton nuclear missile right up your ass!"

"General?"

Silence.

"Son of a bitch!" Brian slammed the phone down. "Codi, you still there?"

"Yes, Brian."

"I'm having trouble getting a response that will fit our timeline," he said, trying to regain some sense of calm.

"I understand." She lowered the phone trying to think.

"Seven minutes," Joel mumbled. "I have an aunt in Chicago. She's really cool too. Makes these coconut macaroons that are to die for."

"Joel!"

The worried energy was getting to him, but Codi's reprimand silenced his rambling. "I'm trying to think here."

A thought that was born out of desperation began to grow. First the seed and then the plant. Codi lifted her phone to her mouth. "Call the FAA," she told Brian.

"I see where you're going with this. Okay. It's a long shot. Hold tight." Brian grabbed his landline and started to dial.

"The Future Farmers of America?" Joel asked.

Codi glanced down at her phone. The last bar was starting to blink. Without looking up she said, "Not the FFA, the FAA—Federal Aviation Administration, dork."

"I knew that," Joel said, properly chastised.

They shared a knowing smile. Then Codi put her arm around him. They were in this together, no matter what. Sink or swim, live or die.

"Sorry about the dork thing," she said.

"It's okay, I deserved it."

25

Twelve Thousand Feet – 6:18 p.m. – Franklin Grove, Illinois

Colleen Simpson was a thirty-eight-year-old mother of three and the bread-winner for her family. She had started a small brick-and-mortar cosmetic store called CosMore in an Internet world where most retail operations were dying. She had focused on customer service and free samples, with plenty of lighted mirrors for customers to try things out. Everyone had told her she was nuts. But in spite of her critics, she had grown the business to a chain of twenty-six stores across the mid-west. Her husband worked as an electrician, and she let him spend his paycheck as he pleased. They'd had their ups and downs, as do most couples, but lately there were more ups.

Colleen had spent so much time going from store to store, that her family was suffering. An inspiration took hold of her a while back, and after several night classes and a few trial runs, she obtained a pilot's license and a near-new Cessna 210. She used it instead of a car, for her commuting, and the time back home had increased dramatically. Three years ago they bought into a community just outside the city with an airstrip shared by all thirty homes in the association. She set up her corporate offices in the space above their four-car garage and could now come and go in her plane right from her house.

Early that morning, Colleen had flown to Cedar Rapids to replace a store manager that was causing more problems than he was solving. She had carefully documented everything over the last two years, but the event was still a nightmare, with screaming and threats, all aimed in her direction. He would probably sue for wrongful termination. Oh well, the cost of doing business, she told herself. The extra drama had ruined her schedule. She was going to miss her six-year-old Chloe's piano recital. Chloe had been practicing her song for the last month, and this was going to be her big moment. Colleen watched as the sun dipped towards the horizon. It would be dark within the hour. She hated to fly at night and was hoping to make it back home before the sun plunged to dusk, just in time to help Casey with his math homework. She smiled at the thought, as mild turbulence bumped her around in her seat. Another ten minutes and she would be home.

Since 911, the US government has put in place several quick reaction programs that get agencies to work together. The goal is to place critical information in the right hands ASAP. The confusion that reigned while terrorists flew our own jets into the twin towers and the pentagon would never happen again. At least, that was the design. Special Agent in Charge, Brian Fescue was not having the success these programs were intended to give. One of them that the FAA had implemented allowed information to be relayed directly through to the air traffic control system. In a last ditch attempt, Brian called the emergency number and explained the problem. The man on the other end got it. *Finally*, Brian thought. He relayed Brian to the lead air traffic controller at Midway International Airport just southwest of downtown Chicago. They quickly brought the controller up to speed in hopes of getting their message out. They needed an actual sighting of the missile. Then they would have the proof they needed. But the problem was time—they were running out of it. The lead controller pressed the transmit button and began broadcasting on the emergency frequency. It was a message they had both agreed upon.

"Codi!"

She heard Brian's voice over the phone.

"Yeah. Hello… Brian? Hello?" She looked at her phone. It was dead. She lowered the phone.

"You did all you could," Ang said.

"*We* did all we could," she said.

Joel looked to the screen with the ICBM's icon as it approached the Midwest. "Four more minutes," he mouthed listlessly.

The tapping on the door was getting erratic.

"Ang, you got any strength left to help me with that door?" Codi asked.

Ang held up a battery-powered metal grinder he had almost tripped over earlier. "I got just the thing."

Codi cut though the welds and Ang pressed the button to open the door.

The large steel blast door slowly swung open. Tenzin stood there, arms raised holding her dented steel caster like a weapon. When she saw Codi and Ang. She lowered it along with a sign of relief.

"*Finally.* I was getting a blister."

After all Codi had been through, she was taken back by her statement. Her forehead scrunched. "A *blister?*"

"Yeah, and I think I chipped a nail too." Tenzin said light-heartedly, as she looked at her finger while stepping into the room. "So, how'd we do?"

"Not so good," Joel said.

Tenzin looked around at the carnage and nodded slowly, understanding the sacrifices that had been made. Now was no time for levity. "I'm sorry," she said.

"You've been shot," she said to Codi.

Codi looked down to see a blood trail draining from a hole in her thigh. She'd been so focused and hopped up on adrenaline that she hadn't even noticed it. She ripped a strip off the bottom of her shirt and wrapped it tight around the wound. "See if you can do anything for Ling," she said to Tenzin.

Ling lay motionless on the floor, his chest red from blood loss. The old woman knelt next to the soldier who had bravely charged the room. "And you too!" she said to Ang.

Ang gestured helplessly with his hand, as if he could have prevented it. His other hand pressed tightly to his injury.

"SOP," Joel said.

"What?" Tenzin said.

"Standard Operating Procedure with Codi. Everyone who works with her eventually gets shot."

"Not everyone," Codi countered.

"Name one."

Codi looked upward trying to think of someone.

Tenzin changed the subject. "So did we stop the bomb?"

Joel pointed to the screen. "Just one minute left and it doesn't look like we did."

They all gathered around the screen watching the final seconds of a catastrophic event they were powerless to stop. Joel reached out and held Codi's hand and she let him.

"Thirty seconds."

Colleen heard a transmission come over her headset. She switched to the emergency frequency of 243.0 MHz. She listened to the distressed voice through her headphones.

"Mayday, mayday, this is Air Traffic Control Midway International Airport. We have an emergency need for a visual confirmation. There is a possible unidentified flying object, possibly a missile coming out of forty-one degrees and seven minutes from the north/northwest. We are needing an immediate visual confirmation. I repeat, we nee…"

Colleen dismissed it as not her problem. As the voice gave the approximate coordinates, she realized she was flying almost that exact course. She tapped her finger on the yoke and thought about her situation. She double-checked her GPS location. Yes, she was right in the area.

"Damn it, I don't have time for this. It's getting dark," Colleen huffed, as she pulled her plane up and around in an arc to get a better look at her six, or rear.

She lifted her head and surveyed the sky as her Cessna made a gradual 180-degree turn. The orange glow on the horizon transitioned to a growing purple sky. She caught a glimpse of something flying at forty-one degrees and seven minutes out of the northwest. She corrected her path to get a better look. It was a small spec on the horizon but was moving incredibly fast. There appeared to be a significant jet trail growing behind it, reflecting off the setting sun. Her jaw dropped and she pressed the transmit button on her plane's yoke. "This is Cessna N2815P. I have a visual on your missile."

Her hands began to shake as the rocket quickly grew in size.

"Roger that, Cessna N2815P. Can you give us a location?"

"I'm just over…" She quickly peeked out the window. The missile was even bigger now.

"I'm just over Waterman. And it looks about ten miles away, moving incredibly fast."

"Waterman. Oh my God, we're too late." The Lead Controller went silent after his unintended exclamation. They all knew there was no time to do anything more than a quick prayer.

"Is this for real?" Colleen asked.

"I'm afraid so, mam. God speed. Attention, all aircraft, this is not a drill, redirect immediately to–"

Colleen went numb as the emergency broadcast continued on. She was looking at the beast as it grew on the horizon.

"… may the Lord have mercy on us all."

Codi and her team watched as the missile icon moved towards the city. She was done hoping for a miracle. And besides, something was shaking the building. She stepped through the open blast door into the burned-out security room. Like a moth to a flame she walked out into the light. It was another beautiful morning as though this part of the world had no idea what was about to happen. As she looked up, three military helicopters came swooping in, fully loaded and armed. One, a Mil Mi-26 heavy transport with a detachment of fourteen armed men. The other two were WZ-10 attack helicopters.

I guess they saw the SOS fire, she thought.

The heavy transport landed, sending dirt and debris flying into the air. The two attack copters patrolled the air, their guns locked and loaded.

Could this day get any better, she thought while shaking her head.

Smartly, Codi knelt down and clasped her hands behind her head, the international symbol for I give up because I just don't give a shit.

Within moments her entire team was zip-tied and thrown to the ground like a sack of potatoes. Soldiers ran back and forth trying to make heads or tails of the situation.

26

Undisclosed Location – 8:34 a.m. – Wuzhou, China

The sound of rifle fire woke Codi with a start. She squinted at the rush of light as the door to her cell screeched open. Two military guards goose-stepped in and dragged her out into the hallway. It took her a moment before she was able to stand and walk along with them. It felt like every muscle in her body was in protest. The partially dressed bullet wound in her leg throbbed with every step. Her brain screamed for relief, but her mouth was too dry to relay it. Her tongue was stuck to the roof of her mouth and felt like it was made of wood. She cracked her head to the left and recognized Joel. He was walking stiffly next to her, also held by two guards. He looked like hell, and she could only imagine how bad her reflection might appear.

They had been taken at gunpoint from the silo. There were no questions, only orders, and they were followed to the letter. All four of them had been forced to lie face-down in the bed of a metal troop truck with their hands bound behind them. The truck then proceeded to bounce over rough terrain for the next two hours. Finally they hit pavement and the ride smoothed out. The vehicle stopped with a lurch, and a hasty unloading of the prisoners commenced. With guns locked and loaded, pointed in their direction, Codi and Joel were forced to march straight to a dark cell, with a concrete bench for a bed.

Codi had managed to doze off and finally get some much-needed sleep. There'd been no sign of Ang or Tenzin since they'd been imprisoned. Codi assumed they had either been shot or had talked their way out. Perhaps they were waiting for them, wherever they were now going.

She tried to get her mind back up to speed for what might come next, but she was feeling completely hung-over. It was amazing what a lack of everything could do to one's self. Normally, she would have to do some serious hard drinking to feel like this.

The procession exited the building into a dirt courtyard, where a line of several more soldiers waited. Joel looked at his current situation and started to fight against his guards, but their iron grip was no match for a beat-down, sleep-deprived, dehydrated, all-out exhausted federal agent. His struggling stopped almost as quickly as it started.

The guards released Codi and Joel. They turned and joined the others in formation. Codi's hoarse voice squawked to Joel as she took in their surroundings. There were nine soldiers all armed standing in a line in front of them. The concrete wall behind them was covered in bullet holes and the ground was a mixture of straw, dirt and blood. "It's been real, Joel."

Joel looked at her, and back at the armed soldiers, staring at them with a crazed twitch. A forced chuckle escaped his throat. This was not the way he had hoped to die. Where was the sleep and the bed?

The soldiers just stayed in formation, rifles on their shoulders. Codi and Joel stood in front of them, each looking at the other, daring one side to make the first move. No one spoke, some didn't even blink. Joel, exhausted, bent at the waist and put his hands on his knees, too tired to stand erect any longer. Codi glanced once more at the bullet holes and blood stains on the wall behind them. There were tell-tale drag marks on the ground going off to the left. She and Joel had been through the ringer and had somehow come out the other side, but even she had a breaking point. She took a moment to run her fingers through her hair and straighten her shirt. If she was going out, it would at least be on her terms. She rubbed the top of her shoes on the back of her pants and tugged her torso to attention. She was ready.

The rocket had no fear, only ones and zeros flowing through its circuits. It was simply a mechanical organism that followed a preset list of instructions guiding it forward to its target. It followed the guidance computer's feedback, making micro adjustments to its position based on wind, elevation and GPS. It took no notice of the cobalt blue sea below it, or the verdant fields that followed. Once it reached its apex, its programming triggered a gradual path back to earth. It continued to transmit its unique frequency signature that would make it invisible to detection. At one-hundred miles out, a pre-arranged sequence of events was initiated, with tests and redundancy checks on all vital systems. At fifty miles from target, the shielding on the plutonium core would pull away and arm the core. At one-thousand feet above ground, an implosion into the core would occur. This implosion would trigger a nuclear reaction that could not be contained, creating a violent detonation that would ensure a maximum destruction radius.

Back in DC, Brian had been following the conversation and FAA broadcast. He was watching helplessly as the webpage sent to him counted down the time to impact. The emergency broadcast had finished by warning all aircraft out of the area followed by a short prayer. Brian slumped in his chair, dazed. How was this possible? How could a missile get through our defenses? The information Codi had given him before her phone died seemed impossible. But she was not known for hyperbole.

The emergency transmission stopped after a brief prayer. Colleen's brow was beaded with sweat as she considered her place in this world. She had but a second to make a decision, one that would change her life forever. She thought of her business and her family. Her family. Little Chloe, Casey, the ever-pragmatic Makenzie, and her loving husband. The years flashed before her eyes in an instant as the tears started to flow. Then uncontrollable sobs took over. With trembling, tear-stained hands she pushed her yoke forward and into the path of the fast-approaching ICBM.

The odds of making contact were stacked against her. There was no explosion as the wing of her plane clipped the fuselage of the rocket, tearing the wing off of her plane. The Cessna 210 began an out-of-control spiral to the earth. Colleen's yell grew to a scream as she plummeted to her death, not knowing if she had made any difference.

The rocket continued on, the small slice in its skin a minor inconvenience. Hydrazine began to leak out of the rip. At first it was just a mist, but soon a dribble, both quickly atomized in the speeding air. As it flowed to the burning jets, a new flame followed the source back towards the damaged skin. The slice spewed flames like a mad blowtorch, causing the rocket to wobble as oxidizer and fuel met outside of their controlled environment. They ignited with a sudden burst, sending parts and pieces of the rocket outward like a roman candle. By a mere five seconds, the atomic warhead had not reached its arming target and therefore had not been allowed to go nuclear in the premature explosion.

Nine thousand feet below, the town of Sugar Grove, just fifty-two miles from Chicago, was hit with a rainstorm of burning debris. It caused many fires and a few injuries. What was left of the warhead fell through the sky and landed in a bowling alley that had been closed for remodeling. The radioactive fallout was contained, but the former site of the 1994 PBA World Bowling Championship would be uninhabitable for many years to come.

The waiting and the silence was too much. Joel was starting to crack. His body began to shake uncontrollably. Codi stood defiantly with her head held high.

"Please, just get it over with. I'm begging you," he pleaded.

As if on cue, the soldier on the far left of the formation barked out something in Chinese. The other soldiers all in unison grabbed their rifles, and with a frill, spun and twirled their guns before coming to rest across their chest.

Joel held a hand out in front of himself. "I was kidding."

It was the weirdest firing squad maneuver Codi had ever seen. It looked more like something you would see at a parade. It just needed a marching band and some cheering fans.

"Joel, keep it together," she whispered.

Two black limos pulled up and stopped between the soldiers and the two agents. Two officers with medals adorning their chests exited the rear limo and stepped next to the prisoners. They gave a curt bow and shook hands with both Codi and Joel.

"Congratulations," one of them said. "You save many lives."

A photographer ran up and snapped a few photos. The prisoners honestly seemed confused by it all.

"Wait. What is he talking about? Did they stop the missile?" Codi asked the man who had spoken.

"Yes. Missile stopped. You did good job."

The two officers shook hands with the Americans once again.

Then the front passenger side of the limo opened, and Corporal Ling slowly exited. He was using a cane to move, and he had one arm in a sling. He was dressed in a Lieutenant's uniform and a smile. Joel was speechless as his injured friend slowly moved up to him and shook his hand. "Hey."

"I, I thought you were... Hey," Joel replied. He grabbed Ling's hand and shook it a bit too hard. It made Ling flinch in pain. But the smile on his face was electric. Ling gave him a salute, and Joel returned it.

He then shook Codi's hand, and gave a mutual bow, which caused severe pain.

After a moment, Codi and Joel were escorted into the first limo. It moved out of the courtyard, spitting dirt, straw and blood from the rear tires. Sitting across from them was Ang. He had a weary smile that seemed to match their mood, and a white sling holding his injured arm. Joel and Codi each grabbed a bottle of water that was sitting in the small bar. They drank like they hadn't been given water in three days, which was true.

"I thought they were going to shoot us," Joel said as he crushed his plastic water bottle and pointed it at Codi like a gun.

"Easy there, muscles," Codi said.

But Joel was worked up after what had just transpired. "Shoot us, right then and there. And you! 'It's been real, Joel?' That's all you had to say? After all we've been through. And

Ling, a friggin' colonel. We get thrown in the slammer and he gets promoted? I thought he was dead. Dead! I cried for him. *Shit.*"

Joel then pointed the crumpled bottle at Ang. "The things we've done for this country! I'm calling bullshit right here and now."

"Lieutenant, not colonel," Ang said.

"What??"

Codi and Ang both started to smirk. This pissed off Joel even more and his rant elevated.

"It's not that I don't like being shot at, kidnapped, arrested, and drowned, but the least they could do is say thanks or something. I mean where's my medal..."

That set off Ang and Codi even more and a giggle turned into full delirium as they drowned out Joel's monologue.

Soon all three were laughing at the ridiculousness of it all, and for the first time, Ang had become one with the crazy Americans.

After a few miles they fell into silence.

Codi found the strength to break it. "So what happened? Where's Tenzin and how the hell did we stop the missile?"

Ang sat up in his seat and scratched something behind his ear. "She could talk her way out of the Minotaur's Labyrinth, I swear. She dropped back into that southern dialect that no one can understand, all hunched over and frail. She was out and released the next day."

Codi smiled at the memory of the quirky old woman who had helped save so many lives. "Probably back in Tibet planning her next infiltration."

"Yes, she is really something," said Ang. "As for the missile..."

Ang filled them in on the events that transpired after they'd been taken prisoner.

"It took three days for me to convince the authorities that

we were not part of Chow's operation. Really, it was Ling who set them straight. They were ready to bury us and this whole thing six feet underground."

Ang paused for a moment remembering all that had transpired. "For the first time in my life I am glad to see the politicians get involved. They will spin-doctor this whole thing right under the rug."

It was always the way. Whenever things in the world got too intense for the masses they were given the vanilla version. It kept them in check and promoted that thin illusion of security the public needs to believe in, because without it markets would crash and riots would rule.

Matt ran for the entrance to the terminal. The call had just come through ten minutes ago. Codi was alive and being transported to the airport for her return to the states. He had rinsed his face and brushed his teeth while using his free hand to put on his socks and shoes. After a cab ride and an early exit due to stopped traffic, Matt had come across a florist. He dashed inside and purchased two-dozen red roses.

He held them like a baton as he sprinted the last few blocks to the airport, leaving a fragrant trail of blossoms behind him.

Supervising Special Agent Brian Fescue was on a similar mission. He had been at the embassy working with the state department to get some word of his agents' disposition. After the failed attack on Chicago, Brian had been a sudden focus and the adoration of his superiors. He had used this leverage to get back involved in the case.

He had taken the time to update Matt and they both hopped a flight to Hong Kong. SSA Brian Fescue was assigned a state department lackey. The woman had no horsepower and fewer connections, but Brian's expertise in China was nil, so he had to use what he was given to move things along. Matt, on the other hand, was stuck playing the waiting game and it was killing him.

They had finally gotten word that Codi and Joel were being held at a PLA base in Wuzhou but were refused any contact or additional information.

Brian and Matt both found a flight to the Wuzhou Changzhoudao Airport and a hotel with fast Internet. They had pushed and pleaded as much as they could, but this squeaky wheel was being ignored. It had been the culmination of extreme frustration after what Brian had been through back in the states. This was no way to run a case: agents disappearing, being pronounced dead, and then phoenix-ing back in time to help stop a nuclear strike. It was crazy. And now being held prisoner when they should be given big-ass medals.

It was an unexpected call from the embassy that had set them both in motion. Brian from the Wuzhou police station, and Matt from his hotel room.

Matt dodged cars and bicycles as he turned the corner that led to the terminal. He was suddenly struck with the thought of what he would say to Codi. He hadn't given it much attention and there was no time like the present to figure that out.

He thought about all the hiccups they had experienced recently and it all seemed so trivial. He knew in his heart that he loved her. Now all he had to do was figure out how to tell her. His distracted thoughts cost him dearly, as he did not see the vehicle pulling out of the alleyway. At full speed, Matt went over the hood and crashed to the gutter on the other side. He popped up amid honks and yells from the driver. He hobbled away with a severe limp. He grimaced in pain as the driver behind him berated his character. He had a nice gash on his shin and a knot on his cheek, but he held tight to the roses.

Brian opened the door to the limo as it pulled to the curb.

He felt a wave of relief overwhelm him as Agent Joel Strickman and Agent Codi Sanders exited the vehicle. One look told him all he needed to know—bruised, battered, but still going. They looked like they'd been run through a spinning industrial dryer filled with ball bearings.

They took a moment, and then shared a professional hug. Codi introduced Ang, and they all made ridiculous small talk.

Joel brought the conversation back on point. "So let me guess, as far as both governments are concerned, this never happened."

"Yeah, that about sums it up," Brian said. "There's a hell of a debriefing waiting for us back in DC, and then the case will be closed and sealed."

"So much for your medal, Ang," Joel said.

Ang raised his one good hand in an *oh well* gesture. "I'll always have this to remind me," he said, referring to the sling that held up his bullet-wounded shoulder.

"I know what you mean," Joel said "I told you, everyone who works with Codi gets shot. Last time it was my turn."

Codi shook her head in mock defiance. "Not!"

The conversation finally died out to a moment of awkward silence, which left an opening for a subject change.

"Ok, I have a plane waiting. Let's get you two back home," Brian said.

Those words sounded wonderful to Joel. They all shook hands and watched as Ang got back into the limo and sped off.

"I could really do with a good burger and a brew about now," said Joel. "Oh, and some quality coffee too," he added.

Brian let out, "Oh almost forgot…"

"Codi!" A hoarse shout bellowed.

They all turned. Matt ran up the sidewalk and stopped. He was heaving, completely out of breath and looked like he might throw up any second. His clothes were tattered and covered with stains and dirt. His hair was disheveled and had something brown clinging to one side. He had several cuts and scrapes on his arms and face. And he was absently holding out several smashed and shabby flowerless stems that were once twenty-four beautiful roses. He finally caught his breath enough to speak. "Codi." He huffed several more breaths. "I got these for..."

He couldn't finish without a few more breaths. He held out the flowers, unaware they were nothing but stems.

Codi was taken aback. She had no words for him. How had he gotten here? What had happened to him? And... "Matt?"

She rushed to him and held him for all she was worth. Tears mingled with dirt as emotion consumed them both.

Joel nodded his approval and then put his hand on his boss's shoulder. "I'm taking a week off."

"But the President has asked to see the both of you right away. Plus the debriefing. It's at the Joint Chiefs of Staff," Brian said.

Codi loosened her grip on Matt and called over her shoulder. "Make that two weeks,"

EPILOUGE

Gray clouds that hid a waning sun threatened to drop rain. Codi was standing next to Joel, both were dressed in their FBI formals, suit and tie. The previous two weeks were behind her and there was great promise for her future. Her bullet wound had been superficial, and with the proper care was now almost pain free. She and Matt were back in a healthy and growing relationship. They had made standing plans to get together every other weekend with the hope of something more permanent in the future.

The turnout was supposed to be moderate, with only a few invitations given out. But once word of its political importance leaked, the number doubled overnight, in spite of it being a closed, private affair.

The president knelt before the empty casket and paid his respects. He was followed by a cavalcade of the Who's Who in DC, each trying to one-up the other. Codi watched the display with a knowing disdain.

The Speaker of the House gave a short speech, some of it pertinent to the occasion. He was followed by a general, who was part of a flag-folding ceremony that ended with tears. They handed the triangle fold to the widower standing next to his three motherless children.

Codi looked over at the broken family. She could see the sorrow in their faces, but strength as well. She knew from experience that it would be a long road, but that they would be okay in time.

Colleen Simpson was a true American hero. She had sacrificed everything to save so many lives. It was an act born of desperation and love. Love for her family and love for her country.

The press continued to drone on about a satellite that had malfunctioned and spread its contents across the city of Sugar Grove, Illinois, but the reality was still safe with the few.

Once everyone had his or her moment to shine, the empty casket was ceremoniously lowered into the ground. The pastor finished with a solemn prayer, and the crowd started to dissipate just as the first few drops of rain began to fall.

"Good to see you again Agent Sanders."

Codi turned to see the President standing right behind her. "Twice in one week, sir."

They shook hands.

"I wanted to thank you again for all you have done. The country owes you a great debt." He leaned in a bit closer and lowered his voice. "And if there is ever anything I can do for you..."

He let the sentence fall off, gave her a nod, and turned to leave. One of the secret service agents stepped up and handed Codi a card. She looked down and saw the presidential seal on one side and a hand-written number on the other. Codi slipped it into her pocket.

She had met with the man just four days previously as she, along with Joel and Brian, had received unofficial commendations for their efforts. It was a small ceremony held in the oval office behind closed doors. No pictures or records were taken, but it's the thought that counts, right?

Now he owed her a favor. Her mind spun with the

possibilities. All the things a president could do for her career, for her future. It was staggering.

But Codi was a creature of habit. She liked to do things only one way, her way. She pulled the card from her pocket, turned it in her hand, and dropped it in the grave as a shovelful of dirt followed behind it.

She felt a load lift from her shoulders, as she ran to catch up with a receding Joel. "Hey."

"Hey."

After a moment of silence Joel spoke. "I've been giving this a lot of thought, even did some calculations. Do you know what the odds are of a Cessna 210 traveling at 230 mph hitting an ICBM moving towards it at 15,000 mph?"

Codi looked over at her partner as he demonstrated the collision with his hands.

"Let's just say it's an impossibility. How she managed to get her plane in front of that missile. Was it skill or dumb luck? The odds are less than–"

"Joel. You know better than to play the odds. This is *us* you're talking about. Plus, in all your calculations did you ever stop to consider a higher power?"

"You mean like God?" he asked.

"Yeah. Some things just can't be explained. I believe that and I've seen that. It takes a little…faith."

"Okay. Let's say God had a hand in it and intervened. Why didn't he do it back in China and save us a whole lot of drama?"

"Fair enough. But drama, that's what makes life interesting."

Joel just shook his head. His partner was one of a kind.

"Hey," she said, "how 'bout a slice of pie? My treat. David Mamet said, 'stress cannot exist in the presence of pie.'"

"Okay, but I get to pick the place."

"Deal."

"Somewhere with good coffee."

"You mean great coffee."

"Precisely."

The rain intensified. Codi and Joel moved off together with the confident gait of experience, and one chapter in their lives laid to rest.

IF YOU LIKED THIS BOOK

I would appreciate it if you would leave a review. An honest review helps me write better stories. Positive reviews help others find the book and ultimately increase book sales, which help generate more books in the series.

It only takes a moment, but it means everything. Thanks in advance,

Brent

AUTHOR'S NOTE

This is a work of fiction. Any resemblance to persons living or dead, or actual events, is either coincidental or is used for fictive and storytelling purposes. Some elements of this story are inspired by true events; all aspects of the story are imaginative events inspired by conjecture. *Blind Target* was a true labor of love. Like life, the writing process is a journey, one meant to be savored, and to me it's more about the pilgrimage itself than the destination. I learned a ton while writing this book, and I hope it's reflected in the story and the prose. Only you, the reader, can be the judge of the results. Drop me a line if you have feedback or just want to say hi.

Brent Ladd Loefke, 2019, Irvine CA

INTERESTING FACTS

For more facts go to my website and see as well as read these details. brentladdbooks.com

DEW Line or Distant Early Warning System
The DEW Line was a string of radar stations in the far north Arctic, from Canada to the Aleutian Islands of Alaska. It was set up to detect incoming Soviet bombers during the Cold War. It provided early detection and allowed Strategic Air Command time to scramble jets to intercept. The 63-base Line reached operational status in 1957 and was eventually decommissioned in 1988.

Nikolski Bay on Umnak Island
Umnak is one of the Fox Islands within the Aleutian chain of islands. It is mostly volcanic and there are no trees that grow there. The town of Nikolski is located on a small southern inlet. It is reputed to be the oldest continuously-occupied community in the world, with a current population of 18. Archaeological evidence from Ananiuliak Island, on the north side of Nikolski Bay, dates as far back as 8,500 years ago.

LeTourneau Sno-Freighter
Alaska Freight Lines had the contract in the early 1950's to transport supplies for the construction of DEW Line. They commissioned heavy equipment specialist Le Tourneau

Technologies to build a land train capable of fording semi frozen rivers and deep snow. Powered by two Cummins engines generating 800 HP the Sno-Freighter was able to pull 150 tons of material through temperatures as low as minus 68 degrees Fahrenheit. Much like a rail based locomotive the diesel engines powered electric motors located on each of the 24 combined wheels of the power unit and the trailing wagons.

Sludge Ice

Ice the consistancy of honey is called sludge ice. This is water that is in an early stage of freezing. It offers little resistence at first but can be a deadly trap as it will often times quickly solidify, without warning.

Tupolev TU-16 Bomber - Badger

The Soviet Union was strongly committed to matching the United States in strategic bombing capability. Their first bombers with frontal aviation entered service in 1954 with the TU-16 service designation. It had a large swept wing and two Mikulin AM-3 turbojets. It could carry 20,000 lbs. in warheads and was still in service until the early 1990's.

NORAD, or the Cheyenne Mountian Complex

Cheyenne Mountian Complex is a military installation and defensive bunker located in unincorporated El Paso County, Colorado. Formerly the center for the US Space Command and NORAD—North America Aerospace Defense Command. The Complex is built under 2,000 feet of solid granite. It boasts a full city floating on springs and a twenty-five-ton blast door. The overall facility is built to deflect a thirty-megaton nuclear strike.

D.B. Cooper

D.B. Cooper is a 70's icon that was the most successful

skyjacker in US history. He extorted $200,000 in ransom and then parachuted out of a passenger jet to an unknown fate and certain fame. The FBI's case has over 60 volumes of information, but has never been solved. Years later, a young boy did discover a wad of cash along the Columbia River with matching serial numbers.

The Abittoir

The Abittoir is an old meat processing plant that is still standing in Hong Kong. It has been long abandoned and is considered by many to be haunted. It is currently a popular destination for urban explorers.

Fenghuang China

Fenghuang is a truly magical town that time has forgotten. It has colorful buildings with stilts holding them up all along a lazy river that rolls past. There are several bridges connecting the two sides of the town and a stepping stone crossing made of stone columns. Even Chongde Hall is located in the city, built in the 1700's by the town's wealthiest resident.

The Southern Great Wall or Miaojiang Great Wall

The Southern Great Wall is a lesser known structure to the Great Wall of China. It was built in the mid 1500's to protect the Chinese against the Mio people in the south. It stretched over 190 kms. and housed over 5000 soldiers. Much of the Southern Great Wall has been lost to time.

ACKNOWLEDGEMENTS

With deep appreciation to all those who encouraged me to write, and especially those who did not. I wanted to thank the following contributors for their efforts doling out their opinions and help to keep my punctuation honest. Jeff Klem, Kristin Woodruff, Natalie Call, Brad Simmons, Carol Avellino, and Wade Lillywhite. A host of family and friends who suffered through early drafts and were kind enough to share their thoughts. My lovely wife Leesa, who is my first reader and best critic. And my editor Cathy Hull.

A special thanks to my publisher, Archway Publishing, who helped make this all possible, as writing is only half the total equation. Finally, to Patrick Fitch for the cover design.

As many concepts as possible are based on actual or historical details. Special thanks to the original action hero—my dad, Dr. Paul Loefke.

Lastly, writers live and die by their reviews, so if you liked my book, *please* review it!

More Codi Sanders coming soon! – BrentLaddBooks.com

ABOUT THE AUTHOR

Writer Director Brent Ladd has been a part of the Hollywood scene for almost three decades. His work has garnered awards and accolades all over the globe. Brent has been involved in the creation and completion of hundreds of commercials for clients large and small. He is an avid beach volleyball player and an adventurer at heart. He currently resides in Irvine, CA, with his wife and children.

Brent found his way into novel writing when his son Brady showed little interest in reading. He wrote his first book making Brady the main character—*The Adventures of Brady Ladd*. Enjoying that experience, Brent went on to concept and complete his first novel, *Terminal Pulse, A Codi Sanders Thriller*—the first in a series, and followed it up with *Blind Target*.

Brent is a fan of a plot driven story with strong intelligent characters. So if you're looking for a fast paced escape, check out the Codi Sanders series. You can also find out more about his next book, and when it will be available. Please visit his website – BrentLaddBooks.com

CPSIA information can be obtained
at www.ICGtesting.com
Printed in the USA
BVHW080816030719

552580BV00004B/158/P

9 781480 878433